# KID PALOMINO: OUTLAWS

Outlaw Bill Carson and his gang ride into Fargo knowing that the sheriff and his deputies are out of town. Carson has inside information about the bank and banker, which the ruthless killer intends to use to his advantage. What Carson and his equally bloodthirsty gang do not know is that the deputies have returned early. Kid Palomino and his fellow lawman Red Rivers notice the strangers in town and decide to find out who they are. All hell erupts as the lawmen confront the outlaws . . .

MICHAEL D. GEORGE

# KID PALOMINO: OUTLAWS

*Complete and Unabridged*

**LINFORD**
*Leicester*

First published in Great Britain in 2017 by
Robert Hale
an imprint of The Crowood Press
Wiltshire

First Linford Edition
published 2019
by arrangement with
The Crowood Press
Wiltshire

A catalogue record for this book is available
from the British Library.

ISBN 978–1–4448–4208–1

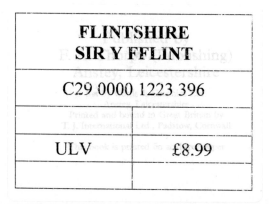

*Dedicated to my grand-daughters*
*Alexia and Skye*

# Prologue

The town of Fargo was quiet. Most of its inhabitants had been asleep for hours as the sky slowly began to show the first glimpses of light. The sun was about to rise but five riders were already wide-awake as they slowly steered their horses into the sleepy settlement. Merciless outlaw Bill Carson led his band of fellow outlaws through the back streets toward the Fargo Bank.

Like his followers, Carson sported a long dust coat which hid their arsenal of weaponry from curious eyes. He led the Brand brothers, Luke and Amos through the shadows like a mute army general. Poke Peters and Jeff Kane trailed the trio like obedient guard dogs. It was their job to watch out for any sign of trouble that might raise its head and start fanning their gun hammers in their direction.

Yet Fargo was a law-abiding settlement. Trouble rarely entered its boundaries. Until this day it had only had to cope with drunken revelry but as the heavens slowly grew lighter above the roof shingles, all that was about to change. Had it been later in the day, the streets would have been filled to overflowing with people going about their rituals.

Bill Carson had chosen the moment of their arrival with perfect accuracy. He knew that the moment between night and the birth of a new day was when all towns were at their most vulnerable.

The outlaw leader kept tapping his bloody spurs into the flanks of his powerful mount. Carson was known for his prowess at robbing even the sturdiest of banks and was wanted dead or alive in three states and two territories. Yet no one in Fargo had ever set eyes upon him before. He had travelled more than a hundred miles from his usual hunting grounds in order to strike at Fargo's seemingly impenetrable bank.

Unknown to his four deadly underlings,

Carson had been given inside information concerning not only the bank itself but also its owner. All the brutal Carson had to do was follow his instructions and the money was as good as his.

The five riders continued at their slow pace and as far as Carson was concerned, everything else would fall neatly into place. His hooded eyes glanced over his shoulder at the men riding behind him. They were all hired killers and wanted by the law just like he was. The only difference between them was that Carson demanded total obedience and would kill even them if they did not follow his orders.

Carson had two rules that he demanded his followers abide by without question.

The first was to kill anyone who got in their way and the second was not to show any mercy. Carson had earned the high price on his head. He had left a mountain of dead bodies in his wake. Women and children fared little better than men when it came to the hot lead he and his men dished out.

Carson glanced at the cloudless heavens and continued to jab his spurs into his walking mount. Blood dripped from the metal spikes. He watched the sky turn pink as the distant sun was about to rise.

The bank stood like a fortress in the middle of Fargo. It towered over the many other buildings. Not one of the numerous outlaws who had passed this way before had even dared to try and rob it. Its red brick and cement walls were enough to scare most of the lethal outlaws away. The iron bars that covered every one of its windows looked impossible to penetrate, as did its reinforced doors.

Yet Bill Carson kept jabbing his spurs even though he knew the bank was virtually impregnable. His eyes darted from one shadow to the next as he led his four followers deeper into the sprawling town. The empty streets satisfied the merciless Carson as he glanced at the gigantic edifice.

'Keep riding, boys,' he growled.

The five horsemen rode slowly past the massive structure and glanced at the ominous sight. Fargo was getting brighter with every heartbeat but Carson did not seem to be at all concerned. The confused riders who trailed the veteran bank robber considered the reason why the ruthless Carson continued to jab his spurs and turn into another side street.

The Brand brothers glanced at one another and silently began to wonder why they were now riding away from the very thing they had travelled two days to rob. Amos Brand looked over his shoulder at Peters and Kane. They too could not understand what was going on.

But no matter how curious they were they did not dare to question Carson's motives or reasoning. They just followed and left the thinking to the lethal outlaw.

Bill Carson turned up what appeared at first glance to be a dead end, yet the narrow lane led to a secluded street of four very expensive houses. Carson drew rein and stopped his mount as his gang flanked him.

'What's this place, Bill?' Luke Brand asked as he surveyed the properties curiously. 'Why'd we come here?'

'I thought we were here to rob that back there,' Kane added as he steadied his mount.

Carson did not answer. He simply pulled out a long thin cigar and bit off its tail. He spat at the ground and then placed the black weed between his teeth. Then the outlaw struck a match and cupped its flame and sucked. When his lungs were filled with acrid smoke, Carson slowly exhaled and tossed the match at the sand before them.

He pointed at the end house. 'See that house sitting there, boys?'

The four riders nodded.

'What's so important about that one, Bill?' Kane asked.

'A certain Stanley Hardwick lives in that fine house,' Carson informed his curious men. 'And Hardwick happens to be the man who owns that big red brick bank.'

Peters rested his hands on his saddle horn and looked blankly at Carson. 'That's real nice, Bill. But why do we wanna know where that varmint lives?'

Carson tilted his head, pulled the cigar from his mouth and tapped ash at the sand. A cruel smile etched his hardened features as he glared at Peters and then the others.

'Hardwick don't live on his lone-some,' he said. 'He got himself a wife and a fifteen-year-old daughter.'

His men were still no wiser. They looked at their leader with bemused expressions. Carson shook his head and sighed heavily.

'I happen to know this because a certain party told me all about the banker, boys,' he explained. 'Hardwick will do anything to save them females from being harmed. Now do you savvy?'

'Who told you, Bill?' Luke Brand asked.

'The man who plans all my jobs for me, Luke boy,' Carson sucked more smoke into his lungs. 'A critter that I've

7

never even met but he's the smartest bastard this side of the Pecos.'

'What's his name?' Kane wondered.

Carson grunted with amusement. 'I'll tell you his name when the job is all done.'

Peters steadied his mount. 'I heard that they got themselves a pretty good bunch of star-packers in Fargo, Bill. What we gonna do when we have to face them critters?'

The outlaw leader muffled his amusement.

'I've bin told that they're out of town, Poke.' Carson grinned and concentrated on the house again. He looked at the affluent structure. 'They've got a retired old lawman holding the fort. He ain't gonna trouble us.'

A sense of relief drifted through the men behind Carson's wide shoulders. Amos Brand edged his horse closer to the older man and looked at Carson.

'You mean that Kid Palomino ain't in Fargo?' he asked nervously. 'That critter is said to have killed more lawbreakers than most. Are you sure he's out of town with the sheriff, Bill?'

Smoke drifted from Carson's mouth. 'I'm dead sure, Amos.'

'Phew,' the outlaw exhaled. 'I sure didn't hanker taking on Kid Palomino.'

Carson gathered his reins in his gloved hands.

'C'mon. We'll tie our horses around the back of that mighty fine house and then pay Hardwick a visit,' he said.

The sound of spurs filled the quiet street as the five horsemen encouraged their mounts on toward the banker's home.

# 1

Apart from the sound of distant roosters hailing the arrival of a new day, the five horsemen were totally alone in the quiet section of Fargo. The caravan snaked along the neatly maintained street and turned up behind the most imposing of all its houses. Carson was first to drop to the ground from his trail-weary horse and lash its long leathers to a white upright close to the rear of the banker's home. As his gloved hands tightened the reins his underlings dismounted around their merciless leader.

Bill Carson had learned long ago that it did not pay to have a regular gang of fellow outlaws. For even the best outlaws could and would betray their more famed leader given the chance. Each job required different skills and Carson always prided himself in choosing the right men for the right job.

So it was as the first rays of the day raced across the cloudless sky above Dry Gulch. The seasoned killer of untold numbers of men, women and children checked his pair of matched Remington .45s and glanced at his men.

His eyes were like emotionless ice. Their glare could cause most grown men to freeze when they focused upon them. The four hired guns he had recruited only a week earlier were no different. They each knew that Carson would kill any or all of them should he want.

'Take off your spurs,' Carson snarled quietly.

The four dust-caked men behind his wide shoulders did exactly as they were commanded and placed their spurs in their saddle-bags just as Carson had also done. He gave a nod of his head and turned on his heels.

The fearsome Carson led his men to the rear door of Hardwick's home and grabbed the door handle with his left hand as his right clutched his six-shooter at hip level.

The door was unlocked.

A wry grin etched his face as Carson looked back at his four followers.

'Folks are mighty trusting in Fargo, boys,' he hissed. 'Reckon it's time we taught them how dumb that is.'

The five hardened criminals entered quickly and spread out through the quiet house. None of the quintet had ever seen such obvious wealth before as they moved around the interior of Hardwick's home. It was everywhere they looked. Expensive paintings adorned the walls and lush imported carpets covered the highly polished floorboards.

Peters and Kane signalled to Carson that there was nobody on the ground floor as the Brand brothers glanced up the staircase like rabid wolves. The thought of the two females upstairs made both the depraved outlaws eager to get their hands upon them.

'Wipe the drool from your mouths,' Carson ordered the brothers. 'You can have your fun when the time's right and not a damn second before. Savvy?'

Both Brand brothers reluctantly nodded. Their desires were not as great as their fear of the veteran outlaw. Even though they had never worked with Carson before, they both knew of his reputation and it frightened them.

They nodded in silent obedience.

Carson moved between Amos and Luke and pointed up the carpeted staircase to the landing.

'Get them,' he ordered. 'Bring them down here and don't go using them hog-legs. I don't want any shooting to wake up this town.'

'We don't need our guns to round up a banker and his brood, Bill,' Amos said as he placed a boot on the first run of the steps.

'Get them,' Carson repeated.

As Peters and Kane moved back to the side of Carson, the Brand siblings slowly ascended the carpeted staircase. The thick pile of the carpet absorbed any sound of their hefty footwear. A few moments after the two men entered the bedrooms the noise of startled outrage

14

filled the large house.

'I still can't figure out why we come here and not the bank, Bill,' Peters said as he stared up at the landing. 'Not unless this Hardwick critter has got himself a safe in this house.'

Carson raised his eyebrows. 'You'll understand soon enough, Poke.'

The noise of the younger female was the loudest but was soon muffled by the palm of one of the Brand brother's gloved hands.

Carson holstered his gun and listened with amusement to the activity up upon the landing as Amos and Luke rounded up the three members of the Hardwick family and began forcing them out of their bedrooms and toward the staircase.

As the sound of startled adults and the child grew louder above him, Carson's attention was suddenly drawn to the kitchen. His eyes narrowed.

'What was that, Bill?' Kane whispered.

Carson said nothing as his eyes narrowed and focused on the rear door in the kitchen. He turned and moved quickly into the large cooking area as the rear door was pushed open and a well-rounded woman entered. Her arms were full of parcels of differing shapes and sizes as she waddled toward a table.

It had not occurred to Carson that anyone as wealthy as Hardwick would have people working for him. His information had not gone into that sort of detail. The lethal outlaw pressed his back against the wall behind the rear door as the female shuffled across the tiled floor.

Elvira Baker was a woman in her mid-fifties. She had worked for the banker as his cook and cleaner for nearly a decade. She knew her duties and nothing had ever interfered with them.

Until now.

Now her entire world was about to come crashing down.

Elvira stopped and placed the groceries on to the rectangular table unaware of the intruders within the lavish house. As she placed the provisions on the table her attention was drawn to the muddy footprints on the tiles. Elvira stopped and stared at the floor in bewilderment.

'I only scrubbed them tiles last night,' she pondered as her mind raced. 'Who on earth dragged in that mud?'

The sound of the door being shut behind her filled her with a mix of fear and curiosity. Her eyes widened as she slowly turned around.

The sight of the tall outlaw standing across the door sent a chill through her.

'It's a bad habit talking to yourself,' Carson sneered. 'I'm told they lock folks up in asylums for less.'

Elvira's eyes widened as she stared in horror at the figure clad in the long dust coat. He towered above her petite form. She was about to speak when she noticed the gun belt and the gleaming .45s hidden beneath the protective coat.

The cook tried to swallow but it was impossible. Fear gripped her throat like a noose. She rested her hip against the table and tried to steady herself as fear washed over her startled shape.

'Who are you?' she managed to ask as

her entire body shook with growing alarm.

The hideous smile grew wider across Carson's face. He began to approach her slowly. 'It ain't none of your business, woman.'

Elvira's eyes flashed. She turned and started to make her way across the kitchen. After only three steps she saw the ominous figure of Poke Peters blocking her way into the living area of the house. She abruptly stopped as Carson continued to track her every step behind her.

She turned and looked up into Carson's narrowed eyes.

'Who are you?' she asked fearfully.

'I'm just someone who's got business with your boss,' Carson replied in a low drawl as he strode across the tiled floor and placed a hand on her shoulder. She looked up into his cold, calculating eyes as he smiled. For a moment the tone of his emotionless voice calmed her down.

'The master never said that he was expecting visitors,' Elvira stammered. 'It's awful early. He don't get up this early unless it's important.'

Carson touched her chin. 'He's up.'

Elvira stared into his hypnotic eyes. 'He is?'

The last thing she had expected was the long blade of a Bowie knife to be thrust up under her ribcage and twisted. A look of total disbelief washed over the face of Elvira Baker as the taste of blood filled her mouth. Carson moved his gloved hand and covered her face.

Her eyes rolled upward.

Carson pulled his knife free and then wiped the gore from its blade on his dust coat sleeve. The small female fell heavily on to the floor as Carson slid his knife back into its leather sheath. Within seconds a pool of blood spread out across the tiles. Carson stepped over the body and marched back toward Peters into the living area of the house.

The brutal outlaw had only just reached the foot of the stairs when the Brand boys forcefully dragged their three captives down into the heart of the house. Amos pushed the banker and his wife on to a couch as Luke physically wrestled with the young female.

Carson glared at the older of the brothers. His look said everything without him having to utter a word. Luke Brand released the banker's daughter. She rushed to her parents and threw herself between them.

Petra Hardwick had only just celebrated her fifteenth birthday and as her heart pounded, she began to doubt she would see another. The females whimpered like whipped dogs as they huddled close to the night-gowned Hardwick.

Mustering every scrap of his resolve, the banker stared at the five heavily armed intruders and shook his fist at them.

'This is an outrage,' he boomed. 'I'll have you locked up for this.'

Carson shook his head and strode to a table. He opened a fine silver box and withdrew a fine cigar. He sniffed it and then bit off its tip and placed it between his teeth.

'Keep your voice down, Hardwick,'

the leader of the devilish men said as he scratched a match across the highly polished table top. 'We've got a little business to do and then we'll be out of your hair.'

Beth Hardwick looked at her husband. 'Do you know these animals, Stan?'

'I've never met them before.' The banker shrugged.

'But he says you have business to do,' she added.

'Don't go burning his ears, ma'am,' Carson interrupted as he exhaled a long line of grey smoke at the floor. 'Stan don't know anything about the business we've got to do. This is kinda like a surprise.'

The three members of the Hardwick clan sat in their night clothes and watched the merciless outlaw as he savoured the fine cigar and paced around the living room.

Hardwick leaned forward.

'What's all this about?' Hardwick raged before Peters stepped aside and allowed the banker to see the body of the innocent cook. Hardwick gasped as his wife and daughter buried their faces in their hands. The banker stared at the pitiful corpse and then looked in terror at the five dust-caked men who had invaded his home. 'You've killed Elvira. Why?'

Carson grinned. 'I figured it would hone your attention, Hardwick. I reckon I was right. You sure look attentive to me, *amigo*.'

The distraught banker went to stand but Jeff Kane pushed him back on to the couch. Beth clutched his arm to prevent him from attempting to rise again.

'They've killed Elvira, Stan,' she whispered into his ear. 'Don't give them an excuse to do the same to you.'

Hardwick patted her hand. 'You're right, Beth.'

Carson inhaled on the fine cigar and then stared down into the banker's eyes. He pulled the Havana from his mouth and pointed at the overweight man.

'Your woman got sense, Hardwick,' he growled. 'Listen to her and you'll live to see another sunrise.'

The banker gulped. 'What do you want? I don't keep any cash here. My money is in the bank just like everyone else's.'

Carson stepped closer. 'I know that. I also know that you own that big red brick structure down yonder. Nobody can question you coming and going, can they?'

'I don't understand.' Hardwick frowned. 'What exactly are you talking about? Of course I can come and go to the bank. I have the only key.'

Carson screwed up his eyes.

'Then that's exactly what you're gonna do.'

Hardwick started to understand the outlaw. 'You want me to get you into the bank safely?'

Carson leaned over and blew smoke into the face of the banker and then grinned. 'Damn right. Me and my boys don't need to bust into that building if you got the only key. Right?'

Hardwick nodded in agreement. 'Correct.'

Bill Carson sat on the arm of the couch.

'First you're gonna go get dressed and then you, me and a couple of my boys are gonna go visit your bank,' the outlaw announced before patting Hardwick on the back.

Hardwick clutched his wife and child as close to him as he could. He could not stop himself shaking as the acrid aroma of cigar smoke and sweat-soiled clothes filled his nostrils.

'What about Beth and Petra?' the banker croaked. 'If I do what you want, you shall not harm them. Do you promise?'

Carson stood and swung on his heels to face the terrified trio. He laughed at them and then grabbed Hardwick's side whiskers and dragged the banker to his feet. The lethal outlaw pulled him close. So close that the stout banker could feel the heat of the cigar in Carson's gritted teeth burning his cheek.

'Your womenfolk will be fine as long as you obey my orders and don't get smart,' Carson said quietly.

'It don't pay getting smart with Bill, mister,' Poke Peters told the wealthy banker. 'Believe me. If you try to cross Bill he'll do things to these gals of yours that you wouldn't believe.'

Hardwick nodded. 'I'll do anything as long as you do not harm my wife and daughter.'

Carson released his grip and pointed to Amos Brand. 'Take this varmint to his room and watch him get dressed. Then bring him down here.'

Amos Brand grabbed Hardwick by his nightgown and led him up the staircase as if he were taking a dog for a walk. Carson moved slowly around the couch and stared down at the two females. He then paused above the younger female.

She was a cut above the females that the outlaw leader usually encountered. Even her youth could not hide her beauty from the ruthless Carson. Young Petra was like a rose just starting to bloom.

Petrified by his spine-chilling attention, she buried her head into the comforting arms of her equally concerned mother and started to sob as fear overwhelmed her. 'I'm afraid, Mother. Make them go away.'

Yet no matter how much she wanted to comply with her daughter's request, Beth knew it was beyond her abilities. There was no way any of the determined outlaws would listen to her pleas. They encircled the couch like a pack of ravenous hounds.

She looked up at Carson. 'Please stop staring at my daughter. Can't you see she's frightened of you?'

Carson pulled the cigar from his lips, glanced around the faces of his hired help and grinned.

'She's mighty smart, ma'am,' he said coldly. 'If I was in her shoes I reckon I'd be scared too.'

'Why?' the older female asked naively.

Carson pointed at the body of Elvira and smirked. 'That's why you both oughta be mighty scared, ma'am. I can get real dangerous when folks don't do what I tell them.'

Beth Hardwick's expression suddenly changed as her eyes focused on the pitiful sight of the dead female. She gently squeezed her daughter's shoulders and looked directly at Carson as he puffed on his cigar.

'But you promised my husband that as long as he did everything you tell him to do, we'd not be harmed.'

Carson raised his eyebrows and poked his thumbs into his gun belt.

'You'd best pray that I ain't lying, ma'am,' he drawled.

# 2

The main thoroughfare of Fargo slowly warmed as the long shadows gave way to the creeping sunlight. It was still early as acting sheriff Charlie Summers slowly made his way through the streets of Fargo toward the office he had occupied since Sheriff Ben Lomax had taken his deputies, Kid Palomino and Red Rivers to nearby Cooperville to attend a trial at the county seat. All three of Fargo's lawmen were witnesses for the prosecution and had to attend to ensure the guilty party did not get away with murder.

In the meantime Charlie Summers was in charge of the normally sleepy town. The yawning old lawman had been retired more than five years and yet his knowledge was still required by the citizens of Fargo. Summers knew that he was well beyond his best but the quiet town seldom had any real trouble that called for his once formidable prowess. Standing in for Lomax was an easy way to make a few much-needed dollars to supplement his meagre pension.

Fargo was seemingly its usual self. A couple of dogs chased their tails as Summers crossed the empty street. He pulled his battered old timepiece from his vest pocket and checked it. It was still early. Real early. He nodded to himself as he climbed the three steps up to the boardwalk outside the office and paused.

After slipping the dented watch back into his vest pocket, Summers entered the office and raised its window blinds. Sunlight streamed in and the old timer glanced around the twelve-feet square room. He knew that as Lomax and his deputies were due back at any time, he had better clean up.

The old timer blew dust off the rifle rack and then waddled to the cluttered desk. He scratched his neck and pushed his battered hat onto the crown of his balding head.

Charlie stacked the posters into a neat pile and then dusted the newly exposed section of the desk. He paused and yawned again before looking at the stove. He moved to it and opened its iron jaws. He looked in and placed a few crumpled posters into the void. Then he picked up the last of the kindling on to the paper and struck a match. As the paper caught alight and started to envelope the kindling he added more wood until he was happy that he had a fire going.

'That should do it.' Summers clapped his hands together and closed the stove door. He then ladled some water from a bucket into the blackened coffee pot and added a handful of coffee beans. He closed the lid and placed the pot on the stove's flat top. 'Reckon that coffee should be ready in about an hour or so.'

Old Charlie sighed. Nowadays he found that even the slightest effort left him breathless. He squinted out into the quiet street and then returned his attention to the desk. The chair looked very welcoming but the veteran lawman knew that if he sat down he would sleep until noon. He straightened his loose gun belt and rubbed his whiskers.

'Hell, that's enough hard work,' the elderly man reassured himself before walking out on to the boardwalk and resting his bones on the weathered chair. The gentle breeze which looped under the porch overhang was just enough to keep Charlie awake. He pulled out his pipe, tapped it against his boot leather and then started to fill its bowl with tobacco. A solitary buck-board quietly turned the corner and made its way to the feed store.

Summers acknowledged the wave of the driver and then looked down at his pipe. He used his thumb to push the tobacco down into the bowl and then closed the pouch and returned it to his shirt pocket.

'I sure hope Ben and the boys get back today,' he muttered before striking a match along the side of his pants leg and placing it above the bowl. He sucked a few times on the pipe stem and watched as the flame disappeared into the bowl. As smoke filled his mouth he tossed the match at the street and slowly closed his eyes. 'This job is plumb tuckering.'

As the old timer rested, two hundred yards away Bill Carson escorted the terrified banker into the main street and toward the impenetrable red brick edifice. Amos Brand and Poke Peters walked a couple of yards behind the odd pair. Hardwick was wearing his usual hand tailored suit and brown derby. The affluent banker was in total contrast to the three men escorting him in their trail-weary dust coats.

If there had been anyone on the street they might have noticed that the men beside Hardwick were carrying empty saddle-bags across their shoulders. They might have also noticed that the stranger beside him had a firm grip on the elbow of the pale-faced banker. Carson was steering the portly man to the bank to make a hefty withdrawal.

'You'll never get away with this,' Hardwick said as they closed in on the bank.

'Just keep walking and remember that Luke and Jeff are back with your good lady and handsome daughter, Stan,' Carson muttered. 'If there's any trouble, they'll snuff out them gals' candles permanently.

'Savvy?'

The banker nodded.

As Carson helped the banker turn the corner into the main street his eyes darted across the dozens of shuttered store fronts. Barely any of the businesses were open at this ungodly hour and the infamous outlaw knew it. Carson glanced back at Peters and Brand.

'Keep alert, boys,' he commanded.

The outlaws both nodded in reply.

'This is crazy,' Hardwick whispered to his chaperone. 'It'll never work. Folks in Fargo will figure out what's happening and stop you.'

Carson tightened his grip on the

elbow of his walking companion. 'You'd better pray that they don't start poking their snouts into this, Hardwick. Just do as I tell you and everything will be OK.'

Even though the banker was probably the wealthiest man in Fargo, there was nothing more precious to him than his wife and child. He would willingly give everything he owned to prevent Beth and Petra suffering the same fate as had befallen Elvira. As the four men trooped to the bank, the terrified and confused banker glanced upward at the church spire that loomed over the far smaller structures at the far end of Fargo. His heart raced. Hardwick had seldom entered the whitewashed church at the end of town but as he and his escorts drew closer to the towering red brick edifice, he began to silently pray.

# 3

The key which opened the reinforced door was returned to the pocket of the banker as Hardwick turned its handle and led his three companions into the dark interior of the bank. Banks of such impressive dimensions were a rarity in this region and none of the men with Hardwick had ever entered such a structure before.

Carson secured the door behind them and then placed his left hand upon Hardwick's shoulder. He leaned down to the far shorter man and growled into his ear.

'You told me that there's a night guard in here, Stan,' he started as his eyes flashed through the unlit depths of the bank. 'Where is he?'

Hardwick felt his heart pound inside his starched shirt as he slowly raised his shaking hand and pointed to their right.

All three of the outlaws looked beyond the polished stone pillars to a door set in the corner. The door was totally in sympathy with the rest of the handsome bank. Even in the darkness Carson and his fellow wanted men could see the brass fittings.

'That's his room,' Hardwick stammered as he rubbed the sweat from his features. 'He stays in that room throughout the night and only patrols the bank every hour until the tellers arrive.'

Carson pulled out his pocket watch and checked the time. He showed the timepiece to the banker.

'When does he venture out?' he asked.

'Any moment now,' the banker replied.

Bill Carson returned his watch to his vest, inhaled and then nodded to himself. He looked at Peters and Brand in turn as he drew one of his Remingtons. He cocked the weapon's hammer until it locked into position and pointed to both sides of the door.

'We don't want any shooting,' he hissed at his men. 'Take up positions to either side of the door and I'll try to lure that guard out here. When he comes out, kill him.'

Hardwick gasped in horror. 'No. You can't just kill him.'

Carson pressed the barrel of his gun into the neck of the distraught banker. 'We can and that's what we'll do. Remember, if you wanna see that family of yours again, just keep quiet. Savvy?'

Any concern for the guard evaporated as he thought of his womenfolk. He steadied himself and nodded. 'OK. I'll keep quiet.'

Carson glanced up as both Peters and Brand took up positions to either side of the door. They both waved at Carson who started to push the banker toward the dark-stained door. When both men were ten feet away, Carson halted Hardwick and stepped behind him. He pressed the gun barrel into the base of Hardwick's spine and crouched slightly.

There were no lights burning within the bank. Only gaps around its high windows cast any light into the interior. Spindly shafts of sunlight filtered down into the vast belly of the building.

Even so, Carson did not want the guard to catch a glimpse of him as he hid behind the stocky banker's figure. He gently struck Hardwick in the back with his .45 and hissed.

'Call him,' Carson snarled.

Even knowing that he was about to lure the guard to his death, Hardwick mustered up every scrap of his resolve and called out.

'This is Hardwick, Elias,' he said. 'I've had to come in early to sort out a few things before we open.'

He heard the bolt being slid behind the door and then watched as the trusting man ventured out toward him. 'Howdy, Mr Hardwick. I'm sure glad you warned me that you was in here early.'

Hardwick watched helplessly as both Brand and Peters pounced on the unsuspecting man. The knives in their hands caught the rays of the filtered sunlight as they were plunged into the guard. Bright flashes danced off the polished interior of the bank's fittings.

The banker lowered his head as Brand grabbed the boots of the lifeless man and hauled him back into the small room where he had happily sat less than sixty seconds earlier.

Carson pushed Hardwick toward the pool of blood that trailed the body to where it was deposited. The leader of the merciless trio walked around the banker and patted both men on their shoulders.

'You done good, boys,' he exclaimed before holstering his gun and returning his eyes to the shaking banker. He pointed a finger at Hardwick. 'Now it's your turn to make good our bargain, Stan boy.'

Hardwick looked up. He was filled with shame for his part in the brutal murder of the guard and yet knew that like all family men, he had no choice. He had to comply.

'Follow me,' he said in a faltering

voice as he started walking toward the strong room behind the line of teller windows. 'I'll take you to the vault.'

Bill Carson gritted his teeth and pushed the banker violently between his shoulders.

'Lead the way, Stan,' he drawled. 'Lead the way.'

# 4

The street was getting warmer as the sun slowly crept higher into the morning sky. Charlie Summers had drifted into a deep sleep outside the sheriff's office as he sat stretched out on the old wooden chair beneath the porch overhang. Normally the retired lawman would have continued to snore for more than another hour but as the street grew busier, the noise wrestled him out of his dreams.

For a moment the ancient lawman had no idea where he was or how long he had been there. Summers opened his eyes and pushed the brim of his battered old hat off his eyes and squinted at a buckboard as it squeaked along the street. There were a few of the town's womenfolk strolling toward the heart of Fargo with baskets hanging over their arms and brightly coloured

41

parasols resting upon their shoulders.

The elderly lawman blinked several times to clear his eyes and then sat upright. He pulled the pipe from his mouth and spat at the boardwalk.

'That wagon sure needs oiling,' he grumbled as he vainly sucked and blew into the stem of the pipe trying to rekindle it. As was usual with even the finest of tobaccos, it had stopped burning. Old Charlie gave the pipe bowl a frustrated look and then thrust it into his vest pocket.

He was about to stretch his ancient bones when he caught sight of two dusty horsemen moving slowly through the heat haze. Charlie rubbed his tired eyes and stood as he vainly tried to focus clearly on the riders.

'Now who in tarnation are them varmints?' he asked himself cautiously as he rested the palm of his hand on the gun in its holster. 'Whoever they are they sure don't look peaceable.'

Charlie raised a thin arm, rested the palm of his hand on the porch upright and rubbed his old eyes again. 'Why in hell is everyone so blurred nowadays?'

The words had barely had time to leave his lips when he noticed that the riders had tugged on their long leathers and were headed in his direction.

'Ah, hell,' Charlie cursed and stared at the shimmering horsemen. 'They're heading here.'

Just as Charlie thought, the riders were indeed guiding their mounts toward the sheriff's office and the old man who was watching them. Summers nervously scratched his whiskered chin and then polished the tin star he wore with his shirt cuff. He dropped his hand until his finger curled around the holstered trigger of his trusty .44.

Summoning every last ounce of his courage, Charlie walked down the boardwalk until he was at the edge of the porch. He held his hand up in an attempt to stop the riders.

'Hold on there, boys,' Charlie said in his deepest and most authoritative of tones. 'Who are you and how come you're in Fargo?'

The horse continued on toward the valiant old timer. Then the riders drew rein and halted beside the hitching rail.

'Sorry to wake you, Charlie,' one of the horsemen chuckled as he swung his leg over his cantle and lowered himself to the ground.

'Which one of you varmints said that?' Charlie Summers took another step and then grabbed hold of the wooden upright as one of his boots overstepped the edge of the boardwalk.

'Careful there, Charlie,' the youthful voice of the rider sat astride the high-shouldered palomino stallion said before adding, 'You don't wanna break that scrawny neck of yours, do you?'

Summers looked at Red Rivers as he looped his reins over the hitching pole and secured it. He then looked up at the rider straddling the stallion. A smile erupted on the old timer's face.

'I knew it was you boys, Kid,' he chortled. 'I knew it was you boys all the time.'

'No you didn't, Charlie,' Red Rivers argued. 'You thought we were a couple of desperadoes ready to start shooting up the town.'

Summers looked at Red as he stepped up beside him.

'The sun was in my eyes, Red boy. I'd have figured out who you was soon enough.' He shrugged.

'Sure you would.' Kid Palomino smiled as he slid to the ground beside his mount. He tied his long leathers to the twisted pole beside Red's quarter horse and then rested his knuckles on his gun grips. He stared up at the two men.

Charlie looked uneasy at the handsome young deputy. He turned to Red. 'What's the Kid looking at, Red boy?'

'He's looking at you.' Red replied.

'I know that,' Charlie croaked, 'but why?'

Red shook his head. 'Damned if I know.'

'I'll tell you why I'm looking at you, Charlie.' Palomino stepped up on to the boardwalk and placed a hand on the skinny shoulder of the retired sheriff. 'I'm plumb thirsty, Charlie. I sure hope you've got the coffee brewing.'

The eyes of the older man sparkled. 'You like my coffee, Kid?'

'I sure do.' Palomino walked with his two companions into the office. Steam was rising from the blackened pot on top of the pot-belly stove. 'Besides it's too early to go to the café and get a decent cup.'

Summers rustled up three tin cups and spread them out on the desk. He stared at the pot and scratched his beard. 'I must have bin asleep longer than I figured.'

Red glanced at the wall clock. 'It's twenty after eight.'

'Holy crackers,' Old Charlie gasped as he used a cloth to pick up the coffee pot off the stove top. 'Time sure does fly.'

'I guess it flies even faster when you're getting some shuteye,' the Kid remarked as he watched all three cups being filled.

46

Charlie started to chuckle. 'Reckon it does.'

Palomino picked up a tin cup and went to the open door and leaned a shoulder against the frame. As he raised the cup to his lips something at the far end of the street caught his attention.

'What did you say the time was, Red?' he asked as he stared through the steam of his beverage.

'I said that it's twenty after eight, Kid,' Red repeated as he took a mouthful of coffee and swallowed. 'Why'd you ask?'

Palomino glanced at the two lawmen and then returned his eyes to what had intrigued him along the street. 'What time does Hardwick open that big old bank of his?'

Charlie Summers shook his head and glanced at Palomino.

'You know perfectly well that Stan never opens the bank before ten in the morning, Kid.' Charlie sighed. 'What you asking such a dumb question for?'

Palomino downed his coffee and then

tossed the empty cup at his pals. Red caught the tin cup and placed it down on the desk.

'What's eating you, Palomino?' Red asked.

Kid Palomino looked at his companions. 'If Hardwick doesn't open up his bank until ten in the morning, what's he doing with three *hombres* coming out of the place right now?'

'You're imagining things, Kid,' Summers scoffed.

'Hell, I've never seen that rich old dude at this time of the morning, Palomino,' Red agreed with the elderly Summers. 'Bankers don't get up early like regular folks.'

Kid Palomino tilted his head. 'Well he's up and walking this morning. Come take a looksee if you don't believe me.'

Intrigued by Palomino's insistence, Red and Charlie moved to the side of the younger lawman and watched as the four men made their way from the red brick edifice and started heading back toward the corner on their way to

Hardwick's house.

'Ain't that Hardwick?' Palomino asked.

'It sure is and he ain't on his lonesome,' Red agreed.

Palomino pushed the brim of his Stetson back. 'I don't like the look of them three *hombres* with him. They're packing too much iron for my liking.'

'You're right,' Red agreed as he scratched his cheek thoughtfully. 'They're also carrying saddlebags, Kid.'

'Mighty swollen saddle-bags by the looks of them, Red,' Palomino added before raising his eyebrows. 'Now what do you reckon them three *hombres* got in them bags?'

Charlie looked at Red and Palomino in turn. 'I can't see a damn thing, boys. Are you sure that's Stan Hardwick?'

'We're sure, Charlie,' Red nodded.

'Unlock the rifle rack and get me a Winchester, old timer,' the Kid told Summers.

Summers nodded. 'Sure enough, Kid.'

As the old man scooped a bunch of

keys off the desk and moved to the padlock dangling from the line of secured rifles, Red glanced at him.

'You'd best get me one as well, Charlie,' he said.

'Make sure they're loaded, Charlie,' Palomino added. 'I'd hate to confront them *hombres* with empty guns.'

Old Charlie pulled a few repeating rifles off the rack and checked them in turn. The rifles' magazines were all fully loaded.

'Hurry up, Charlie,' Palomino urged. 'They've turned the corner. We can't see them anymore.'

'I couldn't even see them when they was there,' Summers muttered as he staggered to the pair of deputies with three repeating rifles in his thin arms. Palomino took one as Red lifted another. Both men cranked the weapons' mechanisms.

'What's the other rifle for, Charlie?' Palomino asked.

An impish smile etched the whiskered face as the veteran lawman cranked the hand guard of the third Winchester sending a spent casing over his shoulder.

'This'uns for me, Kid,' he winked.

Palomino smiled at the feisty old man.

'C'mon,' he told them. 'Let's go find out what Hardwick and them *hombres* are up to.'

# 5

No riverboat gambler could have looked more the part, but the man in the frilly shirt with its black lace tie hanging down to the silk vest was not what he appeared to be. The white wide-brimmed hat and tailored blue frock coat seemed to scream out that this was a man who made his living at the gaming tables but it was all a well-devised illusion. He was not what he pretended to be.

Everything about him was calculated to deceive, for in reality the gambler was probably one of the most dangerous of people who had ever existed. Danby Deacon had never done an honest day's work in his entire forty-nine years of existence. Men like Deacon had always shunned anything remotely resembling work and found other ways to make their living. He exercised his brain power rather than his muscles.

Although Deacon was never close to the brutal activities he had masterminded, he was never too far away. As long as there was a telegraph office close, Deacon would keep in touch with his underlings.

Deacon had come a long way from the shady streets of his native New York. They had helped to sharpen his skills as a con artist and trickster. Once he realized that he could make more money by planning jobs for others, he had ventured out into the quickly growing West. As towns sprang up and spread like cancers across the vast land, Deacon was usually there.

To most he was just another gambler.

In reality he was something far more lethal. For Deacon had the knack of listening while others talked. When folks talked, they betrayed themselves and others. They allowed men of an unscrupulous nature to work out what was the truth and what was exaggeration.

Years of practice had made him the best there was at his hideous profession.

As he silently played cards he absorbed everything his fellow gamblers said.

Deacon would discover names, addresses and anything else he thought vital to perfecting his plan. Then he would relay the details to the ruthless outlaws who relied upon his detailed information in order to execute his outrageous plan with the least amount of opposition.

It had worked perfectly for years.

Yet even though the meticulous mastermind had made both Bill Carson and himself wealthy men, they had never actually met. Deacon preferred it that way. He knew that those who seek glory seldom live long enough to actually enjoy the fruits of their labours. Yet although Carson knew nothing about Deacon apart from calling him 'the Deacon', the vastly more intelligent Deacon knew everything there was to know about his cohort.

Every scrap of information concerning the notorious outlaw was branded into Deacon's memory. The wild streets of his youth had taught him that knowledge was power and when you were dealing with men like Carson, you needed to be in total control.

Deacon would mail letters to pre-arranged places for Carson to read and obey. All other messages between the two men were sent via the telegraph.

That had proven to be a lucrative arrangement for both parties and meant that Deacon was always well away from the action when it erupted.

For years he had provided some of the deadliest outlaws with vital information that they then used. It was Deacon who had weighed up the banker Stanley Hardwick and discovered what made him tick. He had passed this information on to Bill Carson for a share of the takings the outlaw could get from the banker's seemingly impregnable establishment.

Deacon had passed through Fargo a week earlier and visited every saloon and gambling house in the town until he had gathered all the information he needed.

His habit of quietly playing poker had

once again paid dividends. Men talked freely as they drank whiskey and won hand after hand to Deacon. Their excitement only loosened their tongues more as the card games stretched on into the night and their stacks of gaming chips grew taller and taller.

It was exactly the same in every town Deacon visited.

Deacon had lost count how many times he had repeated the beneficial act. And none of them had ever realized that they were being used. All they could see was the money they were winning from the stranger in their midst.

Deacon would be gracious and bow out when he had discovered everything he wanted to know, and then depart. The victorious gamblers would mock him with no idea that they had just had their mutual knowledge stripped by the best trickster any of them would ever meet.

Satisfied that he had discovered every minute detail concerning the owner of the impressive red brick bank, Deacon had taken the next stagecoach from Fargo and travelled to where he had instructed Carson to wire him.

The small town of Cherokee Springs sat at the very edge of an unnamed desert. It was one of those sun-bleached places that few men ever visited unless they had reason to hole up for a while. Even the law shied away from making the perilous trip across the arid terrain to Cherokee Springs.

Deacon though, knew that it was perfect for his needs. It was an ideal spot to wait for Carson and his hirelings to rob the bank at Fargo. Deacon had alighted from the stagecoach a few days before and rented the best room in the ramshackle hotel.

As agreed, he would send meaningless telegraph wires to Carson in the next town along the stagecoach route and wait for the reply that would confirm the job had done his bidding for him.

Cherokee Springs was twenty hardbitten miles from Dry Gulch. Deacon was a man who favoured good cigars and even better whiskey. The solitary saloon in the small settlement provided both as well as female company.

Danby Deacon would willingly indulge heavily in all the temptations the town offered as he waited for news that Carson had fulfilled his part of the bargain.

Once he had been paid, he would set off for the next large town and start his methodical work all over again. Deacon knew that Bill Carson was a dangerous outlaw who seldom shared out the spoils of his endeavours with any of the numerous men he hired. Only Deacon had always received his cut of the take because even Carson realized that the man who he had never seen was invaluable.

Before responding to a mysterious message from Deacon, years earlier, Carson had been fortunate to survive his attempts at train and bank robbery.

Although he hated to admit it, Carson knew that he could not plan his jobs as masterly as his unknown benefactor. He needed the mysterious Deacon.

They both knew it.

As he waited in Cherokee Springs, Deacon rested his freshly shaven chin on the heaving bosom of one of the town's working girls who straddled his lap. He took a sip of whiskey and savoured its warming glow as it burned a trail down into his gullet.

'What do you do, Danby?' the soiled dove asked as she pressed her heaving flesh into his welcoming face. 'I mean, what do you do for a job?'

There was a long silence as the man who masqueraded as a common gambler considered the question. Her heavily scented flesh filled his flared nostrils as his eyes darted at her powdered face. A wry smile etched his features as her finger curled his side-whiskers. Deacon looked her straight in the eyes and offered her a tumbler of his fine whiskey. She downed the hard liquor with expertise.

'I think and wait, honey-child,' he sighed.

'What do you think and wait for, Danby darling?' she purred into his ear as she nibbled upon it.

'Money, honey-child,' he answered. 'I think about money.'

# 6

A scattering of trees flanked both sides of the street on the way to the half-hidden lane that led to where the banker's elegant residence stood. Bill Carson and his two cohorts were laden down under the weight of their fully filled saddle-bags as they strode through the leafy enclave. With every stride the wanted men kept pushing Hardwick forward as their eyes darted at the neighbouring buildings for any sign of impending trouble.

They need not have troubled themselves. It was still early and the wealthy people who lived in this small section of Fargo did not rise at this ungodly hour.

The four men closed in on the end structure and moved to the rear of the building. Steam rose from their four horses as they walked past them and entered the banker's home.

A blood-chilling sound met their ears

as they crossed the tiled floor of the kitchen. It was the noise that signals the final gasps of life as they succumb to death.

The pitiful body of the maid was still exactly where they had left it. The pool of blood had grown larger and stickier since Carson had ended Elvira's existence. Yet it was not the sight of the brutally murdered female that had drawn the banker's attention. It was what had happened to his womenfolk that enraged the normally peaceful man. Hardwick clenched both his fists in helpless fury when he saw what had occurred in his absence.

His wife and daughter had been brutally assaulted and lay where the two outlaws had left them. Hardwick stared in horror at the bruised throats of both females as they draped the long couch lifelessly.

They looked like porcelain dolls. Every scrap of life and been mercilessly ripped from them. Dignity had been replaced by shock on their dead faces.

'What have you done?' The banker shouted at the satisfied pair. 'What have you done?'

The outlaws glared at the banker as they tucked their shirts back into their belts and then started to laugh at the outraged man.

'Quit belly-aching,' Brand spat at the stunned banker in amusement. 'We give them what they needed.'

'Don't worry, Beth,' Hardwick called to his spouse.

Carson leaned over the shorter man and hissed like a rattler into Hardwick's ear. 'She can't hear you, Stan. Neither of your ladies can hear nothing but the sound of harps now.'

'They're not dead,' the banker vainly insisted. 'They can't be dead.'

'They're dead OK.' Brand laughed as he moved toward the colourless face of the banker. 'Me and Kane seen to that after them gals obliged us.'

'You filthy animals!' The banker went to rush at the mocking pair when he felt the full force of Carson's gun hit the back of his head. Suddenly his eyes only saw a white flashing light. He stumbled and then toppled on to the boards. His face crashed into the floor as he sank into a bottomless pit of total oblivion.

Carson holstered his gun. The infamous outlaw shook his head in anger and glared at Kane and Brand. 'You shouldn't have done that, boys. Them females were screaming fit to burst when we showed up.'

Kane adjusted his gun-belt. 'We couldn't kill them before we had our fun, could we?'

'Why not?' Carson spat and paced around the room and looked out from behind the heavily draped window. 'You're lucky by the looks of it. It don't seem that their howling woke up the neighbours.'

'What if they did wake anybody up?' Brand snarled.

Carson glanced at Brand and pointed a finger at the outlaw.

'Screaming women might have brought unwanted attention here. That weren't in my plans.'

Peters nodded in agreement. 'Bill's right. We need to ride out of Fargo without anybody even knowing we were ever here in the first place. Ain't that right, Bill?'

'Yep, that's right, Poke,' Carson agreed.

Carson stepped over the unconscious banker and looked at the sight of his two hired men as they buttoned up their pants and shirts. His icy stare wiped the satisfied smirks from their rugged faces.

Peters cleared his throat. 'Ain't it time for us to be headed out of here, Bill? We got as much money as we can carry and if we high-tail it now, we'll be long gone before anybody figures that anything's wrong.'

Carson spat as he helped himself to a handful of the banker's cigars, pocketed all but one and struck a match. As its flame ignited the fine Havana he nodded at Peters.

'You're right, Poke,' he answered before pulling his knife from its scabbard and staring at the three figures scattered around the living room.

Slowly Carson removed the heavy saddle-bag from his shoulder and rested the swollen satchels on the edge of the couch. Without uttering a word the merciless leader of the gang stepped to where the

65

bodies of the women were draped and then slid the honed blade across their bruised throats. He then straightened up and wiped the gore from the gleaming blade as he walked across the room to where both Kane and Brand stood.

'Why'd you do that, Bill?' Kane asked. 'They were both dead. They didn't need their throats cut.'

Faster than either of the rugged outlaws had ever seen anyone move before, Carson ran the deadly Bowie knife under their chins. They gulped in terror.

'I was just making sure they were dead and not just play-acting, boys,' Carson laughed as he looked down at the unconscious banker.

Then from behind his wide shoulders he heard the voice of the other Brand brother.

'Quit waving that cutlass around, Bill,' he said.

Carson paused and stared at the nervy outlaw.

'You talking to me, boy?'

'I sure am,' the younger Brand dragged

the saddle-bags from his shoulder and rested his hand on his holstered gun. 'You better not be thinking of sticking my brother with that blade. I'll kill you if you do.'

The half-closed eyes of Carson fixed on Brand's sibling and shook his head. 'Don't even think about drawing that hog-leg, boy.'

'If you stick my brother with that cutlass I'll draw, Bill,' Brand warned. 'Don't make me draw.'

Bill Carson smiled. It was the sickly smile of a man who knew exactly how fast he was and feared no one. He shook his head and exhaled a long line of grey smoke.

'Easy, I ain't gonna kill your brother, boy.' Carson muttered a fraction of a heartbeat before he stepped away from the pair and loomed over Hardwick's prostrate body. His eyes darted between the banker and the riled Brand brother. 'Now quit threatening me before I forget whose side you're on.'

The outlaw relaxed and glanced back

at Peters. He shrugged and then rubbed his rugged features. 'That was close.'

'You don't know how close, Brand.' Peters agreed as he watched Carson look down at the stunned banker as he quietly knelt over Hardwick.

With another swift slash of the knife, Carson ruthlessly dispatched the banker. He stood and looked at the blood spilling out over the floor and smiled. Then he wiped the bloody blade on his sleeve, and stepped back over the corpse and moved to his saddle-bags. He plucked them up and tossed them into the hands of Peters.

'Now we're ready to depart this damn town,' he grunted as his cruel eyes surveyed the outrage. 'We're done here.'

The outlaws gathered around their leader as he savoured the expensive cigar between his teeth. None of the band could figure out Carson. He was like a stick of dynamite with its fuse lit. The trouble was they had no idea how long his fuse actually was.

'Was you figuring on bedding either of them females, Bill?' Kane wondered as he pulled on his dust coat again.

'Nope.' Carson waved the fine Havana around and said dryly, 'I have my fun when the killing and robbing is done and dusted. You should do the same if'n you intend staying alive long enough to spend your share of the loot.'

Peters looked anxious to leave. 'Let's get out of here, Bill. I got me a real bad feeling about this town.'

'OK,' Carson blew smoke into Brand's face before turning and staring at Kane. 'Ready the horses, boy.'

Kane did not argue. He ran from the room and headed out into the back yard.

There was no talking in the large living room for a few moments as Carson walked thoughtfully around the banker. He stared down at the gash across the back of Hardwick's scalp and the pool of blood which now encircled the head.

'You, Luke and Amos take the saddle-bags out to the horses,' he told

Poke Peters through cigar smoke. 'Tie all three of the saddle-bags to my horse, Poke. Two to the cantle and one across the saddle horn.'

'You want me to laden your horse down with all of the saddle-bags, Bill?' Peters checked as he picked the hefty bags off the floor and the Brand siblings did the same. 'These bags are a real load for one horse.'

'You heard me, Poke,' he drawled before eyeing them all in turn and then striding toward the back door. 'Strap all three of them saddle-bags to my horse.'

The outlaws trailed Carson out into the bright yard.

'Have you checked the cinch straps?' Carson asked Kane.

Kane nodded. 'Yep, I checked them all.'

Bill Carson tightened his gloves over his knuckles and then pulled the cigar from his lips. He tossed the spent smoke aside, grabbed his long leathers and poked his boot into the stirrup.

'Mount up, boys,' he hissed as he

looped his leg over the saddle and then gathered up his reins. 'We'll be long gone before anyone knows we were ever here.'

'Where we headed, Bill?' Peters asked as he mounted his high-shouldered gelding.

'We're off to a place call Dry Gulch, Poke,' Carson replied before backing his mount away from the large house.

'Dry Gulch?' Amos Brand repeated. 'What in tarnation are we headed there for? That's in the middle of the desert, ain't it?'

Carson nodded and then pulled the brim of his Stetson down to shield his eyes. 'Yep, it sure is.'

'But how come we're going there?' Kane wondered as he swung his horse around.

'Coz the Deacon told me to go there,' Carson answered dryly. 'And I always listen to the Deacon.'

'How come?' Kane asked. 'Is he the boss?'

'Nope, he's the brains,' Carson corrected.

The five horsemen steered their mounts out from the yard into the blazing sunlight.

# 7

The shadows were getting shorter with every beat of Kid Palomino's heart as he led Red and Charlie across the wide main street and up an alley. It was hot as the bowels of hell and getting hotter. The young deputy knew that the winding alley cut through the numerous wooden and brick structures and led to the side street. Shafts of blinding sunlight burned down on to the exposed confines with a merciless determination that Palomino had grown used to in this part of Fargo.

He pulled the brim of his hat down to shield his face from the hot rays he knew could strip skin from bone. The heat within the alley grew more intense. Sweat ran freely from every pore in his tall frame. He was soaked as though he had been caught in a downpour of rain. Yet no rain tasted like the beads of sweat that negotiated his chiselled

73

features and found his lips.

Palomino licked the salty residue from his lips and glanced back to his fellow lawmen as they tried to keep pace with his long, lean legs.

The Kid rested against a brick wall at the end of the alley, cocked the Winchester and stared out into the blazing street.

By his calculations Hardwick and his three heavily laden companions would have to pass this way in a few moments. As he waited Red and the old timer caught up with him.

'Why'd you stop, Palomino?' Charlie asked as he bent double and sucked in air. 'The way you was moving I figured you wouldn't stop until you got the drop on them fellas.'

Palomino dried his face with his shirt sleeve and screwed up his eyes against the sun which reflected off the white sand at their feet.

'I seen old Hardwick and them strangers turn the corner near the bank,' the Kid sighed heavily. 'I figured they were headed this way.'

'You reckoning on stopping them *hombres* in their tracks, Kid?' Red said as he clutched the repeating rifle to his chest in readiness.

Palomino nodded. 'Yep.'

Old Charlie edged out from the corner and squinted hard into the quiet thoroughfare.

'Are you sure this is the way they was headed, Palomino?' he asked. 'I sure can't see or hear them.'

The face of the young deputy looked long and hard at the old lawman and then pulled him back into the alley. Palomino poked his head around the corner and cautiously stared into the street himself.

Charlie was right. None of the four men they hoped to get the drop on were anywhere to be seen. The Kid returned to the alley and frowned.

'Charlie's right, Red,' the Kid muttered.

'What you talking about?' Red asked Palomino. He had seen the totally baffled look on Palomino's face many times before and it troubled him. He moved closer to his pal. 'You look like a dog that's just lost a bone.'

'I've lost four bones, Red,' Palomino mumbled as he stroked the rifle in his hands thoughtfully. 'Take a look if you don't believe me. They're gone.'

'I mean them galoots ain't there,' Palomino added.

'I told you they weren't there,' Charlie nodded. 'They've up and vanished, Red.'

'They can't be gone.' It seemed impossible to Red as he brushed both his companions aside and carefully peeked around the corner wall into the street. His jaw dropped in utter bewilderment. 'Hell, they are gone.'

'I told you that already,' Charlie nodded.

'Where in tarnation are they?' Red blurted.

Palomino glanced at the sturdy deputy. 'Damned if I know where they are, Red. All I know is that they ain't where they should be.'

Red stared blankly into Palomino's

baffled face. 'How could they just disappear like that, Kid? That ain't natural.'

Palomino rubbed the sweat off his mouth.

'I thought I knew this town like the back of my hand but them varmints with old Stan have just up and vanished into thin air,' the Kid said in disbelief. 'That ain't possible.'

'Are you boys sure that you seen old Stan and them tall gun-toting varmints leaving the bank, Kid?' Charlie asked his younger companion.

'What in tarnation are you gabby about?' Red leaned over the skinny star-packer. 'You seen them too, Charlie. We all seen them.'

The ancient lawman shook his head and waved his finger under the nose of the deputy. 'I didn't see 'em.'

'You must have,' Palomino looked at the feisty old timer. 'You was standing right next to us. I seen them and so did Red. You must have seen them, Charlie.'

'Hell, I couldn't even see the bank

from the sheriff's porch, boy,' Charlie admitted, pointing to his eyes. 'Not with these peepers. All I saw was a blur. All I ever see lately is damn blurs.'

Palomino rested his hand on Red's shoulder. 'I know what I saw and I saw Hardwick and three heavily armed galoots toting saddle-bags.'

Red nodded. 'I seen them too, Kid.'

Kid Palomino bit his lip as his mind raced in search of an answer to the puzzle it was wrestling with. 'They headed this way. That's why I chose to use this alleyway as a shortcut. I figured on getting ahead of them.'

Red rubbed his neck and stepped out into the quiet street as his eyes vainly searched every dwelling and store front for a clue as to where the three unknown men and Hardwick might have gone. Finally he shook his head and rested the Winchester barrel against his temple.

'This is plumb loco,' he growled. 'There ain't no stores along this street that open at this ungodly hour, Kid.

Them *hombres* must have gone some-place else with Stan.'

'But where did they go, Red?' Palomino wondered as he tucked his rifle under his arm.

Charlie Summers shook his head and started to turn. 'I'm headed back to the office and get me some shuteye, boys. You figure it out and then come and wake me.'

Palomino grabbed the scrawny shoul-der of the veteran lawman and pulled him back. 'You ain't going nowhere, Charlie. Not until we find them critters and ask them what they was doing in the bank.'

Charlie looked at the tall deputy. 'Sheriff Lomax will be back soon, Kid. I gotta go and tidy the office before he rides in. That critter is damn fussy, you know.'

Palomino and Red looked at one another and then at the far smaller man. They grinned at the cantankerous old timer.

'You're gonna tidy the office?' Red

repeated his words. 'Exactly how are you gonna do that, Charlie?'

Charlie thought for a moment and then wryly smiled. 'I'm gonna mosey on back and dust the office. The sheriff is partial to a good dusting.'

'Sure he is,' Red chuckled.

Palomino released his grip. 'Go on then, Charlie. Go dust the office while me and Red start looking for Stan and them *hombres*.'

Charlie was about to do as he was told when they all three of them heard the muffled sound of hoofs. Palomino glanced at his two pals and looked around them.

'Do you hear that, boys?' Charlie asked.

'I heard that, Charlie,' Red confirmed as he stepped to the corner and glanced around the empty street. 'I hear horses but where in tarnation are they?'

Kid Palomino bit his lower lip and rested his knuckles on his gun grips. 'Where'd you figure they are?'

The veteran lawman ambled between his two younger companions and squinted hard. Although his eyes could no longer see as they had once done, his hearing was still as sharp as ever. He squinted hard at the mass of trees fifty feet from where they stood. He raised a scrawny finger and pointed.

'Them horses are somewhere over yonder, boys,' he told the deputies. 'I can hear about three or maybe more horses. Can you see them yet?'

Palomino pulled his hat brim down to shield his eyes.

'I reckon you're right, Charlie. It sure sounds like horses walking beyond them trees,' he agreed.

Red shook his head. 'I can't see a thing.'

Palomino frowned.

'Charlie's right, Red,' he said. 'Them horses we can hear are halfway down the street someplace.'

Red slapped his thigh in frustration with himself. 'Damn it all. That's where they built a few real fancy houses for the rich folks, Kid. I plumb forgot about it.'

Before either Palomino or Charlie could reply, Bill Carson led his four hired gunmen out from the confines of the well-hidden alleyway into the side street. As the infamous outlaw turned his head he saw the three star-packers and pulled back on his long leathers. His mount stopped as his four fellow outlaws trailed him into the bright sunshine.

'What you looking at, Bill?' Peters asked as he halted his own horse beside Carson's tall mount.

Carson did not speak. He simply raised a finger and pointed at the three lawmen watching them. The outlaws sat in their saddles and gazed through the shimmering heat haze to where Palomino and his pals were standing.

'Them's lawmen,' Luke Brand spat.

'They're packing repeating rifles, Bill,' Kane added.

'You said they were out of town.' Amos Brand steadied his nervous mount.

Bill Carson shook his head.

'They're meant to be out of town, boys,' he hissed.

Kid Palomino stepped forward. His eyes narrowed as they focused on the lead rider. Carson pulled his reins to his belly and stared along the street at them. The ruthless outlaw had never seen any of the three standing men before but it was not their faces that had drawn his interest.

It was the tin stars pinned to their chests that Carson was looking at. They were gleaming like precious gems across the distance between them. Carson looped the reins around his saddle horn and then slowly placed his hands on his pair of pearl-handled Remingtons.

'What we gonna do, Bill?' Kane asked his merciless leader.

'There's only one thing we can do, Kane,' Carson said in a low whisper as his fingers curled around the holstered guns. 'Lawmen are like Injuns and they say the only good'uns are dead'uns. The same applies to star-packing bastards like them critters.'

83

Poke Peters moved his horse to the head of Carson's. 'I like your thinking, Bill. Ain't nothing more satisfying than killing lawmen.'

The mind of Kid Palomino was racing like a locomotive under a full head of steam. He focused hard on the lead rider and then realized who he was looking at. He looked to both his companions in turn.

'That's Bill Carson, boys,' Palomino stated confidently as he pulled the Winchester from under his arm and readied it for action. 'I've seen his wanted poster a hundred times over the last few years.'

Before either Red or Charlie could respond to the Kid's statement they noticed the horsemen suddenly swing their mounts violently around to face them. As dust rose from the hoofs of the five animals the air began to crackle with fiery lead as the outlaws suddenly unleashed their arsenal on the trio of lawmen.

Red hot tapers cut through the shimmering haze and whizzed by the law officers. Palomino dragged the old man behind a water trough as Red took refuge in a doorway.

Within a few moments the street became deafening as the outlaws kept firing their guns at them. Chunks of wood were ripped from the rim of the trough and flew up into the air. At the same time the side of the doorframe where Red had taken refuge also began to disintegrate as bullets tore into its lumber.

Red pressed his back against the door. He waited for a brief lull in the vicious attack and then blasted his Winchester at the outlaws. Yet for every shot he managed to fire at Carson and his gang, at least six bullets were returned. Red was trapped and he knew it. Bullets continued to gnaw away at the wall beside Red's shoulder until he was covered in burning sawdust.

Crouching behind the cover of the water trough, Kid Palomino and the startled old timer were also pinned down.

'This is getting serious, Kid,' Charlie piped up.

'I'm starting to get mighty riled.'

Kid patted the veteran lawman on his skinny shoulder.

'Don't get riled, Charlie,' he said from the corner of his mouth. 'I'll try to fend the bastards off.'

The young deputy primed his rifle and then moved around the side of the trough. He fired repeatedly until the Winchester's magazine was empty and then moved back beside Charlie.

'They're still shooting at us, Kid,' the old man sighed and exchanged rifles with his companion. 'Here, use this'un.'

'Thanks, Charlie.' Palomino cranked its mechanism.

Just as he was about to turn and fire another volley of lethal lead at the outlaws he felt a scrawny hand grip his arm. He looked at the whiskered face.

'Try and hit some of them this time,' Charlie said.

'I'll do my best,' the Kid answered as another barrage of bullets ripped into the fabric of the water trough. 'You can reload my rifle for me.'

As the older lawman started to remove bullets from his gunbelt and push them into the rifle's magazine, Palomino turned and rested on both knees. The blinding sun mixed with the ever increasing smoke coming from the outlaw's gun barrels made it tough for even his young eyes to find a target but the Kid was determined to try.

Flashes of deafening gunfire lit up the eerie street and drilled into the trough as Palomino gripped the Winchester firmly and raised its metal barrel. He focused along the gun sights at the fiery flashes and then fired.

Within seconds bullets came at him from the riders' arsenal of six-shooters. The ground around the trough was peppered with lead. A cloud of choking dust flew up and forced Palomino to retreat to the side of the grumbling old timer.

'You'd best start killing them varmints before they kill us, Kid,' Charlie sniffed.

'I'm trying, old timer.' Palomino rubbed the dust from his face as they felt the trough behind their backs rock under the deadly onslaught.

Charlie raised his bushy eyebrows. 'Try harder.'

Flabbergasted by his elderly pal's attitude, Palomino decided to try harder. He crawled over the skinny legs of the old lawman and immediately started firing the rifle from the opposite corner of the trough.

Shafts of lead criss-crossed the length of the street. The outlaws had the three star-packers trapped and they knew it. Slowly they began to edge their mounts closer to their cornered targets. The entire street was engulfed in red-hot tapers and enough noise to shatter eardrums.

Palomino exhausted his rifle's ammunition and crawled back to Charlie's side. He thrust the smoking rifle into the old timer's hands and grabbed the fully loaded weapon.

Red fired three swift shots from his place of cover. Then he was forced back behind the bullet-ridden wall as every one of the horsemen fired at him.

'Are you OK, Red?' the Kid yelled out above the relentless din of gunfire.

'I think so,' Red gasped as yet another half-dozen shots tore even more of the wooden door frame apart.

'I've had me enough of this, Charlie.' Kid Palomino cranked the hand guard of his rifle and then swiftly swung around and began to empty its venom at the approaching horsemen. 'Now I'm getting darn sore at Carson and his gang.'

Charlie Summers clapped his hands. 'Hallelujah! Now maybe we'll send them bastards to Boot Hill.'

Bullets ripped into the trough that the Kid was shielded behind. Water sprayed up over the defiant deputy as he continued to fire his Winchester at the horsemen.

The toxic mix of gunsmoke and hoof dust did not make the task of hitting any of the targets Palomino had chosen to shoot at any easier. Yet the simple matter that he could not see any of the outlaws did not deter Palomino.

The Kid knew that if you couldn't see the men you were aiming at you looked for the bright flashes their six-guns spewed out. His eyes narrowed as he quickly blasted the Winchester every time they fired their guns.

His lethal accuracy began to pay off. He heard one of Carson's men yelp like a kicked hound.

Red stepped out on to the boardwalk and fired his own rifle into the men masked by choking gunsmoke.

'Get behind the trough, Red,' Palomino urged as he continued to fire the smoking rifle into the depths of the dust cloud. 'Take cover with Charlie.'

'Quit gabbing and start picking them varmints off, Kid,' Red said as he fired from the boardwalk.

Then the five riders emerged from the dust. Their mounts reared up in terror as their masters blasted more and more bullets at the lawmen.

One bullet ripped the hat from Red's head and he doubled in pain. He fell on to his knees and clutched his head and crawled back to the doorframe.

With the sound of firing still echoing

in his ears, Red stared at the blood on his gloved hand. He rested on one knee and began reloading the smoking rifle.

'I've bin grazed, Kid,' Red shouted.

'It's a good job you ain't my height, Red.' Palomino leapt over the trough and crouched down at its side as he exchanged his empty Winchester for the one Charlie had just reloaded.

Charlie tugged on Palomino's sleeve. He drew the youngster's attention.

'I'm all out of bullets, boy,' the elderly lawman said. 'Make 'em count.'

'I'll try my best.' Palomino checked his own belt. He had only a few bullets remaining himself. He then inspected his handguns and shook his head. He hadn't reloaded the two matched Colts since last using them. He had only three fresh bullets in the weapon's dozen chambers. 'Reckon I'll have to stop missing, huh?'

'Good,' Charlie sighed rolling his eyes. 'At this rate we'll end up throwing rocks at them.'

Palomino cranked the hand guard. A

spent casing flew from the rifle's magazine as the deputy raised the Winchester and eased its stock into the groove of his shoulder.

Carson's men suddenly transferred their lethal lead in Red's direction. Window panes shattered sending fragments of glass all over the boardwalk. Lumps of wood were torn from the side of the door frame forcing Red to press his backbone against the door.

'Keep drawing their fire, Red,' Palomino shouted as he levelled the rifle and rested its hot barrel on the rim of the trough. 'Keep drawing their fire.'

Within only a few heart-stopping moments the air was thick with acrid gunsmoke as Palomino tried to hit the horsemen who were shielded by the swirling mist. Shot after shot came at the Kid as he held his nerve and waited for a clear target.

Then he saw one of the Brand brothers emerge from the dense smoke. As Amos Brand sat on his nervous gelding and forced fresh bullets into the magazine of his carbine, Palomino squeezed gently on his trigger.

The rifle shuddered in his hands as a flash of flames and smoke erupted from the Winchester's barrel. As he rocked on his knees he knew that he had finally hit one of them.

Amos Brand lifted off his saddle and crashed heavily into the dry sand between the other horses. Palomino pushed the hand guard down and then dragged it back up. Another metal casing flew over his shoulder as the young deputy squinted through the heat haze and smoke at the lifeless body upon the sand.

'Good shot, Kid,' Red praised.

The lawman was about to smile when he heard the nerve-shattering noise only grief can muster. Palomino swallowed hard but his throat was dry. There was no spittle. He glanced down at Charlie.

'What in tarnation is that, Kid?' the old lawman asked.

'I ain't too sure,' Palomino answered.

Then another sound filled the street. It was pounding hoofs as a horse came thundering out of the mist and was being driven straight toward them.

Kid Palomino stared straight into the eyes of Luke Brand as he got closer and closer. The outlaw was fuelled by rage and grief unlike anything the deputy had ever witnessed before.

'Holy smoke,' Palomino gasped as he watched the rider lash his long leathers across the tail of his horse and charge away from Carson and his cronies toward the trough.

Red tried to fire his rifle but its red-hot mechanism jammed. The deputy screamed at Palomino.

'Kill him, Kid,' Red called out as another volley of bullets bore down on him.

Charlie poked Palomino in the ribs. 'You heard him, boy. Kill that varmint before he kills us.'

The unearthly sound of revenge had burned into Palomino's mind like a branding iron. He had never heard anything like it before. Brand's vocal curses echoed around the street. Desperately Palomino raised the rifle to his shoulder again but it was too late.

Luke Brand suddenly burst through the dust with his six-gun blazing. Obeying its rider's thrusting spurs, the horse jumped and cleared the water trough. The outstretched hoofs of the outlaw's mount hit the rifle clean out of Palomino's hands. The Kid ducked as the hefty horse and rider landed just beyond the startled deputy. Brand dragged his reins back and charged at Palomino. The startled lawman was knocked violently off his feet and careered headlong across the sand as the avenging outlaw fired down from his high perch.

Palomino came to an abrupt halt when he hit the edge of the boardwalk. He shook the dust from his face and rubbed the blood away from his grazed features. To his horror he watched as the horse cornered and blocked his escape as Brand straddled the gelding and reloaded his smoking six-shooter.

'You're gonna pay for killing my brother, boy,' Brand snarled at the dazed young Palomino. 'Pay with your life.'

Still unable to see anything but a colourful blur, the old lawman staggered up off the ground beside the trough and squinted hard at the snarling rider. Charlie knew that the Kid was in trouble and needed help.

'Quit yelling like a dried-up old school-marm,' the veteran shouted as his hand found his holstered old six-shooter and pulled it clear. 'If'n you wanna shout at someone, shout at me.'

Luke Brand pushed the reloaded cylinder back into the heart of the smoking gun and secured it. His eyes glanced back at the intrepid old man as Charlie pulled on his trigger and unleashed a rod of deafening flame.

The bullet passed well over the horseman's head.

'That was your last mistake, old man.' Brand's thumb pulled back on his hammer and then aimed his .45 at Charlie. He fired and watched as the skinny remnant of a once sturdy lawman staggered and fell backward. A wave of water lashed over the sides of the trough as the old man sank into its shallow depths.

The water in the trough turned a sickening shade of scarlet. Only bubbles escaped the watery tomb.

It seemed like an eternity to the bruised and battered Palomino but it had been less than sixty seconds since Brand's horse had leapt over the trough and crashed into him. The dust still hung in the bright sunshine as it had not had time to settle.

Blood trickled from Palomino's mouth as it slowly dawned on his dazed mind what had just happened. His attempts to get up off the sand were futile as Brand's horse crashed into his already bloodied body. No matter how desperately he attempted to get back on to his feet, the outlaw denied him. The sturdy quarter horse lowered its head and knocked Palomino off his feet again.

Palomino glanced at the trough. The old lawman was nowhere to be seen. Then he recalled the shot and sound of splashing and realized where his cantankerous pal was.

'Charlie,' the Kid called out. There was no reply.

With blood running from his nose and mouth, Palomino attempted to find his pair of match six-shooters. The horse was unwilling for its master's prey to succeed. The Kid raised his arms to shield himself from further injury as the powerful horse reared up and lashed out with its hoofs. Every instinct in Palomino's soul wanted to fight but he was reduced to merely defending his already battered body.

The young deputy was forced into a huddle as his hands searched for his guns. Then the snorting horse lowered its head and butted him. He coughed and spat blood at the sand as he tried to escape the continuous attack.

The sound of haunting laughter rained down on him. He glanced up at the face of Luke Brand. The horseman was determined to make him pay for killing his brother and Palomino knew that his death would not be swift. Brand intended to draw every scrap of life from his victim before he finally killed him.

The Kid managed to force himself up to his feet but his victory was short-lived. Brand drove his spurs into the flanks of his horse and the animal charged into Palomino. The deputy crashed down against the rim of the boardwalk. He fell on to his face and gasped for air as the devilish Luke Brand levelled his weapon at him.

'You ready to die, star-packer?' Brand's words dragged the Kid back into consciousness. He stared up with glazed eyes at the horseman as Brand added, 'Are you busted up enough?'

'I've had worse,' Palomino lied as he felt the horse's breath on his grazed face. His mind raced to find a way to turn the tables on the outlaw. No matter how hard he searched for a solution, all he could do was stare into the gun barrel trained on him.

No cat had ever tormented a mouse

quite as much as Brand mocked Palomino. All thoughts of avenging his brother had vanished from the outlaw's mind. Now Luke Brand was content to keep torturing his helpless victim to the very last drop of the deputy's blood.

'I've got me six bullets in this hog-leg, boy,' Brand snarled. 'I reckon I'll use every damn one of them before finishing you off.'

Kid Palomino had been in quite a few tough scrapes in his life but none of them like this. His eyes narrowed and stared up at the face of the horseman as he heard the hammer being locked into position once more.

'That's fine with me,' Palomino sighed heavily.

'Say your prayers, star-packer,' Brand growled as his finger curled around his trigger and aimed down at his trapped prey. 'This is for killing my brother Amos.'

Once again time appeared to have come to a standstill as the Kid stared up at the still-smoking gun barrel that was aimed at his head. His hand wiped the blood from his face and he defiantly looked at the man who intended to be his executioner.

'Are you sure you don't wanna get a tad closer to me?' Kid Palomino forced a pained laugh. 'I'd hate for you to miss.'

Brand's expression changed as a storm fermented inside his ruthless guts. His hand was shaking with rage.

'I'll wipe that smile off your face with lead.'

'Shoot then,' Palomino spat. 'I ain't scared.'

A gruesome smile etched the outlaw's face as he leaned his bulk over the neck of his horse.

'Anything to oblige,' Brand hissed.

A thunderous shot echoed along the street.

# 8

The sound of a shot rang out in the street and echoed off the surrounding structures. Palomino had gritted his teeth as he awaited death, yet death did not visit the young deputy. The Grim Reaper had chosen another target for his inevitable wrath. The startled Kid watched as the outlaw arched on his saddle and gave a sickening grunt.

The gun curled on his finger and hung for a few moments as the sound of the solitary shot resonated in the Kid's ears. Then it fell from Brand's trigger finger and landed upon the churned-up sand as the brutalized horse backed away from Palomino.

Confusion filled the deputy's mind. He watched as the outlaw rocked on his saddle. Palomino steadied himself and stared at the outlaw. Brand's expression was one he had seen many times during his life as a lawman. It was the look only death can paint upon a face.

Hollow eyes looked down with unseeing bewilderment at the bullet hole in his chest. Blood squirted from the devilishly accurate wound in the middle of his chest as Brand slowly slid off his high-shouldered mount. The outlaw hit the ground yet one of his boots remained hooked in the stirrup. The skittish horse cantered down the street, dragging Brand beside it until the boot finally was pulled from the foot.

Palomino watched as Brand rolled like a rag doll on the sun-drenched sand before coming to a rest.

Red staggered through the gunsmoke and dropped down beside his young pal. He holstered his six-gun and then helped Palomino to his feet before glancing across at his handiwork.

'Don't look so damn surprised, Kid,' the older deputy said as he moved to the lifeless Brand and kicked sand in his face before returning to his pal. 'I told you that I could shoot.'

Palomino looked up at his friend.

'I sure wish you'd done that a whole lot earlier, Red,' the Kid sighed as he rubbed his aching ribs. 'I almost got kicked to death.'

Red raised his hands and shrugged. 'My damn rifle jammed, Kid. I tried to draw my gun but Carson and them two other varmints had me penned in.'

Palomino shielded his eyes against the sun and stared down the street. Only the body of Amos Brand remained beside his horse. Carson and his hired guns were gone.

'Carson high-tailed it?' he asked.

'Yep, they just whipped their horse's tails and rode on out of here a couple of minutes back,' Red replied as he looked all around them and then rubbed the nape of his neck. 'Where's Charlie?'

The Kid's eyes widened as horror etched his face.

'Hell!' Palomino swung on his boot leather and ran to the trough. He stared down into the murky water and felt panic overwhelm his bruised form. 'Help me get him out of here.'

Red rapidly moved to the opposite side of the trough and reached down into the water. They gripped the old man's arms and legs then fished him out.

Ignoring his own painful injuries, Palomino carefully scooped the bedraggled Charlie up in his arms and steadied himself. He forced himself away from the trough and started along the blisteringly hot street.

'I'm taking Charlie to the doc's,' the Kid gasped.

'What happened, Kid?' Red asked as Palomino staggered with the limp body in his arms. 'How'd Charlie get in there?'

The young deputy continued walking as best he could. 'This brave old critter tried to draw that bastard's fire away from me, Red.'

'Holy cow.' Red trailed his friend toward the home of Fargo's only medical man. 'Charlie sure drew that varmint's fire OK. He looks dead to me.'

The younger deputy's eyes darted at

his pal. There was a fire burning within them.

'Charlie ain't dead,' the Kid insisted before adding, 'not until the doc says he's dead anyway.'

Red did not dare utter another word. He knew that Palomino was right. Nobody was truly dead until the doc said so.

Kid Palomino kept walking even though every sinew in his bruised and bleeding frame told him that it was useless. He knew that if Charlie had not drawn Brand's attention away from himself for those precious few seconds, the outlaw would have simply shot him as he had intended.

As they reached the small house at the end of Fargo's main thoroughfare Palomino sucked in air, stepped up on to the rickety boardwalk and kicked the small gate off its hinges.

The shooting had awoken most of the town's citizens but Doc Black's front door was still shut. The Kid paused and was about to kick it out of its frame when it swung open and the elderly medic ushered him into the building.

Red rested his wrists on the picket fence and stared silently into the darkened interior of the wooden structure. After what felt like a lifetime, the Kid wandered back out into the sunshine.

Red rubbed his unshaven jaw and watched as Palomino brushed past him and sat down on the edge of the walkway. The young deputy looked down at the sand at his feet but said nothing.

It was obvious to Red that he had been correct about Charlie, but not to his young pal. Palomino had to have time to let the truth sink in. The older deputy was about to speak when the sound of movement behind his broad shoulders drew his attention back to the small house. Red turned and stared at the old medical man as he approached the open door and looked straight at him.

The grim face of the doc answered the question that was burning in his craw. Doc Black shook his head and then sorrowfully closed his door.

'Charlie's gone, Kid,' Red sighed heavily.

Seated on the dusty boards, Palomino nodded in acceptance of the gruesome fact. He then got back to his feet and exhaled loudly.

'C'mon, Red.'

'Where we going?'

Palomino paused and looked straight at his friend's face.

'We're going to get our horses,' he snorted. 'We got some outlaws to round up. We got a score to settle.'

Even though Red knew that they should wait for Sheriff Lomax to return to Fargo, he also knew by experience that it was never wise to argue with Kid Palomino.

Not when he was hurting and the Kid was hurting real bad.

As they made their way back to their awaiting horses outside the sheriff's office, Palomino stopped and stared to where they had first set eyes on Bill Carson and his hirelings.

'I reckon we'd best go check on Stan Hardwick, Red,' the Kid said. 'Him and his ladies might need our help.'

Neither Palomino nor Red could imagine the horror they were about to find as they casually strode up to the elegant house and entered.

Their gruesome discovery only a few moments later within the confines of the banker's home would spur both battle-weary lawmen to avenge the shocking outrage. They retraced their steps and paused in the rear yard for a few moments. They looked as though every drop of colour had been drained from their faces.

The Kid glanced at Red. 'Let's get back to the office and get our horses ready.'

The older man nodded. 'I'll call in the funeral parlour on the way, Kid. He can sort this mess out.'

Palomino tightened his gloves.

'I'll leave a note pinned to the billboard for the sheriff,' he drawled angrily as he vainly tried to dismiss the sight that was branded into his mind.

'I'll tell him where we're headed and ask him to rustle up a posse to follow.'

Red nodded and thought about the brutal slayings they had just discovered. 'How can anyone do something like that, Kid?'

'I don't know,' Palomino answered. 'But I swear by all that's holy, Carson and his boys will never do nothing like this again, Red.'

Both lawman headed back into the heart of Fargo.

# 9

The sight that had greeted the deputies had chilled them to the bone. Neither lawman had ever seen anything like the savagery they had discovered in the home of the banker. It was clear to Palomino that the notorious Bill Carson was probably far worse than even the law realized. The Kid wondered how many other times had Carson simply dispatched all the witnesses to his lurid crimes in a similar fashion, so that they could never be linked to him.

Palomino hooked his stirrup over the horn of his saddle and tightened the cinch strap as his fellow deputy came out of the office with two fully loaded Winchesters and a box of cartridges. He stepped down into the sunshine and slid one of the rifles into the mount's saddle scabbard. He lifted the leather flap of his saddle-bags and pushed the ammunition into the satchel.

The Kid lowered his fender and caught the repeating rifle his pal threw to him. He pushed the gleaming barrel into his own scabbard and then looked over his high-shouldered stallion.

'Are we ready?' he asked Rivers as he pulled his long leathers free of the hitching pole.

'We got us a few extra canteens of water and some vittles,' Red replied as he patted his quarter horse and ducked under its reins. 'We got rifles and enough bullets to fend off the 7th cavalry.'

'That should do.' Kid backed the palomino stallion away from the office and then grabbed the horse's cream-coloured mane and stepped into the stirrup. He mounted in one fluid action and then gathered up his loose reins and watched as his friend duplicated his actions.

Palomino leaned on to his saddle horn and stared at the now busy street that faced them. He tilted his head and looked at his partner.

'Which way did them bastards head, Red?' he asked.

Red pointed. 'They was headed for the desert, Kid.'

Palomino grimaced and then sighed, 'The desert is gonna be mighty hot at this time of day but I reckon I know it a whole lot better than they do.'

'It ain't even noon yet, boy,' Red remarked. 'That desert is gonna get hotter than hell before it starts to calm down again.'

The Kid patted the neck of his handsome horse and shrugged as he steadied the powerful animal beneath his saddle.

'As long as we've got enough water for these horses I ain't worried, Red,' he stated firmly.

'You figure we can catch up with them *hombres?*' Red asked as he swung the quarter horse around and trotted to the side of his friend. 'They've got a mighty good start on us, Kid.'

Palomino nodded. 'Yep. We'll catch

up with them though.'

Both horsemen glanced around the wooden structures and the tall red brick bank before steadying themselves on their hot saddles. It was something they always did without even knowing that they were doing it. It was as though they were taking a last look at the settlement in case they never returned from their often perilous missions.

'Nugget's ready,' Palomino told his pal.

Red leaned over the neck of his mount. 'Are you ready, Derby?'

The quarter horse shook its head. Both men raised their eyebrows and gave out a mutual yell. The horses thundered through the shimmering heat haze in the direction that Red had pointed to a few moments before.

The determined duo stood in their stirrups and thundered between the countless people who now filled the street as the sun slowly rose in the cloudless blue heavens.

It would get hotter, just like they

figured. Hotter than hell in more ways than anyone might imagine before the day was through.

# 10

The rattling chains of the stagecoach echoed off the scattering of buildings, which were known collectively as Dry Gulch. Those who were not sleeping during the unrelenting sunshine sat on weathered hardback chairs and pondered the shadows that slowly indicated the passing of time. Dry Gulch was a place that only survived at the edge of the desert because of its deep wells and crystal clear water. Yet the overwhelming heat had always kept the population to a bare minimum.

Shaded by porch overhangs the onlookers puffed on pipes and watched as the Overland Stage came to an abrupt halt outside the solitary saloon. The Busted Wheel was by far the largest building within the confines of Dry Gulch. It oozed a powerful aroma of stale perfume, spilled liquor and tobacco smoke.

The driver beat the dust off his clothing and wrapped his reins around the brakepole. He leaned over, looked down at the side of the coach and bellowed.

'Dry Gulch.'

The carriage door opened and the well-dressed Deacon disembarked with elegant ease. He held his ivory-topped cane under his arm as the driver handed down his canvas bag.

'Thank you, driver,' he said touching the brim of his hat and turning to face the large saloon. 'Do they have rooms to rent here?'

'Yep, and they also got females to rent as well,' the driver chuckled and then carefully descended to the board-walk and pushed his way past the man who looked like a gambler in his rush to quench his thirst.

Danby Deacon smiled to himself and then followed the bearded stagecoach driver into the saloon. The smell greeted him before his eyes adjusted to the far dimmer interior. It was in total contrast to the blazing sun of the street. The driver had already finished his first whiskey before Deacon had walked across the sawdust-covered floor.

The bartender looked long and hard at the elegant Deacon as he slowly walked with bag in one hand and the other swinging his cane to match his stride.

'What in hell is that?' the bartender asked the driver as he poured the thirsty man another full glass of whiskey.

The driver glanced over his shoulder at Deacon and then returned his attention to the glass in his hand.

'A gambler,' he sniffed as he filled his mouth with the fiery liquor and swallowed. 'Picked him up in Cherokee Springs. Why in hell anyone would wanna come here beats me.'

The scrawny bartender shook his head as he polished a glass with his apron bib.

'He sure looks awful neat, even for a gambler,' he remarked. 'I ain't ever seen a gambler look quite so neat before. It just ain't natural.'

'And he's a lousy poker player, Hyram,' the driver noted. 'I sure don't know where he gets his money from 'coz it ain't from being able to play cards.'

A wry smile came to the bartender's face. 'That's mighty interesting. I might challenge the dude to a few games of stud.'

'He dresses up a storm though.' The driver sighed. 'He's got himself a gold stick pin holding down his bib.'

Danby Deacon reached the bar counter, glanced at the stagecoach driver and smiled.

'Cravat, my good man. It's called a cravat,' Deacon corrected and patted the dusty driver on the back. He coughed as a cloud of trail dust wafted over the counter and then placed a fifty dollar gold piece down on its wooden surface. 'A bottle of your best sipping whiskey and a box of your finest cigars. If this establishment has such items.'

'We got 'em, mister,' the bartender said.

The driver looked at Deacon. 'That's a lot of whiskey for one man to guzzle on his lonesome.'

Deacon nodded in agreement. 'Two bottles of whiskey, barkeep. One for my friend here.'

The stagecoach driver beamed. 'Well thank you kindly.'

'My pleasure.' Deacon looked at the bartender as the man placed two bottles of amber liquor down on the wet surface and then plucked a box of cigars from a shelf at his side. 'Anything else, mister?'

Deacon smiled and glanced around the tobacco-stained interior of the Busted Wheel. 'Where are the whores?'

Both men chuckled.

'They'll be here soon enough, dude.' The driver winked as he picked up one of the bottles and tucked it under his coat and turned on his heels. Deacon watched the driver sway as he walked back toward the bright street. 'You'll smell them before you see them.'

Danby Deacon turned to the man

who was still polishing glasses on the other side of the counter.

'Where's he going?' he asked the bartender.

'He's got to drive the stage to Poison Flats.'

Deacon rubbed his jaw. 'He's going to drive a six-horse team in that condition?'

'Hell, he can drive even when he's sober,' the lean bartender replied before testing the gold coin with his teeth and then pocketing it.

Deacon raised his eyebrows. 'Keep the change.'

'I already have.'

# 11

The tracks left by the Carson gang's horses' hoofs were easily followed in and around Fargo but the further north they ventured toward the arid desert, the harder it was for the intrepid pair of deputies to follow. Every mark left in the white sand soon disappeared. It was so fine and dry its granules filled in every impression a few seconds after it was made.

Yet somehow young Kid Palomino seemed to instinctively know where the three riders were headed. He kept encouraging the tall golden stallion beneath his saddle on, to the bewilderment of his pal.

'Admit it, Kid,' Red said nervously as he trailed his determined friend deeper into the unfamiliar terrain. 'Them *hombres* could have headed anywhere. We ain't got a chance of catching them.'

Palomino had been strangely quiet since they had discovered the bodies of Hardwick and the three females. The young deputy had a gritty determination festering in him that refused to even consider defeat. He glanced back at his pal and slowed his mount so the smaller horse could draw level with him.

'Stop fretting, Red,' he snapped. 'I know exactly where Carson and his men are headed. I figured it out before we even left Fargo.'

Red mopped the sweat from his face with the tails of his bandanna and exhaled loudly. 'I ain't calling you a liar, boy, but you ain't yourself. You're dripping with revenge and its messing with your head. Nobody could find them in this inferno. It just ain't possible.'

Palomino grinned. 'Nothing's impossible, Red.'

Red shook his head as the horses headed up a slight rise of soft sand. Both men had to stand in their stirrups and urge the lathered-up mounts up the slope. With every step an avalanche of loose sand rolled down the ridge they were climbing.

As the exhausted horses reached the flat top of the ridge they eased back on their reins and stopped the animals. The top of a dune offered them a panoramic view of the arid terrain they had doggedly ridden into. Yet wherever they cast their attention all they could see was a desolate ocean of golden sand. The distance was blurred by a curtain of boiling air that rippled and played tricks with their tired eyes, yet Palomino was still confident that he knew exactly where their prey had headed.

Red Rivers did not share his partner's enthusiasm. He was scared and it showed. The veteran lawman had faced many heavily armed outlaws in his career but the blistering sun and the arid landscape frightened him.

'We'd best turn back, Palomino,' Red sighed as he checked his canteens nervously. 'They ain't nowhere to be seen and we're running low on water.'

'Easy, Red,' the Kid said as he removed his hat briefly to wipe the sweat off his brow. 'I know where they've gone.'

A tormented expression filled Red's features. 'How can you tell which way they've gone? There ain't nothing out there but sand and nowhere to take cover from the sun. I'm as riled up as you are but I ain't hankering to commit suicide trying to catch them throat-cutting bastards. We just gotta head back to Fargo while there's still time.'

The Kid dismounted and dropped his hat on to the ground and then poured a good ration of water into the upturned bowl for his mount to drink. He stared at his friend who carefully slid from his saddle and watered his own mount.

'This is loco, Kid,' Red muttered as the horses drank their meagre ration of water. 'You're gonna get us killed on a hunch.'

With wisdom far beyond his years, Palomino scooped up his hat and returned it to his head and shrugged. The droplets of water trapped within the bowl felt good as they cooled him.

'I know exactly where they've gone,' Palomino said bluntly and then poked his boot in his stirrup and dragged himself back on to his saddle. He waited for his partner to do the same and then tapped his spurs against the creamy flanks of his mount. 'You coming or are you gonna turn-tail and ride back?'

Red thought for a moment and then urged his quarter horse to follow the majestic stallion of his friend. 'Hold up, Kid. I ain't finished gabbing yet.'

The younger deputy glanced at his partner. 'I've finished listening to you moaning and groaning, Red. I tell you I've figured out where they're headed and I'm headed there too.'

Red Rivers lifted his wet pants off the sweat-filled saddle and glanced at Palomino as they continued to allow their mounts to walk between two steep dunes. No matter how hard he racked his brain, he could not figure out how Palomino could possibly tell where the outlaws could have ridden in this terrain.

'How can you know where Carson and his galoots have gone, Kid?' he asked before sitting back down. 'Tell me, how can you be certain where they're headed?'

'You'll figure it out just like I did,' Palomino said as his unblinking eyes stared into the shimmering heat vapour before them.

'My brain's boiling inside my head, Kid,' Red grunted. 'My figuring ain't so good in this temperature.'

They steered their trusty mounts down through a narrow canyon of bleached rocks. The heat grew more intense as they travelled the winding course. Both men could feel the merciless rays of the overhead sun bearing down on them as they rode side by side into the sickening abyss.

Yet Palomino continued to lead them as though he had travelled this route many times before. Red could not fathom how the younger horseman was able to negotiate this unfamiliar place. Had Palomino noticed something that his partner had failed to observe? Thoughtfully, Red chewed on the tails of his bandanna and watched as the Kid defiantly continued to lead the way.

The shimmering heat haze bent the air before them. Nothing was exactly as they imagined it to be. It was as though they were looking into a powerful water-fall and not blisteringly hot air.

Suddenly as the horses turned a rugged corner of bleached rock, they both saw the very thing that the Kid had spotted two hours earlier.

A line of poles stretched from one horizon to the other held together by telegraph wires marked a dusty road. The wires glistened in the unforgiving sun as they swayed back and forth between the weathered poles. The dusty road was between the riders and the poles.

Palomino drew rein first and leaned back against his cantle. Red slowly halted his mount and stared at the poles in bewildered awe.

'If that don't beat all,' Red sighed.

'That's how I know which way they went, Red.' The Kid picked up one of his canteens and took a welcome swig of its warm contents.

Red turned his head. 'Telegraph poles?'

'Exactly,' Palomino confirmed. 'Telegraph poles.'

'How the hell do they tell you where Bill Carson and his gang have gone, Kid?' Red growled. 'Go on, tell me how them poles can possibly tell you where them bastards have gone.'

Palomino smiled and handed his canteen across the distance between them. The older horseman grabbed the canteen and took a long swallow of the precious liquid.

'Feel better?' the Kid asked as he accepted the canteen and returned its stopper to the leather vessel's neck.

Red sighed heavily. 'I'm obliged for the drink, Kid, but this is driving me plumb loco. I just don't understand what you're getting at.'

'To my knowledge, Carson and his

cronies ain't ever bin in this territory before, Red,' Palomino explained as he hung the canteen beside the others next to his cutting rope. 'This is mighty dangerous country and not to be taken lightly. Think about it, Carson and his men knew who owned the bank back in Fargo and they knew where Hardwick and his family lived. They must have bin given this information by someone else.'

Red screwed up his eyes. 'I'm with you so far.'

'It wasn't an accident that Carson rode in here and knew where Hardwick lived. That gang rode into Fargo and followed detailed instructions so that they wouldn't run into any trouble robbing the bank,' the Kid continued to explain. 'They would have gotten away with it if they hadn't have run into us when they were making their escape. It stands to reason that they were also instructed on how to get out of this territory.'

Red stared blankly at his pal. 'But what have these telegraph poles got to do with you being able to figure out where them *hombres* are headed, Kid?'

Palomino indicated to the poles. 'The telegraph wires head on out of Fargo, don't they? Then they split into two sections. One section heads east and the other heads west.'

Red Rivers pulled out his tobacco pouch and started to roll a cigarette. 'I know that. So what?'

'The wires head east to Cherokee Springs and west to Dry Gulch.' Palomino watched as Red struck a match and lit his cigarette. 'Cherokee Springs is too far away from Fargo to ride to with saddle-bags full of money, Red. You'd have to travel there by stagecoach but Dry Gulch is only just over that rise.'

Red stared through his cigarette smoke. 'It is?'

Palomino nodded. 'It surely is. I reckon it's only a few miles away from here.'

The wily deputy looked long and hard at Palomino.

'How'd you know that, Kid?' Red sat up on his saddle and frowned. 'I know for a fact that you ain't ever ridden out this way before. How'd you know that Dry Gulch is only a couple of miles away?'

Kid Palomino shook his head in frustration and checked his pair of matched Colts. Then he glanced at his bewildered pal.

'Ain't you ever looked at the big map on the wall in the telegraph office back in Fargo, Red?' Palomino gathered up his reins again and looked at the daunting terrain still ahead of them. 'That map has got all the poles marked on it. That's in case they gotta send out linemen to fix them.'

'They got a map in the telegraph office?' Red asked as he sucked the smoke through the cigarette and then blew it at the cloudless sky.

'A real big map for all to see,' the Kid nodded and then guided the high-shouldered palomino stallion to the rough road of compacted sand.

Red tossed the cigarette away, tapped his spurs and navigated the distance to the dusty trail. He looked down at the road and observed the wheel grooves cut into the ground.

'You can see the ruts where the stage-coach travels up and down this road, Kid,' he said before noticing that his partner was staring down at something else marked in the sand.

Palomino eased his tall stallion beside his pal's horse and studied the sand carefully. He raised a hand and pointed down at fresh hoof tracks.

'There,' he muttered before dismounting and kneeling beside the tracks. He could not contain the sense of gratification he felt in finding the fresh tracks.

Red leaned over the neck of his mount. 'What you doing, Palomino boy?'

The Kid straightened up and then grabbed the mane of his mount. He threw himself back up on to his saddle and mopped his brow with his shirt sleeve.

'Fresh hoof tracks,' he pointed out.

'That's the stagecoach horse's tracks, Kid,' Red sighed.

'No they ain't. These tracks weren't left by the stage team.'

Palomino pointed at the deep hoof marks six feet away from the wheel rim grooves. 'They're the hoof tracks of three horses that were headed west.'

'To Dry Gulch?'

Palomino grinned. 'Yep, to Dry Gulch.'

'Why'd you figure they're headed there for, Palomino?' Red wondered.

The younger deputy glanced at his pal. 'I bet it's to meet up with the *hombre* who planned the bank robbery and split their ill-gotten gains, Red.'

'The what?' Red raised his bushy eyebrows.

'The loot, Red,' Palomino said slowly. 'They've gone to Dry Gulch to split the loot.'

Finally it dawned on the older lawman what his partner was talking about. 'Now I get it.'

Kid Palomino rolled his eyes. 'I'm sure happy that you now understand what I've bin talking about for the last few hours.'

'Next time talk clearer, Kid,' Red scolded. 'How's a body meant to know what you mean when you keep gabbing about telegraph poles?'

The Kid silently frowned.

Then without warning Red suddenly slapped the sides of his quarter horse with his boot leather and galloped away from Palomino. The older lawman glanced over his shoulder and shouted, 'What you waiting for? C'mon, Kid. Let's go get 'em.'

Kid Palomino steadied the handsome stallion. 'Catch that old rooster, Nugget.'

The powerful horse bolted into action and chased the quarter horse. The Kid rose off his saddle, balanced in his stirrups and cracked the tails of his long leathers in the desert air.

Within a few heartbeats the stallion had caught up to the far smaller horse. As Palomino drew level he looked at his old pal and winked. Red Rivers touched his hat brim and nodded as their horses defied their exhaustion and kept thundering on to Dry Gulch.

Neither of the deputies had any idea of what lay ahead of them in the aptly named Dry Gulch. All they knew for certain was that they were closing in on the merciless outlaws. Men of Bill Carson's formidable reputation were all cut from the same cloth.

They would fight to their last drop of blood and take as many innocent folks with them as they could before they succumbed. Their evil breed did not die easy.

Soon there would be a clash of titanic proportions within the arid town the deputies were quickly approaching, for neither Kid Palomino nor his sidekick Red Rivers had ever shied away from a fight when they knew that right was on their side.

The lawmen rode on.

# 12

A growing worry was gnawing at the mature outlaw's innards as his eyes kept glancing at the wall clock hanging from a rusty nail in the small office. He knew that time was quickly passing and wondered how much of it was left before the law finally showed up in the remote town.

Bill Carson was sat opposite Jeff Kane and Poke Peters inside the Dry Gulch telegraph office waiting for the pre-arranged message from the Deacon. Yet as the clock ticked loudly there had not been any indication that the message was going to arrive.

The gang had been there for over an hour and were getting more and more anxious. The grim-faced Carson rose from the hardback chair, strode to the wooden counter and glared over it at the small figure sat beside the telegraph key pad.

A fury was brewing inside the notorious killer as he clenched both his fists and watched the weedy man, who only seemed to awaken when a message caused the crude machinery to start tapping like a frantic woodpecker.

Poke Peters stood and moved to the side of Carson. He rubbed his throat and shook his head before turning to the stony-faced Carson.

'I thought you said that the Deacon would send us a message, Bill,' he asked the statuesque outlaw before glancing back at the still seated Kane. 'Me and Jeff figured he was totally professional but this don't sit right in my guts. What are we meant to do?'

Beneath the wide brim of his Stetson, Carson's eyes darted at Peters. 'Something feels mighty wrong to me about this, Poke. You're right.'

Peters nodded in agreement.

'I don't like this hanging around,' he said. 'We should have left this cesspit by now. Every damn minute we wait in here, the closer the law is getting, Bill.'

'Yeah.' Carson knew that Peters was correct.

They were wasting time and time was the one thing they were mighty low on.

Kane got to his feet and strode to where his fellow outlaws stood. He tilted his head and stared between the pair at the sleeping telegraph operator.

'Them telegraph keys ain't made a sound since we arrived here, Bill,' he commented before resting his hands on his holstered guns hidden beneath his long dust coat. 'Maybe it's busted.'

Carson and Peters looked at Kane.

'How would you know if it's busted?' Peters asked.

The older and far more dangerous of the men stroked his unshaven jaw and narrowed his icy glare. 'You could be right. For all we know there might be a break in the wires. The Deacon might have sent me his instructions but his instructions ain't reached here.'

Kane and Peters looked troubled by the prospect.

'What'll we do, Bill?' Kane wondered.

'We can't hang around here waiting for a message that might not even arrive.'

Peters leaned closer to his fellow outlaws and drawled in a low whisper. 'I got me a feeling in my craw that them star-packers back at Fargo will be rounding up a posse when they find the banker and them women.'

Bill Carson nodded in agreement. 'Yeah, you're right.'

Peters glanced briefly at the dozing operator and then returned his attention to Carson.

'What do you figure we should do, Bill?' he asked nervously before pacing to the office windows and looking out into the sunlit street. 'We've already wasted over an hour in this damn town and if they do send out a posse from Fargo we're in real big trouble.'

'They could arrive here at any time,' Kane swallowed hard.

'I ain't scared of any posse,' Carson snapped viciously at his hired guns. 'But you're right. We have wasted a big chunk of time here and no mistake. If there is a posse looking for us they'll be getting mighty close.'

Kane looked at Carson. 'Let's high-tail it, Bill.'

'Jeff's right,' Peters nodded. 'I reckon we should split the takings and ride. It ain't our fault the Deacon hasn't sent you a message, Bill.'

'It ain't his neck them star-packers will be itching to stretch,' Kane added. 'We gotta get out of here.'

The grim-faced Carson stared at the sleeping old man beyond the counter. 'The Deacon said that we should sell our horses and take the stagecoach to Yuma like ordinary folks. Trouble is there ain't no stagecoach.'

'I ain't selling my horse,' Kane announced.

'Me neither.' Peters spat at the floor.

The fearsome Carson rubbed his jaw and looked at the telegraph operator as he slumbered on a note pad. The outlaw slammed his fist down on the wooden counter. The noise shook the building and caused the small man to wake. His bleary eyes squinted through his spectacles at the three awesome creatures facing him.

'Are you boys still here?' he yawned.

Carson pointed a gloved finger at the bony old character.

'Check that your telegraph is working, old timer,' he ordered.

The telegraph operator raised his eyebrows. 'What on earth for? It's working just fine.'

Furiously, Carson lifted the wooden flap and walked toward the still sleepy old man. As he reached the desk he drew one of his six-shooters and cocked its hammer. He pushed the cold steel barrel under the nose of the seated man.

'Humour me and do what I tell you,' the outlaw growled. 'Test that the lines are OK. I'll blow your head off your damn neck if you don't. Savvy?'

The old man gulped. 'I savvy.'

Carson watched and listened as the operator tapped on the keys. Within a few seconds the office resounded with the distinctive noise of the keys replying. The outlaw rose to his full height and holstered his gun.

'It's working just like this old fossil said it was, boys,' Carson muttered at his men. He then glanced down at the terrified figure with his fingers poised in mid-air. 'When's the next stagecoach to Yuma due?'

The old man was still shaking as he gathered his thoughts.

'There's one due through here at sundown, sir,' he croaked. 'Yes, that's right. Sundown.'

Carson marched back to his men. 'We're going to the saloon and have us a drink. I gotta think.'

The telegraph operator watched as Carson grabbed the door handle and pulled the door toward him. Kane and Peters stepped out on to the boardwalk as Carson paused and glanced back at the frightened old man.

'If you get a message for Bill Carson, bring it straight to me at the saloon,' he demanded.

The fragile old timer nodded. 'I'll

bring it to you as soon as it arrives.'

As the door slammed shut the operator opened a drawer and pulled out a quart of whiskey and pulled its cork. He guzzled half its contents and then shook his head. There was something about looking into the eyes of the merciless Carson, which few men had ever done and lived to tell the tale.

The elderly telegraph operator downed the remaining half bottle of fiery amber liquor and glanced at the empty vessel in his hand.

'I sure hope it's good news that he's expecting,' he stammered in terror. 'I don't hanker giving him anything that might upset that varmint.'

# 13

The Broken Wheel saloon was like numerous others in the more desolate portions of the west. It towered over the other sun-washed structures so that anyone with a hankering to quench their thirst, lose their wages or get their itch scratched knew exactly where to go.

Bill Carson and his two dusty cohorts marched purposely across the parched sand toward the welcoming building. Carson stretched his long legs and stepped up on to the building's board-walk. He paused for a few moments under the shade of the porch overhang as his fellow outlaws caught up with him. As Kane and Peters stepped up on to the boards, Carson ran a match down the wooden upright and cupped its flame as he lit the cigar between his teeth.

Like a sidewinder studying its next

victim, his eyes darted around the virtually deserted street. He filled his lungs with the strong smoke and then shook the match before flicking its blackened remnants away.

Kane was edgy. Sweat dripped from his chin as he watched the deadly Carson staring at the saloon's hitching rail where they had tethered their mounts upon entering Dry Gulch and heading for the telegraph office. Kane had made no secret of the fact that he wanted to be paid his share of the proceeds and ride. Carson looked at the hefty bags secured to his mount and then looked at Kane.

'You get them bags and tote them into the saloon,' Carson ordered and then pointed a gloved finger at Peters. 'And you help him, Poke.'

There was no argument from either Peters or Kane. They stepped down into the blazing sun and started to undo the leather laces that kept the saddle-bags in place.

As his men did what he had told them to do, Carson placed a hand on the swing doors of the Busted Wheel and entered. The saloon was a lot cooler than the street but the outlaw did not appear to notice.

The half dozen souls within the weathered structure glanced at the tall figure as he strode across the sawdust-covered floor toward the bar counter.

Hyram Smith had been a bartender for years and always recognized trouble when it raised its ugly head. He picked up a glass and started to feverishly polish it with his apron as Carson slowly approached. With every step that the outlaw took, the bartender's heart pounded inside his chest. It was facing the Grim Reaper to watch Carson approach.

'Howdy stranger,' the terrified barkeep managed to say.

Carson did not utter a word as he walked toward the bar counter. He placed his boot on the brass rail and then rested one hand on the damp surface of the counter as he plucked his cigar from his lips.

'Whiskey,' he drawled through a

cloud of smoke. 'A bottle of your best with an unbroken seal.'

The bartender nervously nodded and swiftly lifted a bottle off the shelf behind his narrow shoulders and placed it down before the rugged Carson.

'Is this brand to your liking?' the nervous bartender asked, as he carefully took a thimble glass from a pyramid of identical vessels and set it beside the bottle. 'This is the best in the house.'

Carson studied the label and then looked up.

'It'll do for now.'

Hyram Smith relaxed and continued to polish glasses as the swing doors were flung apart again. He stared at Kane and Peters as they entered toting the saddle-bags. The bartender felt his throat tighten again as he watched them.

'Those bags sure look heavy,' he commented innocently.

A mere heartbeat later, Carson drew and pushed the barrel of his six-shooter under the chin of the bartender. Their eyes met as the leader of the greatly diminished band of outlaws started to shake his head.

'You ain't seen no saddle-bags,' Carson growled before turning to face the rest of the seated saloon customers. 'None of you have seen no saddle-bags. Savvy?'

Every man within the Busted Wheel nodded in agreement. Carson returned his attention to Smith and started to stroke the seven-inch steel barrel across the feeble man's face.

'You ain't seen anything, have you?' Carson repeated before adding, 'You ain't seen no swollen saddle-bags and you ain't seen us. Remember that and you'll live a whole lot longer but if you start recalling this, you'll surely die.'

'I ain't seen nothing,' Smith stammered.

Carson smiled and holstered his gun. He glanced at Kane and Peters as they reached a table and placed the bags on its green baize surface.

'Howdy, gents,' the bartender greeted them.

The attention of Carson went from

the bartender to his men as they rubbed the sweat from their grimy faces and strolled to the bar counter.

Suddenly the sound of giggling females above them on the landing attracted all their attention. The outlaws stared in amused disbelief at the sight of the elegantly attired man with his arms draped around the bargirls' shoulders.

'What in tarnation is that?' Kane grinned in amusement by the sight above them.

'Whatever it is, it's sure fancy,' Peters chuckled.

'It's just a gambler,' Carson dismissed the sight and broke the paper seal of the whiskey bottle. 'Don't pay him any heed, boys.'

Danby Deacon stepped to the top of the staircase and cleared his throat. Every eye in the saloon glanced at the man who seemed to want the attention of the three outlaws.

'What about me?' he called out. The two powdered females continued to giggle as Deacon lowered his arms and adjusted his cuffs as he smiled down at

Carson and his men. 'I've seen the three of you desperados and those well-stuffed saddle-bags.'

'You'd best forget or you'll die, dude.' Carson sucked on his cigar and stared at the unusual sight of the man he had never before met. When his lungs were full of smoke he removed the cigar and dropped it into a spittoon at his feet. A loud hiss echoed inside the brass vessel as Carson pushed his coat tails over his holstered weaponry.

'Is that right, Bill?' Deacon started to walk slowly down the steps toward the older of the outlaws. He kept on smiling as he tapped his cane on the boards. 'You'd kill me just for having a good memory?'

Carson glanced to either side at his equally dumbfounded men as the immaculate Deacon continued to descend the staircase toward the bar.

'He called you by name, Bill,' Kane said.

'How does that dude know you?' Peters wondered.

Carson raised his thumb and scratched his chin. 'I don't know how that fancy hombre knows my name.'

Deacon laughed, 'We're old pals, boys.'

'Pals?' Carson repeated the word. 'I ain't ever set eyes on you before. How could we be pals?'

Deacon could see the hands of the notorious outlaw start to twitch as they hovered above his holstered guns. He kept smiling though.

'We've known each other for years,' the man who resembled a riverboat gambler announced. 'Haven't we, Bill?'

Peters and Kane could not believe their eyes or their ears. They had never seen anybody face up to Carson before and it confused the pair.

There was something about Deacon that made Carson focus hard on him. It was as if they already knew one another and yet the outlaw could not recall ever meeting this flamboyant figure before. Deacon was not the sort of man anyone ever forgot once they had encountered him.

Carson gritted his teeth and squared up to the dandy who seemed totally unaware how dangerous it was to argue with obviously hardened outlaws.

'You know who I am, dude?' Carson raged.

Deacon paused as he reached the bottom of the steps and looked at his questioner. 'I certainly do. You're the infamous Bill Carson if I'm not mistaken, and I seldom am mistaken.'

Kane and Peters watched open-mouthed as Deacon defiantly strolled to the card table and then seated himself. He pulled out a silver case and opened its spring lid. He withdrew a cigar, bit off its tip and spat at the sawdust.

'Sit down, Bill,' Deacon said waving at the empty chairs and looking at the bags on the table before him. 'We've business to discuss.'

Carson glanced at his two cohorts and then dragged out a chair and sat down next to the fearless stranger.

'Who the hell are you?' Carson snarled like a rabid wolf at the smiling man as he watched the cigar being lit. 'How'd you know my name? You wouldn't happen to be a bounty hunter, would you?'

Both Kane and Peters chuckled at the suggestion.

Deacon blew the flame out and tossed the match at the sawdust floor. He inhaled deeply.

'I'm no bounty hunter, Bill,' he said wryly. 'But I know you. We've worked together for quite a while.'

The face of Bill Carson went blank as it slowly dawned on him who this man was. He dragged his chair closer to Deacon and studied him carefully.

'You can't be who I think you are,' he said.

Deacon raised an eyebrow, looked at the devilish outlaw and blew smoke at the saddle-bags. 'I was meant to wire you but I had a little trouble back at Cherokee Springs. So I caught a stage and came here personally.'

Carson looked at the saddle-bags and then at Deacon.

154

'Can you prove that you're him?' he asked.

'Oh, I'm the Deacon OK, Bill.'

The statement was like a lightning bolt and caused Carson to sit back on his chair and stare in disbelief at the man before him. Deacon looked more like a harmless riverboat gambler than the man who had planned the outlaw's most daring of robberies.

'Hell,' Carson cursed. 'You are the Deacon.'

Deacon raised his hand and indicated to the bartender. 'Bring that bottle and four glasses over here, friend.'

Hyram Smith did as instructed.

The females cooed like doves up on the landing and waved down at Deacon. He smiled at them and watched as Smith placed the whiskey bottle and glasses down between Carson and himself.

'Did it all go as I planned it, Bill?' he asked as he pulled the cork from the bottle neck and filled the four glasses.

Peters and Kane sat opposite the two men who were staring at one another intently. They accepted the two glasses of whiskey and made short work of them.

Carson frowned. 'Things went sour, Deacon.'

For the first time since Deacon had made his unexpected appearance the smile faded from his face. The glass of whiskey was close to his lips but after Carson had spoken he placed the glass down and tapped cigar ash on to the floor.

'What do you mean by that, Bill?' he pressed. 'My plans are always foolproof. How did they go sour?'

The rugged Carson rubbed his jaw and then downed his whiskey in one swift throw. He rubbed his face and then refilled his glass.

'Everything went exactly like you said it would, Deacon,' he started. 'Up until me and the boys left the banker's house and started heading out of town.'

Danby Deacon leaned forward. 'What happened as you were leaving Fargo, Bill? What?'

Carson exhaled and shook his head.

'Star-packers. We run into three star-packers.'

Danby Deacon stared in disbelief at Carson.

'That can't be.' Deacon raised his eyebrows and sucked hard on his cigar. 'The sheriff and his deputies were meant to be out of town. The only lawman in Fargo was that blind old coot who stands in for them when they ain't there.'

'There were three of them OK,' Kane insisted as he poured more amber liquor into his glass. 'They were star-packers and they made a real fight of it.'

Deacon stared at the whiskey in his glass. 'I just don't understand it, boys. It must have been the deputies known as Kid Palomino and Red Rivers. They must have returned early for some damn reason.'

A guilty hush fell over the four men. Then Deacon looked at the three figures and leaned against the back of his chair.

'I thought you were taking four men with you on this job, Bill,' he said as he glanced at Carson. 'What happened?'

Carson spat at the floor. 'Both the Brand boys got killed by them bastards, Deacon. I lost two good men.'

For the first time since his unexpected entrance, Danby Deacon looked troubled. He could not believe that his well-crafted plans had gone bad. He puffed on his cigar and then glanced at the three outlaws in turn.

'My plan would have meant that you could have entered and left Fargo without anyone noticing,' he said thoughtfully. 'By the time anyone figured that anything had happened you would have been long gone, but now things are different. Now there'll be a posse after you. They know what you've done and they'll come hunting to avenge that wrong, Bill.'

'I know, Deacon,' Carson sighed. 'What should we do?'

'Damned if I know.' Deacon shook his head, stood up and puffed frantically on his cigar as he looked down on the three men and the saddle-bags. 'I'm taking the next stagecoach out of here and putting distance between myself and them rope-twirlers. You boys can split my share of the money between yourselves. I don't want any part of it. I ain't getting lynched for what's in those saddle-bags.'

Bill Carson stood beside Deacon. 'There ain't another stagecoach coming through here until after sundown, Deacon. You're stuck here with me and the boys.'

Upon hearing the unwelcome news, Deacon suddenly looked sickly. 'We've got to get out of Dry Gulch before sunset, boys. We can't afford to waste the next couple of hours sitting around here waiting for those star-packers to arrive.'

'Our horses are spent, Deacon,' Carson growled as he grabbed the bottle and drank from its neck. As liquor dripped down his shirt front he lowered it and looked at the elegant Deacon. 'By the looks of it, you ain't even got a horse.'

'I didn't think I'd need one.' Deacon

exhaled a line of smoke and pointed at Peters and Kane. 'Go try and round up four fresh horses for us. Pay anything they ask but get us four fresh mounts.'

Carson glared at them.

'You heard him. Get going and buy or steal us four fresh horses,' he raged. 'And be quick about it.'

Kane and Peters ran out into the brilliant sunshine leaving the two older men standing in the middle of the Busted Wheel.

'Do you reckon they'll find four fresh horses in this shrivelled-up town, Bill?' Deacon asked the notorious Carson.

Carson shook his head. 'Nope, I sure don't, Deacon.'

# 14

Kid Palomino drew rein, stopped the high-shouldered stallion and rested his wrists on the horn of his saddle. The brilliant sunshine bathed Dry Gulch in a daunting glow, which alerted the young lawman that not everything was as it first appeared. The town seemed to be vacant of all life but Palomino knew that was not the case. Places near to the merciless desert harboured a different breed of people. They tended to shy away from venturing out into the rays of the cruel sun and waited for sundown before going about their business. Dry Gulch was similar to numerous others south of the border and the Kid was troubled by its apparent peacefulness. He stared thoughtfully at the small town from beneath the brim of his hat.

Red brought his quarter horse to a halt beside his younger companion and squinted at the array of wooden structures. The tin and wooden shingle rooftops could be seen sparkling in the distance as the overhead sun bore down upon them. The telegraph lines hung from their poles as they made their way to and from the bleached office in the centre of Dry Gulch.

'So that's Dry Gulch,' Red grunted as he steadied his thirsty mount. He was not impressed. 'The damn place looks deserted, Kid. I've seen ghost towns that look better than that.'

Palomino tilted his head and glanced at his sidekick.

'Nope, it ain't deserted, Red,' Palomino disagreed as he spotted two figures searching for something neither of the deputies could fathom. 'Do you see them galoots yonder?'

Red nodded. 'I see them.'

The younger deputy glanced at his partner.

'Now what do you figure them critters are doing running around in this heat, Red?' Palomino wondered as he stroked the lathered-up neck of his stallion.

'My bet is they're looking for something,' Red replied and checked the empty canteens hanging from his saddle horn. 'You got any water left, Kid?'

Palomino shook all of his canteens and then his head as he continued to focus on the fleeting glimpses of the outlaws as they crossed the town's main street. 'Sorry, pard. I'm clean out.'

Both their horses could smell the fresh water within the boundaries of the settlement. They strained at their leathers as both expert horsemen fought to restrain them.

'These nags know there's water real close, Kid,' Red said as he wrestled with his weary animal. 'They can smell it.'

Palomino nodded as his narrowed eyes kept watching the two distant men desperately continue their hunt. 'What in tarnation do you reckon them fellas are looking for?'

'Did you hear me?' Red repeated. 'These horses need water and we ain't gonna be able to stop them for much longer.'

'I hear you, Red,' the Kid sighed. 'What do you suggest?'

'We ain't got no choice, Kid.' Red straightened up on his saddle and pulled the brim of his hat down to shield his eyes from the dazzling sunlight. 'We gotta ride in there to water these nags.'

The Kid used every ounce of his remaining strength to hold the palomino stallion in check. 'I don't hanker riding straight in there and getting greeted by bullets, Red. I figure it might be smart on our part to circle the town and enter from behind them larger buildings yonder. We can use that gully to give us cover and get to water without being spotted by Carson and his cronies.'

Red sighed heavily. 'That's gonna tag another ten minutes on to us getting to water, Kid.'

'That's a whole lot better than getting picked off by Carson and his gang, ain't it?' Palomino turned the head of the tall mount beneath his saddle and tapped his spurs. The handsome cream-coloured horse began to walk slowly down into the long depression that encircled the town. 'C'mon. These animals got themselves a mighty big thirst.'

Reluctantly, the older lawman knew that his pal was right to be cautious. He gritted his teeth and shrugged as his gloved hands gripped the reins tightly.

'You're right, Kid.' Red allowed his horse to follow the younger horseman. They held their horses in check so that neither animal could bolt as the scent of the town's wells grew stronger.

As they journeyed along the sandy gully, they silently recalled the horrific sight that had brought them to this desolate place. Neither lawman had ever set eyes upon anything like the sickening outrage they had stumbled upon back in Fargo.

Images of the innocent people lying in pools of their own blood haunted them and continued to spur them on. The banker and the womenfolk had been slaughtered as though they were

165

mere livestock being readied for the butcher's block.

The unholy memory of innocent, unarmed bodies lying in crimson pools of gore was branded into their minds and was impossible for them to shake off. Those memories would remain embedded in their minds forever.

Both Palomino and Red had silently resolved to get justice for those pitiful souls. It was the spur which drove them on toward their own possible destruction. Every sinew of their aching bodies screamed for them to stop but neither of the peace-keepers could quit now.

They had to prevent Carson and his equally depraved followers from continuing their merciless killing spree, even if it cost them their lives.

The tin stars pinned to their shirts gleamed like beacons in the bright sunlit gully as they secretly circled the small town of Dry Gulch. Palomino was dictating the pace they were travelling at, making sure that they did not cause dust to betray their presence.

'How far are we gonna go along this damn gully, Kid?' Red quietly asked his fellow deputy. 'I'm getting tuckered out holding this horse back, and no mistake.'

Palomino looked over his wide shoulder. 'Will you hush the hell up? I'm listening out for any sign of them murderous bastards, Red.'

They continued to slowly steer their mounts around the back of the few structures erected close to the heart of Dry Gulch. Then the younger deputy hauled back on his reins and stopped the tall stallion.

'What you stop for, Kid?' Red asked as he dragged back on his reins and halted the quarter horse.

'I'm gonna take me a look,' Palomino answered and then carefully balanced in his stirrups and stretched up to his full height so that he could see above the deep gully.

'What do you see, Palomino?' Red asked as he smoothed the neck of his tired horse and watched his friend.

Kid Palomino's eyes were half closed

as they peeped over the sandy rim and observed the area. The back of the telegraph office was roughly twenty feet from the gully. Thirty feet to the side of the office, a far larger building dominated Dry Gulch. There was a full water trough set at the rear of the smaller office. The reflections of its precious contents danced across the wooden wall.

The young lawman lowered himself back down on his saddle and then he turned the palomino stallion to face his pal.

'We're right behind the telegraph office, Red,' the Kid said. 'It's got a trough out back.'

'What else did you see?' Red wondered.

'There's a tall building off to the left,' Palomino replied. 'I figure that must be a saloon.'

'Did you see their horses?'

The Kid shook his head, 'Nope, they must be out front.'

'Have we got cover, Kid?' Red asked.

'Yep, we've got plenty of cover, Red,'

168

Palomino confirmed. 'Nobody will see us approach from here.'

'That's all I wanted to know.' Red tapped the flanks of his mount and rode around his friend. He studied the sandy slope and then jerked his reins hard and fast. The quarter horse cleared the side of the gully and reached the level ground behind the telegraph office. As the scarlet-whiskered horseman steadied his snorting horse, the Kid suddenly appeared right behind his quarter horse.

Palomino pointed at the rear of the smaller structure.

'We can tether the horses there,' he said as the powerful stallion beneath him fought against its reins. 'Right next to the trough.'

Red nodded as they allowed their horses to walk toward the small weathered structure. The Kid dropped from his saddle first and looped his leathers around the metal pump beside the water trough.

Before Red had dismounted and

secured his own mount, the Kid had drawn one of his trusty .45s and was investigating the area carefully.

His eyes darted from one building to another as they slowly headed into the very heart of the remote settlement.

'Seems awful quiet, Kid,' Red said as he stared through the shimmering heat at the array of buildings.

Palomino pressed his back against the side wall of the office and carefully looked around the corner of the sun-bleached building. His attention was drawn to the outlaws' three spent mounts tethered to the saloon's hitching rail.

'What you see, Kid?' Red asked as he leaned against his friend's shoulder.

'I see three lathered-up horses tied up outside the saloon, Red,' he answered before adding, 'I also see two critters in long dust coats. They're still looking for something.'

The bright sun was blazing down on the loose-fitting coats worn by both Peters and Kane. Palomino suddenly felt his entire body go rigid as he spotted the bloodstains on the pale fabric.

The Kid knew that he was looking straight at the blood of the Hardwick clan. He lowered his head and shuddered as he felt his spine tingle.

'What's wrong, Kid?' Red asked his pal. 'You look like you just seen a ghost.'

The younger man looked down at his shorter friend.

'Maybe I have, you old rooster,' he sighed. 'Maybe I have.'

Red glanced around the corner of the telegraph office and watched as the outlaws went from one building to another. He scratched his head.

'What in tarnation are them *hombres* doing?' he wondered.

Palomino inhaled deeply. 'I reckon they're looking for something, Red. I just can't figure out what they're looking for.'

Red suddenly tapped his pal's arm. 'Their horses are spent, Kid. Look at them. They're plumb pitiful. Maybe them *hombres* are looking for fresh nags.'

Palomino considered his friend's words. 'You're probably right. Those horses sure look worse for wear. They wouldn't carry them outlaws far in that condition.'

Red rubbed his mouth on the back of his glove. 'If them two *hombres* are out in the sun hunting down fresh nags, Carson must be in the saloon on his lonesome, Kid.'

The notion of getting the drop on the infamous Bill Carson gave the Kid renewed vigour. A smile appeared from behind the mask of trail dust on his face. 'That's right, Red. He's on his lonesome in that drinking hole.'

'What we gonna do?' Red asked his pal.

The taller deputy swung around on his heels and led his pal back to where they had left their horses. He pointed the barrel of his gun at the side of the saloon. His eyes tightened as he studied the structure carefully.

'What you looking at, Kid?' the older deputy asked.

Palomino indicated to the veranda that encircled the wooden structure. Without answering, he grabbed his cutting rope from off his saddle and slid its coil over his arm.

'I got me an idea,' he drawled.

Red scratched his whiskers. 'What you need a rope for? You figuring on hanging them *hombres*?'

Palomino raised an eyebrow.

'Let's go pay that Carson varmint a visit,' he drawled.

Using the smaller telegraph office as cover the two men circled around the rear of the weathered structure and raced toward the Busted Wheel saloon.

# 15

Red Rivers soon found out what his partner needed his saddle rope for. No sooner had the lawmen reached the high-sided saloon than Palomino uncoiled his rope, swung it a few times and then launched it skyward. The lasso went clear of the wooden trimmings upon the veranda railings and then he pulled and tightened its loop. The slipknot loop constricted around one of the wooden adornments until it held firm. The Kid checked the rope with his weight and then glanced at Red.

'Ready?' Palomino grinned as he wrapped the slack around his arm and shoulder.

The older deputy shook his head and gulped.

'You ain't expecting me to climb up there, Kid?' Red exhaled at the daunting thought. 'Are you?'

Palomino shook his head. 'Nope, I reckon I'm about ten years too late to expect you to do that, Red.'

The older lawman shrugged. 'Then what?'

Suddenly all humour vanished from Palomino's face as he considered the daunting task ahead of them. He tightened the drawstring of his Stetson until it was tight under his chin. He pointed to the rear of the Busted Wheel.

'You make your way around the back of the saloon and find a way in, Red,' the Kid said as he gripped the rope and started to athletically ascend the wall. 'I need you to back up my play. Be careful how you enter this place, Red. Bill Carson can shoot the eye out of a meat-fly at a hundred paces, I'm told.'

'Don't go fretting, Kid.' Red gripped his six-shooter firmly and ran to the rear of the Busted Wheel. He had no idea what Kid Palomino intended to do but knew that whatever the Kid was intending, it was bound to be danger-ous.

The Kid leaned back with the rope gripped firmly in his gloved hands and then started to ascend the wall. Within a few moments he had reached the railings and grabbed hold of one of them. Palomino threw his right leg over them and swiftly followed it on to the balcony. He loosened the rope and then began to coil it again as he stealthily made his way toward the front of the saloon.

Lowering his head so that his face was shielded from the bright sun he saw the two figures of Peters and Kane cross the street and head on to the back of the telegraph office.

'I hope they leave our horses alone,' Palomino whispered under his breath before continuing. He reached the weathered façade, which was nailed to the railings, then heard shouting from down the street. The Kid knew that it had to be the outlaws he had just witnessed heading to where he and Red had left their horses. He dropped on to one knee and squinted to where the

176

raised voices were coming from.

Then he saw them.

Kane and Peters suddenly appeared from behind the telegraph office. As he watched them, the Kid knew why they were rejoicing. Just as he had figured, they had found both Red's quarter horse and his palomino stallion.

'Damn it all,' he cursed angrily as it dawned on him that if he were to unleash his guns on the brutal killers, the horses were in the line of fire. 'Why'd they have to find the horses?'

The Kid chewed on the thumb knuckle of his glove and watched the grinning men sat astride the horses as they slowly rode toward the saloon. Red had been correct. They were looking for replacement horses, just as his pal had guessed.

Palomino narrowed his eyes and glared down on Peters on his precious mount.

'You just made a real big mistake, fella,' he quietly fumed before carefully knotting the rope loop around the back of the railings. Then he frowned at Peters as he drew one of his matched Colts. 'Nobody rides Nugget without my permission.'

Dust drifted up from the hoofs of the walking horses as they steadily closed the distance between themselves and the Busted Wheel.

Suddenly the jubilation both outlaws felt in discovering the two handsome animals evaporated. Jeff Kane hauled back on the reins of the quarter horse as he caught a brief glimpse of the lawman behind the decaying saloon name board. He glanced across to tell his fellow outlaw of what he had just spied but Peters had already spotted the Kid. Kane steadied the muscular animal beneath him as Peters slowly slipped one of his six-shooters from its holster.

'You seen him too, Poke?' Kane asked.

Poke Peters gave a slow nod of his head as he screwed his eyes up tight and watched the vague shadow behind the long name board.

'Yep, I seen the sun dancing off his tin star a few yards back.' Poke Peters pulled back on the hammer of his .45 and then suddenly raised it. 'Whoever that is, he's a dead man.'

The entire town rocked as the bullet flashed through the shimmering heat and punched a fist-sized hole in the façade beside the crouching Palomino.

A thousand red-hot splinters blasted into Palomino's face without warning. It was like being consumed by angry fire-ants. The deputy yelled out in pain and rolled across the floorboards to the end of the Busted Wheel name board. Half blinded by the sudden shock, the Kid lifted his six-shooter and blasted a wild shot down at the horsemen.

Undeterred by the deafening reply of Palomino's wild gunshot, Peters and Kane fanned their gun hammers again, sending chunks of debris rising up into the air from the wooden railings.

The Kid rubbed the side of his face with his gloved fingers until he was able to open his eyes. It was like staring through a waterfall as the singed lawman crawled even further away from where bullets continued to rip the saloon sign apart.

'Do you figure we got him, Poke?' Kane shouted above the deafening din.

Peters shook his head as his eyes searched the length of the balcony. 'Keep shooting until we see the blood dripping, Jeff.'

Like hounds with a cornered racoon, the outlaws refused to quit. They kept firing their guns up at the balcony whilst the Kid dodged the deadly lead like a matador sidestepping a raging bull.

Palomino spat on to the tails of his bandanna and pressed them against his eye in a vain bid to soothe the fire that raged inside it. He blinked hard and could just see the devilish pair as they fired up at him.

He ducked and crawled beneath the red-hot tapers.

The choking smoke from the outlaws' guns hung in the arid air as

Palomino curled his finger around the trigger of his .45. Yet no matter how hard he strained to see clearly, an agonizing pain burned like a branding iron into his eye.

He cursed.

All he could make out for certain was the blurred images of the riders below his vantage point. He moved his barrel away from the golden stallion and toward his partner's smaller mount.

'If I get this wrong, Red can always buy a new quarter horse but if I accidentally shoot my palomino . . . ' the Kid reasoned as bullets continued to keep him pinned down. 'Aim high and you shouldn't hit Red's horse.'

Defying the agony which racked his face, the Kid cocked, aimed and fired his gun at Kane. To his surprise he saw the outlaw buckle as scarlet gore exploded from his back. Palomino ducked as Peters' avenging bullets narrowly missed him. When there was a lull in the barrage of gunshots the Kid fired his Colt at the wounded Kane again. The outlaw jerked violently on the saddle as the second shot finished him off for good. A sickening groan escaped from Kane's deathly lips as he tumbled from the saddle and fell limply into the ground beside the quarter horse's hoofs.

'Jeff!' Peters screamed out in horror as he stared down at the gruesome sight. Yet no matter how loud he yelled, there was no reply. The outlaw dragged the neck of the palomino around and stared up at the long balcony.

He shook the spent casings from his gun before reloading the smoking chambers.

'You're gonna pay for that, star-packer,' Peters raged and then glared through the dazzling sunlight to where he had first spotted Palomino. He hastily started firing again at the saloon sign above him.

Palomino threw himself across the balcony as bullets shattered the glass of the second storey windows. The injured star-packer kept rolling until he had returned to his cutting rope behind the bullet-ridden façade.

He gripped the rope and lowered his head as more choking splinters cascaded over his hunched shoulders. Clouds of black smoke gave the deputy cover as he rose up to his full height and moved with the rope in one hand and his gun in the other.

He cocked his gun hammer and trained it at Peters. The trouble was his weeping eyes still could not clearly see his target. The Kid was just about to fire his smoking six-shooter when it dawned on him that he might end up missing the outlaw and shoot his precious palomino stallion instead.

Another shot came within inches of him. The Kid could feel the heat of the bullet and staggered sideways. He shouted at the top of his lungs at his obedient mount.

'Punch them stars, Nugget boy,' he yelled down at his horse. 'Rise and punch them stars.'

The magnificent stallion did exactly as its master commanded and reared up and kicked its forelegs out just as it had been trained to do. Peters was caught by surprise and found himself toppling backwards. The outlaw dropped his gun and grabbed at the saddle horn. As the palomino stallion landed its hoofs back on to the sand, Peters went to drag his other six-gun from his belt.

It was too late.

Kid Palomino had already launched himself off the balcony holding on to his rope. He swung wide and low through the smoke-filled air.

Both the Kid's boots hit the outlaw squarely in the back sending him flying over the golden mane of the palomino stallion. Peters crashed heavily into the ground with the fearless lawman just behind him. Palomino released his grip on the rope and leapt on to the winded Peters. He grabbed the outlaw's hair and dragged it toward him.

The dazed Peters tried to reach up and grab the deputy but Palomino clenched a fist and smashed his knuckles into Peters' jaw. The sound of knuckle on jawbone echoed along the street.

For a moment the Kid thought that he had knocked the outlaw out but Peters was not so easily subdued. He twisted on his side, wrapped his legs around his opponent's and caused the Kid to fall.

Palomino could not see his foe clearly but he could feel his punches as they pounded into him. The tables had somehow been reversed. Peters leapt on to the Kid and sent a right cross into the deputy's head. He then grabbed Palomino's shoulders and wrestled him full circle.

Both battling men feverishly grappled with one another as they slowly rose to their feet. The Kid grabbed Peters as the outlaw sent punch after punch into his midriff.

Then suddenly the quiet street resounded to the deafening sound of gunfire. The Kid stared over Peters' shoulder and saw the unmistakable figure of Bill Carson standing in front of the saloon's swing doors. Even his blurred vision could not mistake the infamous outlaw as he emptied his gun in his direction.

Without realizing it, the young lawman had somehow positioned Poke Peters between himself and Carson's deadly bullets. He felt the impact of every shot as they drilled into Peters' back. The young outlaw rocked under the impact of the merciless lead. Finally Poke Peters fell into Palomino's arms as his pitiful face looked at the Kid in utter disbelief.

Peters went to speak but the only thing that left his lips was blood. His eyes rolled back and vanished under his lids. He sighed heavily as life departed him and slumped into the arms of the Kid.

Bill Carson stepped down into the sunlight as he reloaded his trusty gun and looked admiringly at the palomino stallion standing in the street beside the quarter horse. He then glanced over his shoulder and shouted at Deacon.

'Looks like we got ourselves some

horseflesh after all, Deacon,' he chuckled in his usual sickly manner. 'A quarter horse for you and a high-shouldered beauty for me. Come take a looksee.'

Danby Deacon reluctantly pushed the swing doors apart and left the confines of the Busted Wheel. He moved after the confident outlaw. 'Has the shooting stopped, Bill?'

Carson snapped the chamber of his smoking gun and spun its cylinder as he glared at Kid Palomino standing behind the bullet-ridden Peters.

'The shooting's nearly stopped, Deacon,' he drawled as he cocked the gun and aimed it at the head of the youthful star-packer. 'There's just one more varmint I've gotta put out of its misery. Then we can ride out of this town with the loot.'

Palomino was holding the lifeless Poke Peters upright with both hands. It took every scrap of his strength. He knew that it was impossible to release his grip and draw one of his guns before Carson fired.

'Tell me one thing,' Carson growled as he closed the distance between them. 'Who in tarnation are you? You've bin a real pain in my arse.'

'He's Kid Palomino, Carson,' Red shouted out from behind both Deacon and Carson as he pushed his way through the swing doors and stood with his cocked gun in his hand. 'Now drop that hog-leg before I drop you.'

Bill Carson lowered his head thoughtfully and then sighed as he stared at the smoking gun in his hand.

# Finale

Deacon turned and ran toward Red with his hands clasped together as though in prayer. He fell on to his knees and pleaded to the lawman, 'Help me. I don't know who this man is, Deputy. He and his cronies ambushed me. They're monsters and I'm just a simple gambler. Please save me.'

As Red considered the outpouring, Bill Carson turned on his heels with his six-shooter at hip height and glared at Deacon in disgust. He glared at the man who until now had never given him any reason to doubt his word.

'You stinking liar,' Carson hissed like a sidewinder and then fired straight into the back of the kneeling Deacon. As the criminal mastermind arched and fell lifelessly on to his face, Red squeezed his own trigger and sent a bullet into the centre of Carson's chest.

The outraged outlaw staggered across the sand coughing up bloody spittle with every step. His vicious eyes glared at Red as he steadied himself. 'You shouldn't have done that, star-packer.'

Red dragged his hammer back with his thumb as he watched Carson muster every ounce of his dwindling energy to raise his gun-hand again.

'Drop that gun, Carson,' Red shouted at the outlaw.

The veteran outlaw did not listen. He cocked the hammer of his gun again and stared with deathly eyes at the man with the tin star gleaming on his chest. 'That was a real big mistake, star-packer. I'm dead but so are you.'

Fearing for the safety of his friend, Palomino swiftly released his hold on the lifeless Peters and drew his own .45 in one fluid action. He repeatedly fanned the gun hammer and sent the last of its bullets into Bill Carson.

The outlaw swayed as his gun fell from his hand and landed in the sand heavily. His eyes snaked between the two men wearing the tin stars. Carson spat blood at the ground as life slowly left his bullet-ridden torso. He flinched in agony while death gripped his torrid soul in its unforgiving fingers. He then stumbled and he fell.

It was like watching a tree falling.

Dust rose around the body and hung in the dry air as Palomino limped across to his pal, patted him on the arm and then sat down on the weathered boardwalk. He removed his gloves and started to reload his gun with bullets from his belt.

'Where's the bank money, Red?' the Kid asked wearily.

'On a card table inside the saloon, Kid,' Red sighed and slid his gun back into its holster. 'I passed it on the way here.'

'How come you took so long?' Palomino asked wryly. 'I nearly got myself killed out here before you showed.'

Red rubbed his scarlet whiskers. 'You told me to be careful, Kid. I was being careful.'

191

Palomino chuckled and pushed the chamber back into the body of his Colt. 'That's true, I did tell you to be careful.'

Red walked to both their horses and led them to the trough next to the outlaws' spent mounts. He wrapped their long leathers around the hitching pole and secured them before resting a boot on the step of the boardwalk.

'By my figuring we got them all, Palomino,' he said as he pulled his tobacco pouch from his shirt pocket and started to sprinkle the contents on to the gummed paper.

Kid Palomino got to his feet as the sound of pounding hoofs echoed around the weathered structures. He leaned over the trough and splashed water into his face to soothe his sore eye. He straightened up and stared at the five horsemen as they entered Dry Gulch.

'Sheriff Lomax is finally here with his posse, Red,' he sighed before stepping up on to the boardwalk and placing a hand on the swing doors. 'C'mon. I'll buy you a beer.'

Red rubbed his chin and poked the twisted cigarette in the corner of his mouth. 'Do you reckon that fancy-looking dude lying in the dust is the *hombre* Carson got all his information from, Kid?'

Palomino scratched a match across his belt buckle and lit his partner's cigarette. As smoke drifted from Red's mouth the Kid tossed the match at the sandy street.

'Yep, I sure do.' He nodded and walked into the saloon with his pal a step behind him.

'Come to think about it I seen him about two weeks back playing poker in Fargo, Kid.' Red pulled the cigarette from his lips and blew smoke at the sawdust-covered floor. 'He sure was a mighty bad poker player.'

'It don't matter none, Red,' Palomino smiled. 'Not where he's headed.'

The posse pulled up outside the Busted Wheel as the two deputies reached the bar and rested their aching bones against its wooden counter. They glanced at the swollen satchels of the three saddlebags on the card table and then Palomino nodded to the tall man polishing glasses behind the bar.

'A couple of tall beers, barkeep,' Palomino told the bartender before noticing the pained expression on his pal's face. 'What's troubling you, Red?'

Red glanced at his friend.

'How come Sheriff Lomax always arrives after the shooting's ended, Kid?' Red sighed as he sucked smoke into his lungs.

Kid Palomino thought for a moment then shook his head and shrugged. 'I reckon that's one mystery we'll never be able to figure, Red.'

Hyram Smith placed the two tall beers down and watched as the deputies lifted the glasses and tapped them together.

'For Charlie,' Palomino toasted.

'Charlie,' Red nodded.

We do hope that you have enjoyed
reading this large print book.

Did you know that all of our titles
are available for purchase?

We publish a wide range of high
quality large print books including:
**Romances, Mysteries, Classics**
**General Fiction**
**Non Fiction and Westerns**

Special interest titles available in
large print are:
**The Little Oxford Dictionary**
**Music Book, Song Book**
**Hymn Book, Service Book**

Also available from us courtesy of
Oxford University Press:
**Young Readers' Dictionary**
**(large print edition)**
**Young Readers' Thesaurus**
**(large print edition)**

For further information or a free
brochure, please contact us at:
**Ulverscroft Large Print Books Ltd.,**
**The Green, Bradgate Road, Anstey,**
**Leicester, LE7 7FU, England.**
**Tel:** (00 44) **0116 236 4325**
**Fax:** (00 44) **0116 234 0205**

Brutally attacked one night in the woods, Steve Karner hadn't been seen in years, and everyone in the Oregon town of Stayton thought him dead. Then the men who tried to kill him start dying, one by one; and it soon becomes apparent that Karner is not only alive, but riding a vengeance trail. But there are many dangers to be faced along the way, including a cunning young million- aire who will use all his family's power to protect his secrets, and a cold-blooded hired killer out for Karner's blood . . .

# DEAD MAN'S EYES

## Derek Rutherford

Ex-train robber Jim Jackson is fresh out of the tough Texas Convict Leasing System, where brutal guards beat all the courage out of him. Now good for nothing except drinking, Jackson is known as 'Junk' by the townsfolk of Parker's Crossing. But Jackson has one thing going for him — he's the fastest gun the Texas Rangers have ever seen. When a series of violent murders terrify the people of Parker's Crossing, it is to Junk Jackson they turn. But can Jackson find the courage to take on the killers?

# OUTLAW EXPRESS

## Gillian F. Taylor

Sheriff Alec Lawson has infiltrated a band of outlaws in order to capture them — but when they kidnap Lacey Fry from the Leadville express, he breaks his cover in an attempt to bring the young woman to safety. Learning of the betrayal, gang leader Bill Alcott vows to find Lawson and kill him. Lawson doesn't know the territory and he doesn't know Lacey. But the chase is on, through snow and bloodshed, until one of the men can run no further — and hunter and hunted finally come face to face . . .

# TAGGART'S CROSSING

## Paul Bedford

John Taggart and Jacob Stuckey are Civil War veterans who operate a ferry on the mighty Arkansas River — but trouble still finds them in the tranquil setting. After robbing a bank in Wichita, Russ Decker and his gang's escape route takes them by way of the ferry crossing. Once there, Decker decides to stop pursuit by putting John and Jacob out of business permanently. But fate decrees that a keelboat full of stolen silver ore will arrive at Taggart's Crossing just at the right moment to create maximum havoc . . .

# BLAZE OF FURY

## Alexander Frew

Tired of being a gun-toting hero to some and a villain to others, ex-bounty hunter Jubal Thorne is looking forward to a peaceful life on his late brother's farm. But when a man has such a past, it isn't long before fate comes knocking on his door. It all starts with a stray bullet that just misses his head, and ends in a blaze of fury. In defence of what is his own, Thorne shows that the bounty hunter might leave his profession, but his profession will never leave him . . .

LOGAN WINTERS

# CROSSROADS

*Complete and Unabridged*

LINFORD
*Leicester*

First published in Great Britain in 2015 by
Robert Hale Limited
London

First Linford Edition
published 2018
by arrangement with
Robert Hale
an imprint of The Crowood Press
Wiltshire

A catalogue record for this book is available
from the British Library.

ISBN 978–1–4448–3633–2

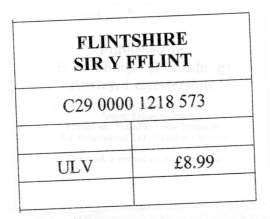

# 1

Crossroads, New Mexico, was what the town was called. K. John Landis came upon it in the middle of the heated day, afoot. His pony had gone down under him the day before and he had been walking ever since, his saddle carried across his shoulder. The day was not only devil hot, it was windy and dust clouded the skies. K. John walked on with his head down, his hat tugged low, looking only for a place in the shade, a place to rest his weary legs.

The town of Crossroads, he found, was short on shade. There was a saloon, of course, farther down the rutted, hard-packed street, but K. John hadn't even a scattering of change in his pocket, and he would not go in without money to stand like someone cadging drinks. His legs were now growing rubbery; he had walked a heck of a long

1

distance. And his shoulder hurt from the weight of his saddle. The hand holding it there was cramped and painful. K. John wanted only to sit down — and then he saw his opportunity.

Next to the saloon was a general store, and through the sift and whirl of the dust, K. John squinted at it. An awning stretched out, shading the plank walk in front of the store. The door to the premises was in the center of the building. It stood open now as two men strode out with various goods and stowed them in the bed of a wagon that stood to the door's right with its two-horse team looking weary and dissatisfied, their heads bowed out of deference to the sand that blew.

At the far end of the walk, just across the alley from the saloon there was room to sit. In fact, someone else was already sitting there in the heat and blow of the day. Bowing his head lower, K. John walked that way. He threw his saddle to the ground and sat down in the ribbon of the shade cast by the awning. It did almost nothing to cool him, but he was grateful for the chance to rest.

'What do you want?' the person next to him demanded, and it was only then that K. John realized that it was a young woman sitting there beside him.

'To sit here. I've just walked most of fifty miles, and I mean to sit here,' K. John answered wearily, but without belligerence. He didn't have the strength to take offense at the woman's sharp tone. He wanted water, but he would find that later. Even in the poorest of towns a thirsty man can find water somewhere. Perhaps when the sun went down he could find a cool place to sleep.

For now he was content to sit quietly on the plank walk. His feet, in his worn-down-at-the-heel boots, were heated and sore. It was good to get off them for a while. Despite his troubles he counted himself lucky. The last time a horse had gone down under him he

3

had found himself alone in the trackless red desert where things like shade and water were only a dream.

'Who are you?' the woman snapped. 'I don't know you! What's your name?'

He was surprised that the woman who didn't seem to care for his company hadn't simply got up and gone about her business. He had thought she might be waiting for the men who were loading the wagon, but just then the men began pulling away from the store. The front door banged shut, the proprietor wishing to keep the dust out. The wind seemed to have lessened some, and the dust was settling to the earth.

He canted his head and looked up at the woman. Not very old — little more than a girl, in fact — she was wearing a sort of brown dress, which gleamed a purplish colour where the stray sunbeams caught it. She also wore a pair of purple boots, which caused K. John to smile. Her hair was dark and glossy. Now slightly disarranged by the wind, a tendril of it dangled past a small pink ear. Her eyes, dark green, were still fixed expectantly on him.

'My name is K. John Landis,' he said, and she turned her head away.

'Did you say 'Cajun'?' she asked.

'No, I said K. John — K, like in 'K', and John like in 'John'.'

'Why?' she asked, without looking back.

'Why? I don't like my first name, that's all. Haven't you ever heard of a man going by his initials?'

'You could just use John, couldn't you?'

'I could, but do you know how many men named John there are wandering around?' He was ready to explain his choice of names, but she was obviously through listening to him. 'What are you doing out here?' he asked.

'I've no place to go,' she said, without embellishment.

K. John nodded, not understanding. For himself, he considered that he was still running in luck, having even found this town. Come tomorrow he could find some sort of labor, whether it was sweeping out a store or shoveling the manure out of a stable, and make at least enough to feed himself. If he kept his ears open, he could probably find a job on some small local ranch eventually, the way men wandered around from job to job out here. He again looked at the woman, who now definitely seemed worried. For a woman life was different, much more difficult. A woman needed more than water and a pile of hay to sleep on.

'Well, where did you come from?' he enquired, taking the chance that she would answer him. He looked again at her face and at her dress, which he now saw had lace along its hem, five inches or so of which was torn free, dangling.

'Right there,' the girl said, just when he had figured she was not going to answer. She tilted her head toward the saloon where now three men exited, talking loudly about the lack of water on the range and someone called Red.

'What do you mean? You work there?'

'I did,' she said, 'until this morning, when my boss got a little difficult.'

'I see,' K. John said.

'No, you don't!' the girl spat, and fell silent again.

K. John shrugged and leaned back, resting his hands on the warm boards to brace himself. It seemed the girl had had a falling-out with her employer at the saloon and had come outside to sulk, nothing more. K. John watched the settling dust, the bits of paper and debris drifting down the street.

'What's your name?' he asked the girl. He thought she was going to decline to answer, but she turned those green eyes to meet his and answered.

'Flower.'

He thought about making an answer, but decided to remain silent. She had questioned him about his name, but he didn't think he should do the same. Had he ever met anyone named Flower before? He didn't think so. He knew that a lot of saloon girls used assumed names, so he supposed that Flower was an adopted name. K. John sat forward again, hands dangling between his knees.

'Why don't you go away?' Flower asked him.

'I've nowhere to go, either. If I had even a nickel I'd go into the saloon and get a beer, that's for sure.'

'I wouldn't!' she flared up. 'I wouldn't go back through that door for all the money . . . for all the money in the world!'

Her bitterness seemed extreme. Maybe whatever trouble she had had with her employer was worse than K. John had believed. 'You must live somewhere,' he said, and her eyes flashed.

'I did! In there.' Her head again tilted toward the saloon where two trail-dusty men were entering, slapping their hats against their jeans.

'And you won't go back in, not even to get your clothes or whatever else you've got in there?'

8

'No,' she said definitely. 'I did have a nickel or two. I would have loaned you one, but I'll not go back into my room.'

'That doesn't seem the wisest way to go about things,' K. John said, and was immediately sorry he had spoken. 'I mean, if you have a little money, you're certain to need it. I'll tell you what,' he finally offered, 'if you like, I'll take you in or go by myself.'

'No,' Flower said, flatly. She looked K. John up and down from the top of his battered Stetson where a few curls of dark hair escaped, down to his faded blue-and white-checked shirt with one elbow out, dusty jeans and down-at-the-heel boots, not missing the Colt revolver with its chipped walnut grips that rode on his hip. She seemed to hesitate for a moment and then said, 'I wouldn't want you to get hurt.'

K. John shrugged again and then left the girl to her own thoughts. He had been in a lot of bad places in his time and had never been afraid to enter a room simply because someone might not like him. Why would anyone want to test him? Then again he considered he might not be getting the entire story from Flower, and he might be walking into a hornets' nest without knowing what he was getting into, or why.

K. John's eyes lifted as a tall man in a gray suit crossed the street directly toward them. The man wore a western hat, which he held on against the still-gusting breeze. His face was square, tough-looking. He wore a long dark mustache and polished boots.

K. John asked Flower, 'Is that your boss?' and she lifted her eyes toward the approaching man. She shook her head.

'No, I don't know who he is. I've seen him in town, but not often.'

'He's got his eyes on us — or on you, more likely.'

'That doesn't mean I know him,' Flower said.

However, the man seemed to know Flower, or at least be intent on talking to her. He strode directly up to them and placed one boot up on the step of the boardwalk. There was a sheen of perspiration on the stranger's forehead, K. John saw; his eyes were dark, hard and confident.

'I've been looking for a couple like you,' the man said.

'We're hardly a couple,' Flower was quick to respond. K. John wagged his head as well. The tall stranger looked surprised.

'Sitting here side by side, both looking like you were a little down on your luck, I assumed . . . look, I haven't much time.' He pulled a brass watch from his vest pocket, opened it and glanced at the time. 'My stagecoach leaves in less than fifteen minutes.

'A couple who answered my newspaper advertisement were supposed to arrive here from Clovis this morning, but they didn't show up. I need a man and a woman — I don't care if you're a couple or not — to watch over my ranch while I take the coach down to Albuquerque. It's extremely important

11

business and I'm late in responding.'

He went on as if the matter had been settled. He pulled a billfold from inside his coat.

'I'm assuming — maybe I assumed too much — from the looks of you two that you would need a little cash and maybe even a place to stay for a while. Tell me if I'm wrong.' He glanced back across his shoulder toward the stage station. All this time he had not stopped thumbing paper money out of his wallet. K. John saw the flash of a gold coin as it was added.

'Look, folks, I'm in a bind here. I have to go, and I have to go now. All I'm asking is for you to stay around the place and watch it for me. My daughter's there and an older woman who cooks for us. And if I don't get to Albuquerque, I stand to lose a bigger fortune than I ever hoped to have in my life.'

His rough hand thrust out the sheaf of bills toward K. John, but Flower intercepted it. 'I think if there's any money in this bargain, I'd better handle it.'

'You're probably right,' K. John agreed. 'Mister — ' He looked at Flower and asked, 'Are we going?' She gave a tiny nod in answer. 'Mister, we don't know who you are or where you live. How to get there.'

'The name's Emerson Masters. My place is the Oxhead Ranch. Anyone can tell you how to get there. You can use my buckboard — I left it at the stable. Can I count on you?'

K. John glanced at Flower, who nodded again. 'You can count on us, Mister Masters,' he said.

'The cook's name is Olive. Tell her I said to roast you a shoulder of good beef.'

This last Masters said hurriedly over his shoulder as he rushed to catch his stagecoach.

'Well, I don't know what you call that,' Flower said, after folding the money and putting it away in a skirt pocket.

'When I was a boy and went to Bible school, they called it divine intervention.'

K. John rose to his feet; his legs had stiffened as he sat there. Flower rose lithely, refusing the hand he extended to help her up. She dusted her skirt, continuing to look back at the saloon.

'That might be a good enough explanation for Sunday school kids, but to me the whole thing seems a little bit strange.'

'Do you know what, Flower? I don't care how strange it seems. A man wanders up, thrusts a wad of bills in our hands, offers us a place to stay for free, the use of his buckboard to get there, and roast beef dinner on top of that. I don't care how strange it might seem. If this isn't divine intervention, it's the next thing to it, and I'll accept the opportunity happily. That is . . . if you still want to get away from this town.'

She stopped, turned toward him and said emphatically, 'I have to get away from this town.'

'Well . . . you've got the money. Let's at least go and see what we've gotten ourselves into.'

# 2

Flower didn't start fussing until they were nearly to the stable where Emerson Masters said he had left his horse team and buckboard. 'All my clothes,' she said a few times, looking up at the rooms above the saloon. 'What am I supposed to do?'

'We can still go get them,' K. John told her. She stopped, looked at him again with her hands on her hips and shook her head as if he had come up short in her estimation.

'No,' she said in a muffled voice, 'we'd better not try that.'

'Well, then,' K. John told her as they entered the shaded, musty heat of the stable, 'you can at least buy yourself some new stuff — I saw the size of that wad Masters forked over. You're a woman of means now. Maybe you can't get a whole new wardrobe, but you can pick up a few things at the dry-goods store.' K. John tugged at the torn elbow of his checked shirt. 'I'd like to have at least a new shirt so I don't show up looking all raggedy at this Oxhead Ranch. We're supposed to be in charge for a while, aren't we? I don't want to arrive looking like a saddle-tramp.'

Which was exactly what he was, K. John knew. He yelled at a passing stable worker, 'Hey, is this Emerson Masters' rig, partner?'

He got a nod in response and K. John swung his saddle from his shoulder to the bed of the wagon. Flower, he noticed, still had not answered him. She stood, sort of biting at her lower lip, watching him as he rubbed his shoulder. He had carried that saddle a long way.

'I hate to waste a cent,' Flower said, finally. 'I don't know how long that money will have to last.'

'I'm sure we'll get paid again when Masters gets back. Didn't he say that he was closing the biggest deal of his life?

He'll be in a generous mood.'

'You don't know that,' Flower argued. 'Maybe the deal, whatever it is, won't work out. We don't know that he's generous, only that he found himself in a pickle and needed to hire someone quick.' She paused. 'We don't even know if he's coming back at all.'

'No,' said K. John, whose own theory had always been spend it while you have it.

'All right, then. I know I need a new shirt. Why don't we just divide that money down the middle and I'll do what I have in mind?'

Flower started wagging her head from side to side. Eventually she said bluntly, 'No, I don't believe I'll do that.'

'You don't believe in clean shirts?' K. John asked, lightly.

'That's not it,' she said, and in the darkness of the stable, K. John thought her eyes looked moist. 'You're a man . . . if I gave you half the money you'd likely run off and find a bottle of whiskey and I'd never see you again.'

18

K. John was silent a moment. Nearby a horse stamped its foot impatiently. At last he asked her, 'Is that what your last man did, Flower?'

She looked indignant, then fiery and finally quite sad.

'It was my father,' she muttered in a voice so faint he could barely hear her.

'All right,' K. John said. He didn't want to hear the story any more than she had wanted to hear about his Bible school days. Just as well — it's better not to know too much about someone you happen to find yourself traveling with temporarily. 'Come with me and buy me a new shirt.' She didn't argue that ladies didn't do that. Instead, she asked 'What color shirt?'

'I don't know. I'll have to see what they have. Does it matter?'

'I was thinking you'd look good in white,' Flower told him.

'Maybe so, but definitely not white. Nothing shows you're wearing a dirty shirt more than a white shirt when it gets dirty.' Also, they made too good a target, but K. John didn't bring that point up with a lady who had likely never been in the sort of situation where that could matter.

'We'll see what they have,' Flower said as if exasperated.

'Hold on a bit. Let's see to getting the horses hitched; then we can drive over to the store with the buckboard.'

'Will they even let us take it?' Flower asked.

'Masters didn't seem to be worried about that.'

'Masters probably wasn't thinking too straight just then,' Flower reminded him.

But the man in charge of the stable gave them no problem. Emerson Masters had mentioned to him that he was expecting a couple to watch his ranch while he was gone. The stable-man eyed them dubiously as if thinking this could not be the couple — he might have recognized Flower from the saloon — but he shrugged as if it made no difference to him, had the team of matched bay horses hitched, and sent them on their way after giving K. John directions on how to get to the ranch.

In the store, K. John changed into a new, very dark red shirt with black buttons, which he liked, and soon he was ready to leave. But Flower had changed her mind — or maybe it was that now she found herself in a store, and being a woman, she could not leave it without buying something. Before they managed to escape, K. John found himself loading a dozen packages into the wagon bed.

'It would have been easier to go get your other clothes,' K. John said, helping Flower on to the spring buckboard seat. She answered him very seriously.

'Oh, no! They would certainly have killed you, K. John.'

Pondering on this, although it no longer mattered to him any more than the town of Crossroads did, he started the team eastward. Flower had bought — or borrowed — a yellow pencil from the store, and she sat beside him, totting up numbers. He glanced her way and, seeing his look, she explained, 'I want to make sure that I don't take anything from your half of the money.'

'Mine when I get it,' K. John said, with a slight edge in his voice.

'When you get it.' She sighed, tucked the pencil and paper away in her skirt pocket.

'You see, K. John, I am quite careful with money and ultimately trustworthy.'

'Whereas I . . . ?'

'I barely know you — no, I don't know you at all! What would have happened if I'd given you your money back in Crossroads? Who knows? You might have gotten drunk, bought a horse and I'd never have seen you again. Where would that have left me!'

'I'm an unturstworthy fool,' K. John said, coolly. All right, he knew now that the woman was insecure, afraid of being alone and penniless on the desert. He supposed he couldn't really blame her, but they had made a bargain, and each had the obligation to fulfil it. Flower did not speak to him, but kept her eyes grimly on the trail ahead.

He nodded toward a trio of roadside cottonwood trees, which cast enough shade to cool them and the horses. There he drew in. The horses blew, poking around aimlessly for grass where there was none.

'Flower, I want to have a little talk with you,' he said. Sunlight filtered through the high reaches of the cottonwoods, dappling the earth around them, splashing moving shadows across her face.

'Yes?' she said innocently although she did not look at him.

'Yes, and it's about things that are more important than me buying a shirt.' He took in a deep, slow breath, and tipped his hat back on his head.

'Such as?'

'Such as this whole enterprise. When Emerson Masters approached us back in Crossroads, we both jumped at the chance of getting ourselves a temporary position and having a few dollars given to us.

'Now, I took it as an easy way to rest up, make enough to replace my horse and be fed for a few days for my troubles. Not a bad deal at all. You, on the other hand, are so dour, you'd think I was taking you to meet the executioner. Why, when all you have to do is watch a house for a while, and you've already been paid? It doesn't have to be forever. Maybe after we've settled in you'll come up with a thought on how to mend fences with your old employer and get your job back at the saloon.'

''Mend fences'!' she echoed explosively in a voice that was partially muffled by sarcastic, snorting laughter. ''Mend fences' with Clyde Willit? Are you kidding? And as for ever entering the Double O Saloon again, I'd have to be out of my mind after . . . '

K. John waited for her to enlighten him farther, but she silently declined.

'You see,' she said, lifting those dark green eyes of hers, turning toward him

24

on the buckboard's seat, 'you see this as a fine opportunity to rest up, be fed, get yourself another horse and ride off to find another cowboying job somewhere.' She adjusted her dust-trailed skirt with a twitch of her hand. 'To me, it's the end of the road. Why do you think I hated to spend any of the money Masters gave us? It might be all the money I'll see again — ever.'

'I can't believe that,' K. John Landis said.

'Believe it. I'm just terrible at roping and branding,' she said.

'But there will be other opportunities,' K. John persisted, trying to smile for Flower.

'Oh, yeah? Where? The Double O was my last chance to save myself from poverty.'

'Don't exaggerate,' K. John said, but the look on Flower's face said she was not.

'All right, then,' he said, changing the subject. 'When we reach this Oxhead Ranch, we don't present ourselves as any kind of a couple — Masters didn't seem to think that mattered anyway. I can sleep in the barn, anywhere. I'm used to no better. We'll have to settle in a little to see what the situation is there, why Masters believed so strongly that he needed someone to watch the place. But you'll have to smile for the people,' K. John added, 'even if you won't for me.'

'Have I been looking that sour?' she asked. K. John nodded.

'You've been looking that sour.' He started the team again and they wound their way down into a long dry valley, following the instructions as he remembered them. It wasn't that much of a puzzle: the trail was there, and it showed the recent passing of shod horses and a wagon — probably the very one they were now using.

He wondered, 'Why did Clyde Willit name his saloon the Double O? It has nothing to do with his initials or anything else that comes to mind.'

'Did you ever play the game of

roulette?' Flower asked as they splashed across a wide, shallow creek. Ahead now, K. John thought he could make out several low structures. He crinkled his eyes and shrugged at Flower's question.

'A time or two,' he admitted.

'Well, you've got about as much of a chance at winning in any game at that saloon as you do of hitting the green 00 on a roulette wheel.'

'I see,' K. John said, thoughtfully.

'No, you don't,' said Flower, stiffly. She was bent forward now, looking into the distance at the buildings up ahead. 'You won't know anything about Clyde Willit until you've had dealings with him — and then it will be too late.'

They pulled into the Oxhead Ranch. The buildings were nicely situated near the base of the surrounding foothills in the shade of a grove of mammoth oak trees. A yellow yard dog came out to meet them, but did not even bark, just slunk away, tail between its legs. It was well into the afternoon now. The shadows were long and the air was cooling. The gusting, dusty wind seemed not to reach here, or else the windstorm had finally blown itself out.

'What do we do now?' Flower asked with a touch of nervousness.

'Pull up and go in. That's what we're here for, isn't it?'

'I'm not sure why I even came here,' Flower muttered.

'Because you had no place else, remember? Now start practicing that smile.'

Her lips twitched into a smile that seemed shy but genuine. K. John halted the rig in front of the house. The porch was wide and white. Six round upright posts supported the awning. K. John was the one who now looked concerned as Flower asked him:

'What is it?'

'I don't know — where are the working men? I haven't seen another soul.'

'There's probably a simple explanation. We'll find out.'

'Yeah,' K. John muttered. He looped the reins to the team around the brake handle and crossed behind the buckboard to help Flower, hampered by her long skirts, get down from the wagon. Now a slight breeze touched them, teasing the leaves in the upper reaches of the oak trees. The old trees rustled dryly. Inside the house there was not a sound that they could hear.

Stepping up on to the porch, K. John dusted off his new red shirt, straightened his hat and knocked at the large, arched front door, smiling at Flower. 'Home for the Holidays,' he said, not getting the amused response he was after. He gestured with his fingers on his own mouth for Flower to smile, and she obliged — sort of. She was obviously worried.

As for K. John Landis, he was feeling fine. The day was already ending better than it had any right to after the morning he had endured. If not flush with cash, they at least had a little. If no one ever answered the door, they were better off than they had been before. He knocked again, hat in hand now.

Suddenly, the door banged open and an almost-pretty blonde glared at them. Wearing a dark-blue dress and her hair pinned up, her face was a mask of tight disapproval.

Her glittering blue eyes searched them judgmentally and found them lacking.

'Well?' she demanded. 'Who are you and what do you want here?'

Flower let K. John do the talking. 'Miss Masters?' he tried. Emerson Masters had said he had a daughter living on the ranch. The woman's frown grew deeper, something K. John would have thought impossible if he hadn't seen it for himself. She answered in a brittle voice.

'Yes, I am Justine Masters — but I asked you who you were.'

'Miss Masters,' K. John replied, trying for politeness. 'Your father hired us to come out to the Oxhead to kind of look after things while he's in Albuquerque.'

'To 'look after things'? What 'things'?' Justine Masters demanded.

'Well, the house and the yard, I suppose,' K. John said, looking around with a weak shrug.

'We have people to take care of those,' Justine said, her voice growing haughty and then derisive. 'I don't think you even know why you're here.'

That was the truth, although K. John wouldn't have admitted that out loud to a woman, particularly this one. Justine continued after a moment's pause for breath.

'My father!' she said with unconcealed disgust. 'Look what he sends to help out around here! A broken-down cowboy and a — ' Justine's eyes raked Flower's clothing, down to the torn lace hem and little purple boots. 'I don't know what you are,' she said to Flower — whose green eyes momentarily sparked with an anger that she managed to contain — 'but I could guess,'

Justine added, unkindly.

Justine sighed as if she were being forced to carry the weight of the world. 'Are you two even married?' she asked and got negative shakes of the head in response. 'I thought not. Get your luggage — or boxes, it seems,' she said, looking past them toward the buckboard, 'and the lady' — she made the word sound like a mockery — 'can have a room in the house. I'll have the maid show her the way. You,' she turned to K. John, 'can Find a place in the bunkhouse — it's empty — or sleep in the barn. Whatever you're used to.'

'Yes, miss,' K. John said with a small nod, the sarcasm of which must have eluded Justine Masters. 'Very good, miss.' Abruptly his tone changed, surprising Flower no less than Justine. 'Your father did tell us that we're in charge here until he returns.'

Justine's mouth opened slightly, silently. She stared at K. John, but he proved to have the harder stare. She spun back toward the house, calling out, 'Olive! Olive, where are you?'

Flower watched K. John with astonishment still in her eyes. 'You could have ruined everything,' she said in a lowered voice.

'I had to shut her up. I was tired of the woman. Let's get your boxes from the buckboard. Here's your guide,' he said, nodding toward the short, stout woman who waited nervously in the doorway, wiping her hands on her white apron.

'Let's get those things to your room, then I'm going to put the buckboard away and take care of the horses. By then it should be time for dinner. Let's not forget to tell Olive that the boss promised us a roast beef dinner.'

They went to the rear of the buckboard and Flower began stacking the boxes in K. John's arms. She said quietly, her eyes going to the house:

'I feel like such a fool, K. John. We don't even know why we're here, what we're supposed to watch over.'

'Oh, I think we do,' K. John said over the tops of the boxes. 'I think we've already met her.'

# 3

K. John was completely content. After supper, Flower had gone off to her room looking concerned, but for K. John Landis this was a small bit of paradise. He had made himself a bed of straw in the loft of the barn. Supper had been a nice cut of roast beef with mashed potatoes and gravy, which had filled his empty stomach with a pleasant warmth and a sense of well-being. The night was cool and quiet. He lay back with a pleasurable relief which only a weary body can find. Below, the yellow yard dog looked up at him hopefully and, if possible, K. John would have assisted the dog up the wooden ladder to share his comfort.

Justine Masters had not joined them at the table and neither had asked after her. They received precious little information from the stout Olive, who worked hastily, fussily, in her kitchen. They did not try to pry into affairs; tomorrow was soon enough.

For now the night was pleasant, the air cool, the bed soft if a little scratchy, his stomach well-fed. K. John yawned — yes, tomorrow was soon enough to get to the bottom of things. Just the night before he had been hungry, thirsty with no place to make his bed but on the desert floor; he felt he was making remarkable progress, even if Flower did not feel the same way about things.

And he could not blame her. Yesterday, she, in contrast to K. John, had been a girl with a job, a room in town of her own, money in her purse, a closet filled with clothes. Tonight, she had been relegated to some sort of housekeeping job with undefined duties and no firm promise of future wages. Flower must have felt as if her life were plummeting into the depths of misfortune.

All of which seemed to have something to do with the saloon-keeper, Clyde Willit. Flower had never told K. John precisely what their dispute had been about. Imagination could provide dozens of answers to that, some of them quite unsavory, but K. John was too tired right now to guess. He rolled over, looked down once, said 'Goodnight, dog,' and drifted off to a comfortable sleep.

Sometime after midnight the dog yipped — only once, but it was enough to wake K. John. Someone was moving about in the barn below. At this time of night?

It could have been some of the Oxhead hands going about their regular, if unusual, business, but K. John did not think so. Their movements seemed furtive; their voices, ragged whispers. The cowhands that K. John had known would not be whispering at their work. They would be grumbling, joking, perhaps cursing if summoned from their beds for night duty of some kind, but never would they be silent in the way these men below were.

There were three of them, K. John could just make out, peering over the edge of the loft. One other thing he noticed was the yellow dog cowering in the corner of an empty stall. Now, the dog might not have been the boldest defender of the ranch, but he would certainly know the men who worked on the Oxhead and would come forward to greet them, not fear them. K. John decided to take a closer look. After all, that was his job — or he thought it might be. The Oxhead was his to run until Emerson Masters returned: that was a large assumption, but he had made it.

Reaching for his Stetson, K. John started toward the ladder, clambering down to the dark floor of the barn. A single lantern had been lit near the open double doors, and by its light K. John could mark his men. They could also see him very well as he walked toward where they stood gathered

38

together, talking.

He could not make out the men's expressions in the darkness, but he saw no smiling teeth, and could only assume the dark looks he must be getting from them.

'Hello, boys!' K. John nodded. 'A little late to be riding, isn't it?'

He half-expected the men to provide some sort of mocking explanation at that. Something along the lines of 'When do you expect the night-riders for the herd to start out — at noon?' Something — anything — that would explain all simply. But the men said nothing, which worried K. John.

He had not been able to make out their expressions before now, but nearing them he could now see they were wearing unanimous deep scowls.

'Who the hell are you?' the bulkiest of the three demanded. He wore all dark clothes, a low-riding Colt revolver and stood hunched forward as he stared darkly at K. John.

'I'm the ranch manager,' K. John said

easily, keeping his eyes on the thick man's hand, which had settled near his holster.

'What do you mean?' one of the others — a younger, narrower lad — asked. 'There ain't no such a thing as a ranch manager for the Oxhead.'

'That's not what Emerson Masters thinks,' K. John said, keeping his tone neutral, his body loose and unchallenging. He didn't want to fight these men; he just wanted to know who they were, what they wanted.

'You mean Mr Masters hired you,' the thicker man asked in a taunting voice, 'and then sent you out to sleep in the barn?'

'Pretty much,' K. John answered. 'He hired me — it was my own idea to sleep in the barn.'

'Have you got a name?' the third man, the one who had not spoken before, asked. He had a broad forehead and squinty eyes.

'Yes. Have you?' K. John asked, not liking the responses he was getting from these men, whoever they were. He no longer assumed they were Oxhead hands. Their manner was too furtive, and when they glanced at each other, their eyes were secretive. He thought about ordering them off the place, but he would be acting on shaky authority — and there were three of them and only one of him.

'Time's wasting,' the leader of the men said suddenly. 'We've got to get about doing what we came for.'

He said this a little too loudly and as he did the three of them lunged forward in a body, driving K. John to the floor of the barn. He started to fight, but there was to be no fight. The man sitting on top of him clubbed him over the ear with the barrel of his pistol and the lights went out in K. John's skull.

★   ★   ★

'K. John!' someone was shouting from the open barn doorway. There was sunshine shafting into K. John's eyes

41

and he winced at the saber-like shards of light. His head was throbbing and he found himself sprawled uncomfortably on the hard-packed floor of the barn.

'K. John!' was shouted again, and he knew that it could only be Flower.

'Right here!' he called back, his tongue thick in his mouth.

'Well, get over here!' she replied a little officiously.

Determining that he had no broken parts, K. John scraped himself off the floor and, after leaning for a minute against the side of a stall, he walked in the direction of Flower's voice, his head pounding.

Flower had changed into a pair of blue jeans and a white shirt. She tapped her foot impatiently as she watched him stagger toward her. He leaned against the door-frame and watched her. There was obvious concern on her face.

'This is a disaster!' Flower said, breathlessly. Despite his injuries, K. John couldn't help noticing how fine she looked. Her hair was worn loose this morning, dark and glossy in the fresh sunlight. Her dark-green eyes were not amused as she looked him over. 'A disaster!' she repeated.

K. John was fingering the lump on his skull carefully. 'It's not that bad,' he replied.

'It's not that bad?' Flower leaned slightly toward him, her breathing coming in short puffs. 'Justine Masters is spirited away in the dead of night and you don't think it's serious?'

'I didn't understand,' K. John said, rubbing his forehead. His brain was still a little foggy. He had assumed that Flower was concerned about the attack on him. 'What happened?'

'What happened? Nobody knows.' Flower looked temporarily abashed. 'I was sound asleep, and you know that Olive and I are the only two in the house besides Justine. There was a note on the kitchen table to her father . . . I opened it.'

'What did it say?' K. John asked, heavily.

'That she was leaving home; that she'd had enough of his controlling ways and needed to find a new life of freedom.'

'That's all?'

'Well,' Flower answered, 'there was something about us, about Emerson Masters wasting his money to hire two incompetents as watchdogs.'

'I see. Well, we seem to have lived up to her impression of us,' K. John said. 'Was there a man involved, a boyfriend? That's usually the first thing you'd consider.'

'I don't know,' Flower said unhappily.

'What about Olive? What did she have to say?'

'Very little outside of 'Oh, my! Oh, my!'' Flower pulled a face. 'But she did say that she was awakened after midnight by what she thought was the sound of Justine's buggy being driven out of the yard. I didn't see how that could be possible — how could she have slipped out here, hitched her horse to the buggy and driven off under your

44

nose? It's not possible!'

'It's possible,' K. John confirmed, dully.

'How? What are you talking about, K. John? You're hard to understand this morning.'

'I know. That's the way it is with some of us 'incompetents'.'

'What are you saying? Let's make an agreement to speak English to each other.' A smile flickered briefly over Flower's lips and then fell away completely to be replaced by worry. 'K. John — what has happened to you? You'd better sit down somewhere.'

There was a chipped and oily wooden bench just inside of the barn and they sat there, K. John holding his head, as he told her about the three visitors the night before.

'I couldn't guess what they were up to,' he said. 'Now I guess we know.'

'No, you couldn't have guessed. I'm sorry, K. John, I should have noticed that you were injured.' She placed her hand briefly on K. John's. 'Do you think those three men . . . maybe it was the boyfriend and a couple of his friends or relatives?'

'I don't think so,' he answered. 'From what I saw of them they were older and hardly the ideal of any young girl's dream, especially a girl like Justine Masters.'

'Stranger things have happened.'

'Not this strange. One thing is for sure,' K. John said, rising, 'Justine had this all planned out. She would make her escape while her father was off to Albuquerque. Emerson Masters must have had an inkling of what was up. That's what he hired us to do — keep watch over the girl.'

'And we've already failed! Not a day into the job.'

'It would have helped if he'd taken the time to tell us what the job was,' K. John commented, 'but with the rush he was in, there wasn't time.' As K. John turned toward the door and the bright sunlight outside, Flower also came to her feet.

'What are you thinking?' she asked, for his forehead was furrowed with thought.

'That we can't just give up. I won't admit that we've already failed at this job, Flower.'

'You're going to go after her?' she asked.

'That's it. I'll borrow a horse — after all, we are Oxhead employees — and get on her trail.'

'I'm going with you,' Flower said with determination.

'You can't.'

'Can I not! Besides, what else am I to do — stay here and help Olive with the cooking?'

'No, I guess not. I just wish someone had told us what the situation was because I still don't know. It's likely as he had informed the couple that was supposed to arrive from Clovis what was up.' K. John paused. 'Well,' he shrugged, 'I suppose it's our problem now. I should be able to cut the sign of four horses and a buggy — or would be if I knew which direction they had gone.'

'I think I already know,' Flower said, and K. John turned to stare down at her.

'What are you talking about? Did you overhear something in the house?'

'No, I didn't. But, K. John, will you believe that I know what is going on around here better than you do?'

'If you say so.' K. John removed his hat to scratch at his head. 'Where is it that you think Justine is going?'

'Why, to Crossroads, of course! Now, shall we saddle a couple of horses and get going?'

Crossroads made sense. K. John couldn't see a young woman in a buggy heading out into the wild country. Flower's guess was a good one, but it seemed to be more than a guess to her. What did she know? He thought that over as he saddled two horses. A long-legged, sleek red roan which might have been Emerson Masters' own, and an alert little paint pony, which seemed eager to leave the barn and go adventuring.

Flower waited impatiently, though why she would be eager to go back to Crossroads he could not guess — the town hadn't treated her well up to now. He asked her once as he finished drawing the cinches on the paint pony but her response was curt.

'I'll tell you along the trail.'

He waited, expecting her to return to the kitchen and come back with some food — K. John was getting downright lean — but she made no such offer. One thing he insisted on: they took four canteens off the barn wall and filled them. The chase might lead them to Crossroads, but it could take a sudden turn, and he would not be left on the desert without water.

He liked little of this, but Flower seemed sure and she was already impatient, dressed for riding, and so K. John swing aboard the roan, feeling slightly like a thief who was abusing Masters' hospitality, but there was little choice and, as the low sun still lit only the tips of the huge oak trees in the yard, they rode away, taking the fork for Crossroads. Glancing back once, K. John saw the stout woman, Olive, watching from the doorway. What was she thinking? What would she tell Emerson Masters when he returned?

Riding away from the ranch, their crooked shadows stretching out long before them, K. John began immediately looking for sign of the escapee's passage. Flower shot him urgent glances. In her mind he was wasting time: she was sure of where they had gone.

'Have to be certain,' K. John grumbled once. 'We can't be riding miles in the wrong direction.'

'No, we can't. Trust me, K. John, this is the way they went.'

About half a mile on where the soil grew sandy, looser, she was proven correct. The tracks of a single horse and buggy along with those of three outriders were evident in the softer soil.

When K. John commented on them, Flower nearly smirked and said, 'Maybe you'll trust me next time.'

'I trusted you this time, but we had to be sure, not ride on hunches. We've already made a mess out of our job.'

'You're grouchy. I suppose you're just hungry,' Flower said.

'You suppose right,' K. John said with little humor. Then, 'You said you would tell me why you were so sure it was Crossroads they were riding to once we were on the trail — well, we're on the trail.'

'I meant to tell you — as soon as you were satisfied by your tracking that I was right.'

'I see.' K. John rubbed thoughtfully at his bristled chin. He had hoped to grab a shave at the Oxhead. He felt obligated to warn her. 'You know, Flower, I don't really like the idea of you riding along. It could turn out to be pretty dangerous.'

'I know that,' she replied, and added

quite seriously, 'I don't think you have any idea yet of how dangerous this might be.'

# 4

The road straightened and leveled; the breeze was light, the morning bright. As they were passing the cottonwood grove where they had stopped to rest the day before, K. John broke the silence.

'All right, you had something to tell me. Why don't you begin now?'

Flower shook her head, thoughtfully. 'It's not a pretty tale, K. John.'

'I didn't ask for pretty,' he said.

'All right,' she agreed with a sigh. 'You see, it involves me, too.'

'You? What do you mean? You can't have known Justine Masters before.'

'No, nothing like that.' She frowned. They were riding close together; her eyes briefly took on a faraway look. 'It concerns Clyde Willit and his doings,' she told him.

'You mean the man who owns the

Double O Saloon?'

'Yes. Well, K. John, you see, Willit is up to other shady business that doesn't include drinking and gambling.'

'You would know, seeing as you worked for him. What kind of thing did you have in mind that specifically might concern Justine Masters?'

'Clyde Willit deals in women,' Flower said, turning her eyes away from his. 'That's how I came to be there in the first place.'

There was a small ringing in K. John's ears that he didn't think was a result of last night's beating. 'I don't know as I understand you,' he said.

'I suppose you wouldn't,' Flower said, returning his gaze. 'You see, K. John, there are a lot of poor families trying to make a living in the basin.' She waved an arm, indicating the entire desert distances. 'Some of them don't even have milk and bread for their babies. It is a desperate land out there.'

K. John nodded his understanding:

the Red Desert was cruel, but what did this have to do with Justine? Or with Flower? She went on:

'My father was one of the dirt-poor farm squatters out here. We had nothing. My mother had died on the land years ago — the heat, loneliness and poverty had driven her to an early grave.'

'I see,' K. John nodded. He had seen more than one such case. A man coming west to look for a place of his own across the barren wastes, not realizing that there was a reason why the land was barren. People shriveled up and died out here, having spent a lifetime of labor to gain nothing.

'Father always believed that if we only had water, our farm would be an Eden.'

'That's what everyone thinks, but no one has water. What has this to do with Clyde Willit, you, or Justine? What has the man got?'

'Money, K. John. Willit has a lot of money. Sleazy money, which he is

55

willing to lend at exorbitant rates. Father went to him and begged for a loan to have a deep well dug on his property. Clyde agreed to lend it. Of course . . . ' Flower hesitated. '. . . he wanted some sort of collateral.'

'Of course,' K. John said. 'What did he want? A share of the property?'

'What use would that be to him? He needed something a lot more useful.' Her expression tightened and she looked away again. K. John came to a realization, a shocking, cold realization.

'You mean you?' he blurted out, unable to control his anger and the sickness he felt. Flower only nodded her answer.

'As Clyde explained it to Father, he would take me in to work for him for three months, at the end of which time he expected Father to repay the loan. Father told me that it was fair enough — I'd at least have food to eat and Mr Willit was doing us a favor by taking me in. Anyway,' Flower shrugged, 'he fully expected to have Willit's money back by the end of the three months.'

'But he didn't have it.'

'He never came back,' Flower said in a voice near a sob. 'He never even came by once to visit me. Never!' She dabbed at her eyes. 'I don't know if he is dead, alive, a victim of the desert.'

'You said that Willit was to hold you for three months as chattel — a guarantee of his loan. What was supposed to happen to you after that?'

'The other girls at the saloon told me. There were a lot of them who were in a situation like mine. After three months, Clyde Willit would just sell them to the highest bidder.'

'What do you mean sell them?' K. John demanded. 'He can't do that; there are laws against it!'

'I know, but who is there to enforce them?' Flower said. 'It wasn't that long ago that bondswomen, indentured servants, were common, and no one thought anything of a man having one. And, K. John, do you know how scarce women are in this country? Cooks are in demand, nurses, housekeepers . . . wives,' she added lastly, stumbling over the word.

'You can't buy a wife,' K. John argued.

'Can you not? That too was once a common practice all around the world, wasn't it?'

'I know, but . . . what do the girls do when they're told of this?'

'Some cry, some rant; some are eager to go — to leave the saloon work for their own home on a prosperous ranch. With their background of poverty and uncertainty, it seems like a great stride forward in their lives.'

They rode on in silence. Ahead, K. John could already make out the squat forms of the buildings of Crossroads. 'You say there's no one to regulate what Willit does. I wonder what he would do if confronted by the law.'

'I can tell you that,' Flower said. 'He'd say that he took in some poor unfortunate young women and gave them work in his saloon. While they were staying there, he would look around for a good situation for them outside of the Double O. It sounds sort of noble, doesn't it?'

'I suppose so, told it that way. The papers the borrowers signed probably had some sort of an agreement to leave the girls with Willit as temporary guardian, so the law couldn't touch him for that. So, your three months are ended?'

'Last week. I told Clyde that I had to stay on to wait for my father; that I'd rather work for the Double O than be sold at auction like an animal.'

'He refused?'

'Yes. Apparently he had some attractive bids for my services.'

'You know,' K. John said, 'I don't really know where Willit would stand legally if this all came out, but I can think of a lot of ugly names for what he's doing.'

Again there was a lengthy silence as they neared the dumpy little town of Crossroads. There was one thing that made no sense to K. John: how had any of this come to involve Justine, who did not fit the pattern of the others? Her father was wealthy and provided her with a decent home. He asked Flower for her thoughts.

'Well, she's going willingly, we know that. She's neat and good-looking enough so that Clyde Willit's interest would be immediately piqued. Maybe Justine is looking for adventure. She may have even heard that the Double O ran a sort of matrimonial agency and that she could find a suitable young man, who are few and far between out here.

'Clyde may be trying to swindle him. Masters is a wealthy man and from what he told us has plans to be wealthier still, soon,' Flower suggested.

'You mean hold Justine for ransom?'

'Not ransom — more like a reward, maybe. I don't see how you could call it kidnapping if she went to him of her own volition.'

'I guess not. This Clyde Willit is one

devious man, Flower. I deeply dislike him even though I've never met him.'

'One thing, K. John, if you don't already realize it, I've never seen the man bully or hurt a woman: they are too valuable. But he has no compunctions about shooting any man foolish enough to try to rescue one of the girls. I've seen it happen.'

'Well, I guess I'm already guilty of that — I've got you.'

'That's the way he'll see it. You've stolen some of his property.'

'I understand.' K. John nodded. They were near enough to the town to smell somebody's wood smoke. 'What I don't understand, Flower, is why you're going back there. You could care nothing for Justine.'

'No more than you — I suppose it's because she is a part of our job. Besides, Justine may be older than I am, better-looking, even smarter ... but the poor dumb boob is riding into a situation she can't possibly understand. We're the only ones who can pull her out of this — for her sake and her father's.'

'And to earn our pay,' added K. John.

'Yes, to earn our pay.'

'You could just ride out, head for home, where your father might be waiting.'

'You could just ride out, too!' she countered, but K. John shook his head.

'I've still got no place to go. I suppose I never have had.'

They entered the town limits and K. John felt that it was time to ask, 'Have we any sort of plan, or are we just riding blindly?'

'I've a plan, though I don't know how good it is,' Flower told him. 'I'll give you a few dollars. You put the horses up and buy yourself a meal somewhere. Later, you can come over to the Double O and drink a few beers while you look around.'

'What are you going to be doing?'

'I'll have a short meal — I'm going to eat crow. I'm going to Clyde Willit and tell him I've been having second thoughts; I've been out on the desert and could see that it was no good my leaving. I'll tell him I want my room back and to work for Double O again, and if he wants to put me in the hands of another man — a good man — I won't fight him over it.'

'I see,' K. John said, not liking the plan but having no other to offer. 'What if Justine recognizes one of us?'

'She won't be down in the saloon tonight,' Flower said, confidently. 'A new girl is always given time alone in a room of her own where she's pampered and served. It settles their doubts.'

'All right,' K. John said, unhappily. They were halted now in front of the stable. Someone shouted inside the Double O across the street and was answered raucously.

'Fun time!' Flower grimaced, slipping from the paint pony's back. When K. John joined her she handed him a few carefully folded dollar bills. 'Get something to eat. I know you're hungry.'

He said, 'Aren't you afraid I'll get

drunk and ride off?' Her dark-green eyes very serious, she looked at him and replied, 'No, K. John. I no longer think you're that kind of man.'

With that, Flower bolted across the dusty street, dodging a tired-looking buckskin horse carrying an even more tired-looking cowboy. K. John watched her go and then turned, leading the horses into the stable.

Glancing around, he saw a little fringed buggy. He did not know if this was Justine's or not, but he recognized the man standing near it, his boot propped on a spoke of the wheel. It was one of his visitors from the night before — the squat, bulky man K. John had taken for their leader.

The man looked his way, but gave no sign that he recognized K. John and stayed fixed where he was, smoking a stubby cigar. From the back room approached the stable-hand K. John had met previously, wiping his hands on a red rag.

'I see you found your way to the

Oxhead,' the man said, perhaps a little too loudly. Had the bulky man heard? He did not turn his head towards them.

'Yes, I did. How did you know that?'

'Pretty simple,' the grinning stable-man answered, stroking the neck of the red roan. 'This here's Emerson Masters' own horse. The paint pony belongs to Miss Justine.' He hesitated. 'I thought maybe you came along with her — but she drove in early this morning with her buggy.'

'I know,' K. John said, without looking in that direction. 'My friend and I were supposed to meet her here.'

'Your friend? Oh, you mean Flower?' The man's face brightened. 'I couldn't think of her name yesterday, but it came to me this morning. Pretty girl! Works at the Double O, don't she?'

'She does,' K. John admitted. He unsaddled the roan while the stable-hand stripped the gear from the pony. Now and then K. John glanced toward the back of the stable where the bulky man still stood as if waiting for someone.

When they were finished, it was with some relief that K. John left the building, striding toward the restaurant up the street. He saw the man's shadow before he fell in stride with him.

'I don't know what you're up to, cowboy,' a menacing voice at his elbow said, 'but you'd have been better off staying on that horse's back and riding on. This town is going to mean nothing but trouble to you.'

Then the man was gone. K. John turned to see the bulky man's back as he ambled across the street toward the Double O.

'Well, I've been warned,' he muttered to himself under his breath, and then continued on his way.

Breakfast at the small home-kitchen-type restaurant K. John visited was substantial, but he really couldn't remember much about his meal. He was too concerned about Flower. Too much could go wrong with this

66

so-called plan of hers.

Would Clyde Willit simply welcome her back into the fold, or would there be some sort of punishment for leaving him in the first place? Even if Flower could see Justine Masters, what good would it do? Justine seemed intent on leaving her father's ranch and striking out in the world on her own. They couldn't just tie her up and take her home. That would do no good in any case. Justine would just leave again at the first opportunity.

Then K. John wondered when Emerson Masters was due back to watch his own daughter. They didn't even know that much.

One thing that was certain was that Masters would hardly reward Flower and K. John for a job well done if Justine remained in the hands of Clyde Willit.

What K. John was to do now — according to Flower's plan — was to go to the Double O and hang around, watching. For what, he did not know.

But at least he would be nearer to Flower if anything were to happen to her. Of course, if the man who had advised him to leave Crossroads were to find him in the Double O, it would probably lead to trouble — assuming the bulky man worked for Willit (which was almost a certainty).

With a sober expression and lowering expectations, K. John crossed the street toward the Double O Saloon. Passing the entrance to an alleyway, a calloused hand reached out, grabbed hold of K. John's arm and spun him out of the view of any enquiring passer-by, forcing his back to thud against the wall of the building there. A hand slipped K. John's Colt revolver from its holster. Holding the weapon expertly, his attacker backed away two steps and panted out his words.

'Where's my daughter?'

'Your . . . what?' K. John was momentarily confused. His attacker was not Emerson Masters, but a much smaller man wearing a thin red flannel shirt and sun-faded jeans. The man's eyes were wide with emotion, his mouth turned down in a sharp frown. His features were shielded by the shadow of his flop hat, tugged low.

'I saw you with her. Now, dammit, tell me where she is!'

'Flower?' K. John asked, still uncertain. The man boomed back at him.

'Certainly, Flower, you knucklehead! Who else would I be talking about? Do you mean you've snatched other girls as well?'

'No, I haven't, I haven't snatched any girls. And I certainly didn't snatch Flower. Mr . . . ?'

'Tremaine. Took a girl and you didn't so much as know her name?'

'She never told me, Mr Tremaine. It didn't seem important at the time.'

'I guess it wouldn't be to someone like you,' Tremaine said, grimly. Glittering eyes studied K. John with disapproval. 'Now, suppose you tell me what you did with my daughter?'

'She went to the Double O.' K. John

jerked his head in the direction of the saloon. Before he could add more, Tremaine erupted. The hand holding the pistol — K. John's own Colt — trembled slightly, but did not move from the man's belly.

'You took her back to Willit, knowing what he is?! He must pay you well. Or are you just some sort of bounty hunter specializing in female runaways?'

Tremaine's blood hadn't cooled any. His rage continued to build.

'You don't understand at all,' K. John said, trying to keep his voice calm. 'Flower only went back to the Double O because it was a part of the plan we have.'

'You have a plan?' Tremaine said, wagging his head. 'What was your part in it supposed to be?'

'Drinking beer in the saloon. That was where I was going,' K. John said, realizing how ridiculous that must sound to Tremaine. 'Look, it's a kind of complicated story, but it's not long. Can't we sit down somewhere, without waving guns, and I'll tell you about it. Then you can tell me why you're here.'

'Me, why I'm here to rescue Flower from that flesh-peddler, Clyde Willit — the very man you just delivered her back to.' After a long pause, Tremaine finally lowered the gun and handed it back to its owner. He agreed to follow K. John to the restaurant he had just left.

# 5

At a quiet corner table where they sat over cups of coffee delivered lethargically by a tired waitress, Warren Tremaine first listened to K. John's rather remarkable tale and then he told his own story.

Tremaine's expression had softened as K. John had spoken of the events leading Flower and himself to the Oxhead and back again. Now the farmer's face seemed to have sagged a bit and he looked exactly like what he was: a tired old man weary from fighting the elements as he searched for a better way of life for himself and his family.

'I knew the proposition was a bad one from the first. But what was I to do?' Tremaine asked, dismally. 'I couldn't even feed myself on the farm without water to grow things. I don't know if Flower told you her mother had died out there, working day after day, trying to survive on what we didn't have.' K. John nodded.

'I couldn't let the same thing happen to Flower!' Tremaine said, powerfully, clenching his hands into fists. He went on more quietly. 'When I heard that Clyde Willit would take girls like Flower in, provide them with food and shelter so long as they worked for him — and at times I'd see Flower scraping the kitchen to look for one thing to eat — well, it only made sense.

'Flower would be taken care of and I would have three months to have a well dug and bring the land back to life. I made the decision. Flower was going to have to be the provider for a while. To my shame I took her to Willit and made the deal. Three months of her labor for a loan of three thousand dollars. There was no other way,' he said, with heavy shame.

'She told me you just got drunk and

rode away after making the deal,' K. John said.

'I did,' Tremaine nodded, sadly. His gaze managed to be steely and ashamed at the same time. 'I couldn't face the girl again. A grief was building up inside me; a grief I tried to soften with whiskey. I could apologize, explain no more to her. I had done what I had to do.'

'How did things work out for you?' K. John asked, still wondering that the farmer had bartered his daughter for a mere loan.

'Fine. The well came in real fine. We raised a big crop of beans and onions. I managed to sell almost all of it to the army.'

'But you didn't tell Flower. She says you never once came to visit her.'

'I couldn't bear another parting,' Tremaine explained. 'I couldn't come back to see her until I had enough money to buy her out of bondage. Profit don't come quick on a farm. It took months to get the water flowing,

74

and more before our first crop came in . . . ' His eyes flickered to K. John's. 'I'm here now, with three thousand dollars.'

'Where'd you put the money?'

'In the bank, of course. As soon as I arrived. Why do you care?' Tremaine demanded.

'I was just hoping that you weren't walking around with it because someone will know you rode in with that much money.'

'I had it — I had it all in my hand when I went to see Willit.' Tremaine finished his coffee. 'He told me I was too late,' he said to K. John, bowing his head. 'I was almost two weeks late. I told him that he was a businessman, he knew these delays happened. The army was slow in paying me. He said that was just too bad.

'I told him I was damned sure taking my daughter, and got a little rough in saying it. He called a couple of his bully boys into the office and told them to throw me out. Once they had me by the arms, he told me that I had defaulted on my loan and damned well knew it.

'Then he said he didn't know where Flower was anyway — she had run off with some wayward cowboy.'

'Which did nothing to cool your temper.'

'It did not,' Tremaine agreed firmly.

While Tremaine had been talking, K. John had been thinking. Clyde Willit was too clever by half. The saloon-owner only wanted everything. He now had Flower back, presumably ready for auction. If Tremaine had not been smart enough to put his money in the Crossroads bank, he would have undoubtedly been relieved of it in some back-alley heist. Even worse, Willit was crooked enough to make a play for Warren Tremaine's land since technically the farmer had defaulted on the loan and, by the farmer's account, that land had grown to a profitable section that could now be sold to someone else.

Simultaneously, Willit had somehow persuaded Justine Masters to join his fold. What sort of a game was he planning to play on Emerson Masters? Nothing straightforward, that was for certain.

'We've got to do something about that man,' K. John said. 'He's planning to ruin you, Flower, and Emerson Masters and his daughter. He's probably got something in mind that will allow him to take control of the Oxhead as well.'

'I don't know a thing about that,' Tremaine said. 'I don't really care. I just want to get Flower back.'

'I don't know if she'd go with you right now,' K. John said, and at that Tremaine's face took on a dark look.

'What do you mean?' he demanded as K. John finished his own cup of coffee and started to rise.

'I mean, the two of us, Flower and me — we were hired to work for the Oxhead, to watch over it for Emerson Masters. Flower seems even more intent on doing so than I am. That's the reason she followed Justine back to the

Double O, as I told you.'

Tremaine's face could not decide whether to be furious or concerned. He asked K. John, 'What should we do now?'

'I think,' K. John Landis said, carefully, 'that you should find a place to lie down for a while and get some sleep. You're obviously exhausted.'

'Maybe so,' Tremaine said. 'I rode all night to get here — a lot of good it did me.

'And you? What are you going to do, Mr Landis?'

'I'm going to stick with the plan,' K. John told him.

'Meaning?'

'Meaning I'm going over to the Double O, drink a few beers, look around and maybe see what I can see.'

The idea was hardly appealing, but that was a part of the hastily contrived plan. He could hardly leave Flower alone. The girl, he thought as he walked toward the Double O, could be a little contrary. She was also moody. But once she had made up her mind to do something, she did it. Flower had gone back to the Double O to rescue a girl who didn't want to be rescued because she had made an agreement with Emerson Masters.

Had Flower learned yet that her father had come looking for her, been rebuffed by Willit? Maybe . . . maybe not. It would depend on which way Willit thought he could bend the truth to his advantage, but K. John was guessing she wouldn't be told of Warren Tremaine's visit.

The day was again hot and dusty as K. John mounted the plank walk in front of the Double O Saloon, then hesitated. The man who had threatened him that morning had warned him out of town. He was certainly a Willit man, and almost certainly the man who had clubbed him down on the Oxhead. He would not be welcomed warmly to the Double O. But what else was he to do? He had committed himself to this course of action, and he owed it to

Flower to remain near enough to render aid if she were threatened.

K. John waited until he saw a group of three cowboys from some local ranch approach the green door of the saloon, happily gibing with each other. He joined their group as they entered the Double O. The cowboys headed toward the bar together and K. John tagged along with them as they arranged themselves along its length. They ordered beer and K. John did the same when the bartender glanced his way.

The cowboys discussed range conditions, their boss, whom they all seemed to like, and the likelihood of rain; then they looked over the dancehall girls, none of whom was Flower, and sipped their beer. K. John found himself envying their genial banter, the life they seemed to lead. He settled in to drink his own beer, which was not as good as the long-anticipated drink he had imagined for days now.

He turned his back to the bar, hooking his elbows over it, mug in hand. There was no sign of Justine or of Flower, no face resembling that of the man who had warned him off. All he saw were the mostly happy faces of men who had found their oasis in the desert. Some were more sober than others, some more boisterous, but the Double O seemed no different from a dozen other saloons K. John had visited in his time.

He did not see Clyde Willit. He had not yet encountered the man, did not know what he looked like, but the saloon-owner would have undoubtedly stood out from this crowd of trail-dusty, work- and weather-hardened men.

'Want to get rid of our money quicker, Ernie?' one of the cowhands at the bar asked another long-jawed rider.

Not understanding at first, K. John looked in the same direction as the young cowboy. Two employees in white shirts were removing the green canvas covering from the roulette table and men were starting to gather around the gaming table, searching their pockets for more money to give to Clyde Willit.

'Not me,' the man named Ernie said, shaking his head. 'I know a man who lost his best cutting horse at that table.'

'But,' another cowhand — older, chubbier — chipped in, 'I know a man who won himself a bride at it.'

K. John glanced at the man. He was not joking, and K. John could see how that improbable occurrence might have eventuated.

'I'm just talking about nickels,' the younger man said.

'Play for nickels, you only win nickels,' Ernie advised.

'And that's all I'd lose,' the kid answered. 'I ride the boss's horses and don't need me a bride. I've got Rosie.'

'I'll go for nickels and dimes,' the older hand said. 'If we get lucky we maybe can drink for free all day. If we don't, well, then we'll just go home.'

'Just watch for that gambling bug. It's got a hard bite,' Ernie said, returning to lean on the bar counter as the other two swaggered off to see how much money they could lose.

K. John heard this all only peripherally. He needed to find Flower if only to make sure she was safe. He knew she had a room upstairs and he eyed the stairway leading that way. At the foot of the staircase sat a wide-shouldered man with a cup of coffee and a belt gun. Willit's posted guard, no doubt. K. John reflected that even if he were to get past the man, he did not know which room was Flower's. His arrival on the second floor could cause someone to raise a real ruckus.

His only thought was to try asking one of the other girls working there where he might find Flower. Looking around, he noticed that most of them seemed very young with here and there what might have been an older matron. Were these girls the slaves of fortune as Flower had been? Their faces were bright only when someone at one of the tables joked with them or made a grab for them as they passed; these were trained smiles — learned, mechanical reactions. When they turned their faces from the patrons they were only pale, expressionless masks, their eyes hollow.

Watching, listening to the saloon noises, K. John guessed that some of the girls would willingly let Willit trade them away as bondswomen, servants, housekeepers. Some would not have an objection in the world to being a purchased wife. This sort of merry drudgery could have no satisfaction for them.

A girl, quite young — perhaps eighteen or nineteen — with dark hair and expressionless eyes approached the bar carrying a tray crammed with empty beer mugs, which she placed on the counter, waiting for the bartender. She wore dark-blue silk and a tiny matching hat. Her blouse was worn off her bare, freckled shoulders.

Stepping up next to K. John Landis she offered him one of her ritual smiles. It faded as he asked, 'Seen Flower today?'

Her dark eyes became curious, alert,

and then faded to an expressionless stare. The question went unspoken between them — *Who are you and why should I tell you anything?*

K. John rushed into the opening her doubt provided. 'I'm a friend of her father. He sent me to try to find her and take her home.'

'I don't know . . . ' The girl hesitated, looking around her. The bartender glanced her way. 'Six mugs for table three, Charlie!' she shouted in a not-unpleasant voice. The bartender nodded and started filling half a dozen mugs as the girl unloaded the empty glasses from her tray. She wiped her hands dry on a bar towel, avoiding K. John's eyes.

'I'm new here, I don't know any Flower,' she said.

'All right,' K. John said, patiently. 'It's just that her father misses her and I'm sure she's ready to go home. I need to find her. Can you tell me which room she might be in?'

'Look, mister . . . ' The girl was

interrupted as the bartender, holding the ears to six mugs of beer, arrived, placing them on the tray as he gathered the empty glasses. 'I don't think I can tell you.'

'What if it was someone looking for you — wouldn't you want them to be told?'

'I can't . . . ' One of the older women, matrons as K. John thought of them, was approaching the bar, wondering at the delay. 'My name's Barbara Casey,' the girl said hurriedly, picking up the tray. 'Meet me in the alley in fifteen minutes.'

She then spun around and walked away under the matron's glare, which adjusted itself to include K. John, who looked exactly like what he was: a rambling cowhand who could not afford the price of one of Clyde Willit's prime herd of women.

From the roulette table a man in a town suit called out, 'Fifty dollars on red,' and the matron switched her attention. This sounded like a more promising prospect for Willit. The man obviously had some money in his pocket.

Ernie, the slim cowhand at the bar, watched with a tolerant smile as his friends whooped and moaned. K. John waited, sipping at his beer. Barbara seemed willing to give him some information — outside of the saloon. When K. John figured that fifteen minutes had passed, he made his way out, still having not seen Flower, Justine or Clyde Willit — though what he would have done if he had seen any of them was uncertain. Maybe after talking to Barbara he could form a better plan.

There was a back door to the saloon, K. John saw as he exited the place and went into the alley, and there in the heat of the day Barbara waited, sketching figures in the sandy soil with the toe of her little shoe. She looked up at him shyly, doubtfully, as he strode nearer. He tried to smile to reassure her.

Three paces on his smile was suddenly erased as something heavy and menacing drove into his back just above the belt line.

K. John chewed on a curse and spat it out as he was driven face-first to the dust, the weight of his attacker on him. He had been set up and stupidly he had fallen for it.

# 6

It was worse than before, much worse. Then the Willit man had just cracked him on the skull with his pistol barrel and sent K. John off to dreamland. He had not fought back then. This time he did, with an impotent fury. There were three of them and they rained down punches on him — jaw, skull, ribs and kidneys. K. John twisted this way and that, trying to fend off his attackers, but it was no use. They beat him into insensibility. Through a curtain of swirling noise, K. John heard their voices.

'Hit him any more, Hammond, we'll kill him,' one of the men said.

'I don't care if we do,' a gruff voice answered — the voice of the man who had previously warned K. John off, now identified as Hammond.

'Maybe not, but I do!' the first man warned.

'You always were soft,' Hammond answered in a growl. One of the men rose from K. John and a second later a boot was driven with violent force into his already-damaged ribs. 'All right, let's go!' Hammond said. 'But if I ever see him again, I'll shoot him dead, no questions asked.'

'What you do then is your business. I just want no part of a killing.'

'I'll say it again, Bean — you're just too soft for this line of work.'

The men grunted, spat and walked away on shuffling feet, their day's work done. K. John's hadn't even begun and he doubted that he was capable of even attempting anything more. Blood mingled with the dust in his nostrils, his mouth. His ribs and lower back screamed out with pain. His skull rang and he had difficulty breathing. Trying to rise, he collapsed immediately, his face again eating dirt. He wanted to roll over but could not. The sun was high, hot and yellow. Someone nudged his boot sole with a foot.

'Well,' a man said, 'he's not dead. Are you sure you want to do this?'

Whoever the man had spoken to did not answer. Maybe a nod was given. K. John could not turn his head to watch, but he heard the sound of an approaching wagon drawn by two horses. What did they mean to do: escort him to the bone yard or simply take him far out of town, never to return?

The hands that scooped him up off the ground were more gentle than he had expected, and as he was placed, face-up in the bed of the wagon, he could have sworn he heard the rustling of skirts.

'Flower?' K. John croaked in a dry voice, but there was no answer. The team of horses was started and the wagon rolled away. K. John had his eyes open, but could see nothing but the back of the head of the man driving the horses. Then they were away from town and, without the shade of the buildings in his eyes, K. John was forced to close them as tightly as he could. He had no idea who these people might be: friends or foes; saviors or members of the same gang that had beaten him? He could do nothing but ride along, his eyes closed, every bone and organ in his body crying out for relief when none could be given. But heading where?

He did not think of that for long; no good destination occurred to him. He only rode on against the hard boards of the wagon, each bump jolting pain through his body. He was going away from Crossroads, which had no use at all for him, and away from Flower, who even now might be in desperate need of his help. His exhausted body wished for rest, but K. John fought not to give in to that desire. A few miles on, his body submitted and he passed into a deep, dark sleep.

★　★　★

Where was he? His mind responded as slowly as his battered body. K. John found that he was in a small room constructed of logs. The room was tiny, dark; the bed beneath him was softer than any he could remember sleeping on. There were frills on the yellow coverlet thrown over him, a few pieces of ceramic figures — a shepherdess and a boy with a bugle among them — on the nearby dresser. There was also a faint scent lingering in the air, of the sort no man ever used.

Had Flower managed to somehow rescue him and bring him home to Warren Tremaine's farm? That was as far as K. John's thinking carried him before the irresistible urge to sleep again overcame him. He drifted off again with one strange memory to accompany him. It seemed to him that when he was nearly asleep a woman had kissed his forehead gently in farewell.

★   ★   ★

He recognized the room from the day before, but did not recognize the girl who was standing near his bed with a blue coffee pot and empty ceramic cup. She was not tall, but slender enough so that she appeared to be. She wore blue jeans and a faded light-blue work shirt. Her hair was a dark coppery colour — Irish hair — worn in pigtails, and her dark eyes were wide and expressive.

'Coffee?' she asked, beginning to pour a cup for K. John.

'Barbara?' he asked, with a sort of weary astonishment.

'It is I,' she nodded.

'Well, I'll be ... ' He struggled, trying to speak and sit up in bed at the same time. He seemed to have enough breath for only one or the other. His ribs hurt, his kidneys as well, but he felt remarkably well otherwise.

Sitting up, bolstered by another pillow, he accepted the coffee, sipped it and asked:

'What's happened? I thought you'd set me up for a beating.'

'I was afraid that's what you'd think.'

'But then ... where am I?'

'On my ranch,' Barbara told him.

'Your ranch?'

'That's what I call it, yes. It's not as big as some of those Texas spreads, but it's fairly large for this part of the country.'

'Well, then, why,' K. John asked, placing his coffee cup aside, 'were you working at the Double O Saloon?'

'That's simple. I don't think we made a hundred dollars last year. I was losing ranch-hands since I couldn't afford to pay them. I was about to lose the property. I hadn't the cash money to pay my taxes. There's only one man anywhere near Crossroads with money to lend. So I went to see Mr Willit.'

'But, you must have known his reputation.'

'Of course I knew! But what were my options? There were none. I figured that within three months we would sell some beef — you know the army is out here now — and show enough increase to pay him back.'

'How did that work out?'

'I don't know. I just got back. I'm riding out with my foreman in a little while to take a look around and count steers.'

'I'd like to go,' K. John said.

'Well, you're not going to. It would be criminal to take you. You are going to stay around the house.'

'But Flower needs me,' he objected.

'She doesn't need you in the shape you're in. You couldn't swat a fly.'

'I suppose not,' K. John was forced to admit. She picked up the coffee pot and cup as if preparing to leave. He had to ask her:

'Barbara what happened yesterday?'

'You don't remember?' she asked, smiling faintly.

'A part of it . . . most of it — before you rescued me in the alley.'

'After I told you I'd meet you outside, I slipped through the kitchen to the back door and went out. I was standing there aimlessly when I saw you walking toward me, and from the other direction I saw Hammond, Bean and

96

Dungee approaching. They fell in behind you and the beating started. I ran away,' she said apologetically. 'I couldn't do much to help.'

'Hammond said he'd make me sorry if I hung around town,' K. John said. 'But how did I get here? You must have had help?'

'Charlie Drummond, the head bartender, helped me. Charlie's not as gruff as he acts. He sent one of his boys for a beer wagon, and when it got there he helped me load you in it.'

'Is he still here? I'd like to thank him.'

'No. Charlie went back last night. They'd miss the wagon, and I don't think he would want to talk to you, anyway.'

'I suppose not.'

Barbara sat on a wooden chair, still holding the coffee pot and cup. She lifted her dark eyes to his and asked, 'Was what you told me about Flower's father having come to retrieve her, true?'

K. John frowned. 'Of course it was. Why would I make up something like that?'

'I don't know,' she shrugged. 'When you live among liars like I was forced to do at the Double O, sometimes you can't recognize the truth any more. At any rate it got me to thinking about what I had done to myself. I had pretty much decided that I was going to come home to the ranch before I had talked to you. You sort of helped me to make up my mind. The way Clyde Willit is treating those young girls, the way he is cheating their families, it's just criminal!' Barbara paused before continuing.

'Now, I hope that the money I was forced to borrow has made a difference here and I can pay him off. And I will. In the meantime, if Willit decides he wants badly enough to sell me for a slave, he'll find me surrounded by some men who are ready and willing to shoot if he tries it.'

'So, you're going to wait him out?'

She nodded. 'That's it. If he wants to

send someone after me, he had better have a badge and a warrant. I'd surrender to the law if it came to that, but I won't be frightened off my ranch.'

Barbara had spunk, that was certain. But none of this was of any help to Flower — or to Justine Masters. He said as much to Barbara, reminding her. 'Flower's time is already up. I'm afraid that Warren Tremaine will just blow up, storm the saloon and get himself killed.'

'Warren?'

'That's Flower's father. The worst thing is, he had the money to pay off Flower's contract, but Willit turned him down because he got there just a few weeks too late with it.'

'What did you have in mind that's any safer than storming the saloon?' Barbara asked.

'Nothing at the time. You never did tell me which room was Flower's, and which one Justine Masters is using.'

'Who?' Barbara looked genuinely

puzzled, but then Justine wouldn't be mingling with the bar-girls yet, according to Flower. K. John described her to Barbara.

'Oh, the prissy one!' she said, nodding her head.

'I suppose so,' K. John said, thinking. 'But she's her father's pride and joy as most daughters are.'

'I understand.'

'At any rate, the girl doesn't deserve to sink into that swamp Willit has developed down there.'

'No, no one does,' Barbara agreed. 'What does Clyde Willit have in mind for Justine?'

'I don't know. I have a few guesses, but nothing to base them on. I only know that whichever way it goes, Emerson Masters is going to get hurt.'

'Financially? Emotionally?'

'Both, one imagines. Flower feels that Justine is her responsibility, and has given back her own freedom to try to help a woman who seems not to want to be helped.'

'She hasn't seen enough of the Double O yet,' Barbara said.

'No, and after she does, she may find herself too ashamed to go home to Oxhead.'

'Oxhead Ranch? Is that where she's from? Why, that's a big-money outfit!' Barbara said, wondering that a woman with all of the advantages of Justine Masters could subject herself to a life like the one she would lead under Clyde Willit.

'Yes,' K. John said, 'and from what Emerson Masters told us, it's about to get richer.'

Barbara shrugged. 'Money isn't everything.'

'No,' K. John agreed, 'but then most people who live in reasonable comfort try to shelter their children from the evils of the world so that their sons and daughters don't even realize how many snakes and coyotes there are prowling around.'

'True, I suppose,' Barbara answered. 'I never had such problems. My mother died in childbirth and when I was five years old my father was killed by a gang of would-be rustlers.'

'It sounds like you had it rough.'

'It was all right. Miles Dietrich — he was foreman here under my father for many years until he recently passed away — and his wife Evette always took care of me. But,' she added, looking more directly at K. John, 'with my father buried out back, you can believe that I knew about the evil in the world.'

'Still you went to Clyde Willit.'

'Yes!' she said, briefly sparking with Irish temper. 'For the ranch. For the brand. For my father. I could not lose this ranch. I will not!'

That was emphatic enough. K. John could sympathize with the woman. This was the only home she had ever had, one her father had built up from scratch in what would have been the rough days. She could not now lose it over one foolish mistake. It was too bad that Justine Masters didn't have the same sort of insight, appreciation — whatever it took.

How much of this had Emerson Masters feared? What did he know of Willit and his machinations? Why had it been so urgent for him to get to Albuquerque? K. John shook his head. It was all too much to think about on this morning.

Finally rising, K. John made his way painfully to the kitchen. Here, as Barbara had promised, breakfast was served by an elderly, hunched woman who had to be Evette, whose husband had been the long-time ranch foreman. Now he was dead and Evette was just one more lonesome widow of the desert.

He ate slowly, gratefully. Evette refilled his coffee cup when it was empty. They did not speak a word between them. What was there to say?

Wandering outside on stiff legs, his side and skull still aching, he found a rattan chair on the front porch and gingerly eased himself into it. Minutes later Barbara rode up, seated on a heavy-legged buckskin horse.

'You're going to stay here and rest up today, right?' she asked, though by her tone she indicated something else. K. John nodded. He was already thinking of Flower, though. Barbara smiled as if reading his inner thoughts.

'If you can't resist the urge to see Crossroads again, you can take either the red roan or the dun pony.'

Then she was gone, whirling her horse away, erect in the saddle, the breeze toying with her reddish hair. 'I heard that!' a peevish voice said from behind K. John.

K. John craned his neck painfully to see a young, slender man with dark curly hair.

'I think maybe you're feeling up to riding right now,' the young man said.

'Not really,' K. John had to answer truthfully.

'I think you are. Take the dun and get out of here. My name's Eric Styles. You might want to remember that name.

I'm ramrod on this ranch now, and Barbara is my woman. I mean to keep her.'

'You're telling the wrong person,' K. John said, looking up at Styles. 'Tell that to Barbara!'

Warily, K. John rose, not because Eric Styles had frightened him off, but because he did need to get back to Crossroads if he were going to help Flower. And he knew that Warren Tremaine would be getting anxious, perhaps anxious enough to do something foolish, especially now that K. John had seemingly disappeared. K. John's fear of the old man rushing into the Double O with a gun to rescue his daughter as he had told Barbara was quite real. Tremaine would only end up getting himself killed, leaving Flower an orphan.

The first thing to do was to find Tremaine and speak calmly with him now that the farmer was rested and presumably over his first wave of anger.

K. John walked stiffly toward the

horse barn. He still hurt everywhere. The knot Hammond had put on his head back at the Oxhead still ached, Oh, well, he told himself, he had ridden many a mile feeling worse than he did now. That was true, but there had been no choice then and he had been younger.

Saddling the patient dun pony was by far the worst of it. His ribs protested violently with each movement. Hammond, who was responsible for all of it, had sworn to kill K. John the next time they met. Now K. John took a similar oath. There would be no choice about it. When a man has vowed to shoot you on sight, in front of witnesses, you had to be ready and willing to return the favor.

The day was no cooler than the previous ones had been. Hot, dusty as K. John hit the trail toward Crossroads, which could be easily followed due to the many horse tracks leading that way. He still had no firm idea of what he meant to do. It seemed important to talk to Flower before making another move. At the breakfast table, Barbara had walked by on her way out and slipped K. John a once-folded piece of paper on which was written 'Room 5'.

Now all he needed was some way to secretly ascend to the second floor of the Double O and get to that room. It was one of those ideas that seemed simple in conception, but was blunted by reality. As he rode, K. John toyed with a dozen ideas — diversions, stealth, bluff — as he rode, but found none of them workable. All right, then, he would just have to tough it out — he meant to see Flower, and that was that.

He wondered about the intent of the man riding behind him. He had spotted him earlier, and now was certain as he continued up the road. Someone was trailing him, perhaps intent on keeping K. John and his meddlesome ways from ever reaching Crossroads.

# 7

K. John could see the buildings of the town when he was a mile away. The land here was nearly flat in every direction you cared to look. Maybe that was the reason the man shadowing him had fallen off his trail. There was no way to disguise the tracker's movements in this country.

K. John stabled up the dun horse, leaving the borrowed saddle there. Then, with his hat tugged low against the desert sun, he made his hobbling way toward the hotel. If he were honest, there were moments when thoughts of simply riding out of Crossroads flickered through his mind. K. John would never make a good martyr, but thoughts of Flower kept him trudging along through the heat of the day.

He found Warren Tremaine sitting in his hotel room, the window half-open.

He was not yet dressed. Sitting on the edge of his mussed bed, he somehow reminded K. John of a scrawny frog. There was a half-empty quart bottle of whiskey on the floor beside him and a glass in his hand. He glanced up morosely as K. John rapped on the door frame and entered the room.

Examining K. John with his froglike eyes, Flower's father said, 'I see you've been in a fight. Did you get Flower out of there?'

'No, I didn't,' K. John answered, seating himself heavily in a chair. 'I haven't been able to find her. Now I think I know where she is.'

Tremaine nodded and poured some more whiskey into his glass. 'Things are moving kind of slowly, wouldn't you say?' he asked K. John. His pursed lips moved in and out soundlessly. Then he took a sip of liquor and asked K. John, 'Do you have a taste for this stuff?'

'Not much. I've never found it be useful for anything except as something to throw your money away on.'

'I used to drink.' Tremaine watched the amber liquid in his glass as he slowly swirled it around. 'Maybe Flower told you?'

'She told me.'

'That was because I lost her mother. This,' he said, holding the glass up, 'is because I'm losing my daughter.'

'You're not, you know,' K. John replied. 'Just be patient. We'll get her out of there and you can take her home.'

'Patient?' repeated the old man, still staring down at his whiskey glass. 'Patience is something that experience whittles away.'

'But you . . . '

Warren Tremaine's eyes flashed. He made a gesture that seemed he was going to hurl his drink away in frustration, but the glass did not leave his hand. Instead, he reached toward one of his boots, fumbling with it. 'Hand me my rifle, son,' he said, his words slurred. 'I'll show you something better than patience.'

'That's the worst possible way of handling matters,' K. John told him, seriously. 'You want Flower back; she needs you back — alive.'

'I can handle that Clyde Willit and any of his boys.' Tremaine scowled, draining his glass. It was now the whiskey that was doing the talking. K. John Landis waited until Tremaine had slapped his glass down on the bedside table and wiped his mouth with his wrist. Then K. John rose and, standing before Tremaine, told the older man, 'I'll take care of Flower's troubles from now on.'

'That sounds as if you mean more than getting her out of the Double O,' Tremaine said in a voice that was growing increasingly indistinct.

K. John pulled himself up short mentally. The way he had phrased that sounded like he had meant something else. Had he? 'I'll take care of things,' he promised.

Tremaine looked as if he were ready to pass out. 'Just because you're younger . . . ' he muttered.

And a lot more sober, K. John thought. Before he had reached the door again, he glanced back to see Tremaine sprawled on the bed, one boot on, one off.

K. John thought about taking Warren Tremaine's Winchester with him, but left it. The aggrieved father could always find another gun if he was determined.

Still moving gingerly, K. John went out into the hall and started toward the stairs. Going down these to the lobby, he passed a man with a familiar face. He started slightly at the glimpse he had of the man named Bean, Hammond's sidekick — the one who had argued against killing K. John — but neither of them spoke. Both continued on their way, but K. John knew that his reappearance in Crossroads had now been noted.

Well, it couldn't have been kept secret for long; not with what he had planned, which was to return to the

Double O. He knew full well that trouble awaited him there, but it was where Flower was hidden — imprisoned? — waiting, hoping for help that could only arrive in the form of K. John.

Feeling not much better physically and a lot less confident than before, if that was possible, K. John started toward the Double O. He couldn't really blame Tremaine for wanting to walk in and start blasting away. Emerson Masters would likely have felt the same way about Justine if he were around. K. John didn't have that sudden flush of red-hot rage that a father must feel when one of his cubs is threatened, but instead carried a slowly simmering dark fire. He would have his revenge, but first he must make sure that Flower was safe. And Justine, for he knew that Flower would not leave without rescuing the Masters girl.

That made everything so damned complicated.

K. John returned to the alleyways,

believing them to be safer than approaching the Double O directly. His pistol, however, was always kept near to hand and his eyes were alert to every shadow and movement. He had not forgotten — could not afford to forget — Hammond's vow to kill him on sight, and this was the sort of frontier town where the law was only something you carried on your hip.

Easing past a cross-alley after first looking carefully around, K. John found himself within sight of his goal. The back door to the Double O was open, and nearby stood something extraordinary. Around the corner, not ten paces from the saloon door, stood a blonde woman in a long, silken, white dress. Her hair was artfully arranged, her eyes bright. The man holding her was smiling, his manner intent.

K. John had to pause to collect himself. He could not believe what he was seeing. The woman was Justine Masters, and the man was — had to be — Clyde Willit. K. John had never seen the saloon-owner before, but the tall man in the neatly tailored gray town suit had to be him. Who else could it be holding Justine in his arms mere steps from the saloon door?

If it was Clyde Willit — and K. John had no doubt that this was the owner of the Double O Saloon — he was younger than K. John had expected. Straight, broad-shouldered, Willit wore a thin mustache beneath a longish nose. K. John started that way without a real plan in his head. Five paces on he was concealed by the corner of the building. He could hear low murmuring from the couple standing just out of his view. Apparently, they were enthralled with each other — or, in Willit's case — pretending to be.

K. John didn't waste any more time trying to figure it out. He stepped on to the sagging wooden porch and walked through the kitchen, which was warm with steam. The place smelled of frying steaks and boiled potatoes, which was probably all that they served and all the saloon patrons would care to eat.

There were three men in the kitchen, but none of them stopped him or said a word as he crossed the room to the inner doorway: they had their own business to take care of.

The saloon, beyond the door, was midday raucous. The roulette table had not yet been opened for gambling, but a few desultory card games were taking place, and a lot of drinking, shoulder-slapping and boisterous laughter. K. John saw no one he knew in the crowded room.

Taking a deep breath, K. John carried on directly to the stairs leading to the second-floor rooms. A man K. John hadn't seen previously was sitting on a chair on guard at the foot of the stairs. He looked infinitely bored, his eyes half-shut. Perhaps he was suffering from a hangover, K. John speculated.

K. John walked directly toward the seated man. 'Mr Willit says for me to get the woman's stuff.'

Even to K. John's ears the excuse

sounded lame and unlikely, but the guard only nodded at him, yawned and gestured with his arm toward the staircase. So was Willit actually planning on taking Justine someplace else? She had been dressed as if for a wedding. With his heart pounding wildly, K. John started swiftly up the stairs, half-expecting the guard to yell out, for Willit himself to appear and demand to know what he was doing. The saloon remained silent, however, except for the constant shouts and gibes of the drinking men. These sounds fell away as K. John mounted to the second floor and turned down the bare hallway. Someone long ago had inexpertly painted the room numbers in white on the doors. K. John moved directly to Room 5, glancing over his shoulder for any sign of interference.

He knocked lightly on the door, getting no response. Was Flower even inside? Had she been moved since Barbara saw her last? Worse, was she lying in there trussed and gagged, unable to move or speak? K. John lifted his hand to knock again, but the door opened just then and an uncertain Flower stood there in her jeans and trail shirt, hesitantly looking up at him, her dark-green eyes sparkling.

'It's about time,' she said, with the faintest of smiles.

'Yes, I guess it is,' K. John responded as he entered the room and closed the door behind him.

'Are you taking me out of here?' Flower asked.

'Yes, I am. I'm taking you out, and delivering you to your father — he's in town, you know.'

'Clyde Willit told me,' Flower said, her voice carrying that bitterness she seemed to reserve only for the saloon-keeper.

'You know about Willit refusing him, then?'

'Yes. Clyde told me that he would let Father stew awhile and then, under certain conditions, release me from my contract.'

'What conditions?' K. John asked.

'What would you guess? A piece of our land and any profits we might make off it.'

'That would put Warren in a real predicament,' K. John said.

'Would it? You know my father? Have you met and talked to him?'

'I have, and believe me he would do anything to get you home, even if it meant losing most of what he has worked for.'

'Where is he now?' Flower asked. She had turned away to look out the window, her arms folded.

'At the hotel — I saw him a little while ago.'

'Why isn't he here? Is he drunk, K. John? Passed out maybe?'

When she turned back towards him there was a hint of fury on her lips, a sneer. Well, the way Flower saw things she had been sold into bondage for three long months by her own father, a man who had never even once troubled to come and visit her.

'Quit being childish!' K. John ordered, a little more firmly than he had intended. 'He wanted to come — with his Winchester. I convinced him that was the wrong way to do things. It would have been twice as hard for two men to sneak in here. He's heartbroken. After his last meeting with Willit, he thought he had the right to get drunk.'

Flower didn't reply. She moved a few steps nearer to K. John and recovered her smile. 'All right! You're here — what do we do now?'

'We get out of here. If you know a way?'

'What about Justine? She's the reason behind this, if you remember?' Flower said calmly.

'Oh, I remember, but there's no way to get her out now — she's already out.'

Briefly, K. John told Flower what he had witnessed outside with Justine dressed up in what for all the world appeared to be a wedding dress.

'Let's get out of here, then — and

fast!' Flower said, with urgency.

'Wait a minute.' K. John grabbed her arm as she started toward the door. 'You can't think that she's really going to marry Clyde Willit.'

'Of course she is. Everyone marries him. This is the third time in the last two years that I know of.'

'But why . . . ?'

'The past unfortunate widows have all had wealthy fathers.'

'You mean he wants Oxhead.'

'Of course,' Flower said, pulling insistently away.

'I see — at least, I think I do. But when Emerson Masters gets back from Albuquerque . . . '

'What makes you think he'll be coming back?' Flower demanded rather sharply. The girl obviously knew more than she had shared with him before. He would have liked to have gone into it, but Flower was right: this was not the time for jawing, but for moving.

'How do we get out of here?' K. John asked in a near-whisper as Flower placed her hand on the brass doorknob. 'Do we try to run some kind of a bluff?'

'There's a ladder nailed up against the outside wall in case of fire. We can go through Gloria's room and get to it. But, K. John,' Flower told him, 'you'll have to keep your eyes closed.'

'Climb down an outside ladder with my eyes closed?' K. John asked in disbelief. It made no sense to him, but then little had lately. Flower slipped out of her room and he followed. A dozen steps along the empty corridor they came to another room — Room 4 — and Flower paused only long enough to whisper to K. John:

'Eyes closed!'

K. John nodded mutely, still not understanding. They entered a room much like Flower's but this was more cluttered with doo-dahs and female clothes thrown willy-nilly about the place. Flower glanced at him and K. John closed his eyes, but not before seeing the reason for her caution. The girl named Gloria was sprawled across her unkempt bed with only a sheet to cover her. Maybe Flower had feared Gloria would not even have that much incidental modesty.

K. John, eyes now firmly shut, felt Flower take his hand and tug him toward the window. She went out first, her little boots finding the rungs of the old, splintered fire-ladder easily. Perhaps she had tested this escape route before.

K. John fumbled with sill and ladder as he swung out into the open air and descended behind Flower.

To meet the man with the gun at the bottom of the ladder.

# 8

'I don't have to ask you to hoist your hands, do I?'

It was Charlie, the stony-faced bartender, who stood there; in his hands, a short-barreled twelve-gauge shotgun — the tool he used to maintain order in the saloon, when necessary.

'Take it easy, Charlie!' K. John replied, his hands raised.

'Just what are you up to?' Charlie asked. 'First Barbara, now Flower. Do you mean to empty the nest of all the little birds?'

'If I could,' K. John answered, without thinking. The bartender's face grew even grimmer.

'Charlie!' Flower interrupted, stepping in front of K. John. 'You have to understand. You know my time was up. Now we've got to try to stop Willit — he's going to get married again.'

124

'The new girl?' Charlie asked, with a little softening of his features.

'Yes. Her name is Justine Masters,' Flower told him.

'Masters?' Charlie's face grew thoughtful. 'Like in Emerson Masters?'

'Exactly like that — she's his only daughter,' Flower said.

Charlie whistled softly. 'The boss has hooked himself a big one this time.'

'He has.' Flower put her hand on his arm. 'Charlie, we've got to try to stop this. Justine won't be left alive long after her wedding day, and you know it.'

'No, I guess not. Mr Willit has had bad luck with his wives.'

'Charlie, you have to let us go,' K. John said. 'The girl is young and naive. She doesn't deserve to die for that.'

'No.' Charlie hesitated and he lowered his shotgun. 'But it's a fool's errand, you know. Hammond, Bean and Dungee will be in the wedding party. They've already proven that they can handle you.'

'I appreciate your confidence in me,'

K. John said, without humor.

'K. John can take care of them all,' Flower said, brashly. 'Just give us a chance to stop this marriage — if it can be called that instead of what it really is.'

'Clyde Willit is my boss,' Charlie ruminated, 'has been for a long time. But I haven't held with a lot of what goes on around the Double O. That's the reason I was willing to help Barbara the other day.

'All right!' Charlie finally decided. 'Go on, then! What do I care if you get yourself killed?' He turned his back on them. 'I've got work to do.'

They watched him stump away. Then Flower grabbed K. John's arm.

'If they've gone, we'll need horses.'

'Why don't you just stay here?' K. John asked, but she ignored him. 'I've got the dun I borrowed from Barbara, that's all,' he said.

'We'll just have to rent another one, then. As you know I am quite careful with money, K. John. I still have some of the advance money Emerson Masters paid us.'

They started off through the heat toward the stable where K. John had left the dun horse. 'Where will they be going, Flower? Do you know?'

'To Judge Baxter's house. He's the one who officiates at all of Willit's weddings. No one knows if he's really even a judge or just calls himself one. We've never had an election for that office. No matter, the girls get to see the trappings of a legal marriage, and they're satisfied.'

Crossing the main street they glimpsed a buggy being driven out toward the south. Behind it were three riders. The witnesses. The Double O gang of thugs. Flower tugged urgently at K. John's arm. 'We've got to hurry.'

Entering the stable once again, K. John saw something he had not been alert enough to notice earlier. The red roan belonging to Emerson Masters and the little paint pony that was Justine's were both still in their stalls, looking sleek and well-rested. K. John had not been interested in looking at horses when he returned from Barbara's ranch. Now, as they searched for a horse for Flower to ride to Judge Baxter's, his eyes immediately fastened on these.

K. John saw the dun, still a little trail-weary, and suggested, 'How about we take those two again?'

The stablehand showed no surprise at seeing these two together again as he strolled toward them. Flower smiled at the man. K. John saw her tuck her little purse back inside her shirt.

'Come to get your horses?' the stablehand asked.

'Yes,' Flower answered before K. John could speak. 'Charge whatever we owe you to the Oxhead account. Mr Masters will be back in the morning to settle up.'

If Flower knew that, she had better sources of information than K. John did. He doubted that she knew a thing about Masters' schedule. She knew more than the stablehand did, however, and he just smiled at her and showed them where he had kept their tack, offering to saddle Flower's horse for her.

'There's my father's bay horse,' Flower said as they outfitted their ponies. On a whim, K. John responded:

'We'll swing by the hotel and pick him up.'

'He's drunk!'

'This will sober him up quick enough. He deserves it, Flower. He's feeling old, defeated and useless. Let's take him along.' Besides, they could use another gun. Flower nodded, doubtfully. It seemed to K. John that she was anxious over meeting her father again; unsure of how to put old regrets behind her.

They rode toward the hotel leading Warren Tremaine's saddled horse. K. John was of two minds about this plan of his. For one thing, he didn't want to lose Willit and Justine as they drove to their wedding. But what was there to do, really, if both were wishing to get married? Break it up at gunpoint? Maybe. But K. John felt it was even more important to get Flower and her father back together, on amicable terms. Tremaine must have worked his head off on the farm, day and night for the past three months, only to arrive and have Willit disappoint him.

Lord knows, those three months had to have been equally difficult for Flower. But they had a chance now for happiness and K. John meant to do the best he could to bring them together, friendly-like. Maybe, he considered, it was because he had never known his own father.

Flower was frowning, and she continued to frown as K. John swung down from his horse and tied the roan and the bay to the hotel hitch-rail. He looked back at Flower, who had not moved, hoping to see some sign of the anger on her face receding. There was none. She sat stonily in her saddle, looking straight ahead.

'Coming in with me?' K. John asked.

'I don't even want to see him,' she said, tightly.

'You're going to in a few minutes,' he said, walking to her horse to look up at her, 'whether you like it or not.'

'I'll not like it, then,' she answered, looking away from K. John. 'Besides you don't know if he wants to come with us. You don't even know if you can rouse him from a drunken stupor.'

'You're a hard woman, Flower!' K. John shook his head, but Flower did not respond. He pushed away from her horse and walked up on to the hotel porch. K. John still had his doubts. They were wasting time here, or so it seemed. Yet, he was still unsure that they could do anything to stop the wedding of Justine and Willit. He had decided to apply his efforts to trying something he thought he could resolve. Angry as Flower was, he thought that bringing father and daughter together again would remedy that. Besides, with Willit and Justine in that slow-moving buggy, with the time the making of arrangements, socializing and performing the actual ceremony would take, K. John believed that they could still catch up if they put their heels to their ponies.

He had Tremaine dressed, up and moving within minutes, although the old man remained groggy and unfocused. K. John handed Tremaine his Winchester.

'You may need this now.'

'What's this you're telling me? Clyde Willit has tricked a young girl into marrying him just to get his claws into her father's ranch?'

'That's the way it seems — get your hat.'

'Hell, yes! I'll ride to stop that. Let me grab one small drink for the road.' Tremaine reached for the bedside bottle.

'Flower's going with us. She's outside, waiting,' K. John said in a soft voice, and he watched the man's hand, which had gripped the whiskey bottle so firmly, fall away again.

'Flower? Here?' Tremaine seemed stunned.

'That's right. Willit's leaving gave me the opportunity I needed to slip into the Double O and get her.'

'Then I'd better . . . ' Tremaine's eyes seemed to be clouding up.

'Then we'd better get going — now!' K. John said, sharply. Tremaine only nodded and shuffled forward, following K. John out the door.

Flower waited, not patiently, but with a sort of grim determination. She had promised herself that she would not speak to her father, would not smile, but as she saw the old man shambling through the door with K. John, her resolve broke and a smile spread across her face. She practically leaped from her horse and rushed to Tremaine to hug him.

So many childhood memories, Christmases, birthdays, picnics and hard times spent together could not be easily discarded.

K. John gave them a moment or two

as Flower murmured small words and Tremaine stroked her hair. When they fell into old meaningless chatter to buffer their present feelings, K. John put a halt to it.

'We've somewhere to be,' he said.

'I don't want my daughter going,' Tremaine insisted. 'She's been hurt. I won't have her hurt again.'

'It's not your decision,' Flower said. 'I'm going, and that's it.'

'Why?' Tremaine asked, in a distraught voice.

'Because, as you taught me, a job begun has to be finished, and a person is only as good as his word. I've taken Emerson Masters' money and swore to do a job for him. It's not the job I expected, but it's mine all the same.'

'Then let's get it done,' K. John said from horseback. 'Time's a-wasting,' he added, even while knowing he was responsible for most of the delay. Watching father and daughter as they rode side by side out of town, though, he considered that whatever time he had wasted had been well worth it.

The sun was hot, the sky bright. After a mile or so K. John began to see fine dust sifting down, and he knew they were not far behind their quarry.

'How far did you say this house is?' he asked Flower.

'I don't know for sure. All I know is it's some distance. I heard the Judge tell Clyde Willit at the Double O that he was grateful to have a place far enough from the rabble that he didn't have to smell them. Clyde told him that that rabble was making him rich and that he could stand the smell for a while longer.'

'What are you planning to do when we get there?' Warren Tremaine asked. He looked woeful and a little concerned. K. John had no answer for him. What was he going to do? It would depend on circumstances; and whatever he decided, it would take more than a bit of luck. He wished again that Flower had not come along, but there was no dissuading the girl.

Just then she chirped up:

'We're taking Justine no matter what!'

Which was easier to say than do. Either Flower had a baseless trust in K. John's ability or an innocent trust in blind faith assisting the righteous. They had come to a stretch of the trail which wound its way across a wooded knoll among scrub oaks and scattered pines of some size. For this part of the country it was a considerable forest. Judge Baxter had chosen the location for his house wisely.

The trail dipped and rose again as it rounded a turn. A man with a rifle in his hands emerged from the woods, hat tugged low.

'You're on the wrong road, friends,' he said, and now K. John recognized him as the thug named Dungee.

'Can't be. We're riding to the Judge's,' K. John said easily, trying to shift in the saddle so that he would have a better chance at his Colt should the gunman start shooting trouble.

'I said you're on the wrong trail,' Dungee warned them again. 'You can turn around now or stay here to get yourself buried.'

'You're one man alone,' the cracked voice of Warren Tremaine said.

'Is that what you think, old man? That would be plain stupid of me, wouldn't it?'

Glancing into the woods, K. John was certain that the man was not bluffing. He spotted the shadowy figure of a second man partly screened by the low brush there.

'Well,' Dungee said. 'I warned you twice.' Then his rifle went to his shoulder.

And before K. John could respond, the Winchester spoke. But it was not Dungee's gun. The shot came from behind and beside K. John, and he looked to see the smoke curling from the muzzle of Warren Tremaine's rifle. Simultaneously, he saw Dungee go to his knees, his rifle dropping free of his hands; saw Dungee bring his belt gun up. And K. John shot him.

The thug pitched forward on his face and remained there in the dirt.

The second gunman burst from the bushes, firing twice. Warren Tremaine's rifle spoke again, and a slug from its barrel hit the man hard, high on the shoulder, spinning him around. He dropped to the forest floor and disappeared from their view. After a few seconds, K. John said, 'I'd better have a look for him. It wouldn't do to have a man with a rifle at our backs.'

'K. John,' Flower said with some worry in her tone, but K. John was already down from the saddle, entering the woods in a crouch, rifle in his hand.

The tall pines appeared as black-painted images against the pale brilliance of the sky.

K. John was circling toward the spot where he had last seen the ambusher, unwilling to walk directly toward him. A squirrel chattered away and bounded off through the boughs of a tree. The pines were laden with drifted dust, their scent heavy in the heated air. K. John shuffled his boots as he walked, to make only whispering sounds and not hefty clomps.

Attentive as he was, nevertheless K. John nearly stepped on the man, sprawled on the ground in the litter of brush; so suddenly did he come upon him. The man was wounded badly. He was trying to staunch the blood leaking from his shoulder, the blood soaking into his bandana, and he was having precious little luck at it. It was Bean, another one of Hammond's sidekicks. He appeared to have lost his rifle, but he still had a Colt strapped to his hip. K. John raised the butt of his rifle to his shoulder. An ashen face turned up toward him.

'Don't shoot, mister . . . oh, it's you!' Bean said. His eyes were wide, miserable, pleading for mercy.

'It's me,' K. John answered. 'Didn't you recognize me before?' Bean shook his head, returning his attention to his bleeding wound.

'You always shoot at men you don't even know?' K. John asked. Bean did not respond. His haggard face had gone almost ghostly white.

'I need a doctor,' the bad man said.

'Yes, you do,' K. John said. He still had not lowered the rifle.

'Look,' Bean said in desperation, 'don't you recall — I saved your life that day in the alley. Hammond wanted to beat you to death and I stopped him. Give me a break. Please, mister!'

'I remember,' K. John said. 'I also remember you were a willing participant in the beating up until then.'

'Just give me a chance!' Bean begged. 'You can't shoot me down like a dog.'

'First, toss that pistol you're wearing aside,' K. John said. The man did so. He felt no real sympathy for Bean, nor did he owe him a debt of gratitude for what amounted to nothing more than Bean not wishing to get involved in a murder back there in Crossroads. But then, he had never shot a defenseless man, and he was not going to start now.

'Go on, get out of here — now!' K. John snarled in his nastiest voice.

'Give me a hand up,' Bean said.

'Get yourself up,' K. John replied, already tired of the man.

'I won't forget this,' Bean said.

'Sure you will. Bean — don't ever let me run into you again! I mean it.'

Bean had reached the trunk of a nearby tree on hands and knees, now he was trying to lever himself to his feet, using the tree as support. K. John paused only to pick up the man's revolver from the ground, and then turned and strode away.

Bean would either make it or he wouldn't make it. For now there were others that K. John had to see to. He emerged from the trees to find his two companions where he had left them. Flower's face still carried concern. Her dark-green eyes were soft, questioning. Tremaine asked:

'Find him?'

'Yes. He won't be bothering us again.'

141

K. John swung back into the saddle. 'Have you seen anything?' he asked.

'There's no sign of the house that I can see.'

Half a mile on there was. The road took another bend or two and came out at the front of the white house of Judge Baxter. The three riders halted their horses.

'They will have heard those shots,' Tremaine believed. 'They'll be staying low, watching.'

'Maybe, that will depend.' On whether they thought that Bean and Dungee had been enough to stop anyone approaching, and maybe, K. John thought, on how close a business alliance Willit and Judge Baxter actually had. Baxter might not like the idea of men hiding out in his house to begin a gunfight.

Flower had been silent. Now she raised a pointing finger toward the house and shouted, 'There she is!'

And there she was.

Justine Masters sat alone in the

142

buggy, which was drawn up in front of the Judge's house, her face looking pinched and angry.

'How are we going to . . . ?' Tremaine began, but Flower gave them no chance to formulate a plan. She had spotted her quarry, and she meant to capture her, even if it meant riding into a hailstorm of lead from the outlaw guns below.

# 9

As Tremaine and K. John watched, momentarily frozen in fear and admiration, Flower rode the paint pony directly at the buggy where the blonde woman waited. Justine's head turned at the sound of the approaching horse.

They could just about hear Flower ask, 'Is this your horse?' and see Justine, startled, open her mouth but say nothing in response. Flower seemed to say something else to the girl, but what, they couldn't make out at that distance. They watched as Flower swung down from the pony, glanced once toward the house, then stepped into the buggy, nudging Justine aside. This clearly angered the rancher's daughter, mightily.

'What's she trying to do?' Warren Tremaine asked.

'She's your daughter — you tell me.'

K. John had almost finished his sentence when they saw Flower grab the reins to the buggy, slap them against the flanks of the bay horse and, with Justine screaming as she held her little white hat on with one hand and gripped the hand-rail tightly with the other, start the horse and buggy running toward the open land beyond.

Oddly, no one emerged from the Judge's house, but K. John was not eager to ride closer to it.

'Better catch up,' Tremaine suggested, with a sort of sour respect for his daughter. 'She's likely to need some help along the way.'

They came upon the buggy half a mile on. No one had yet emerged from the house to give chase. K. John had kept his eyes on the Judge's house. Why the timidity on Clyde Willit's part? He had only one shooter with him — Hammond — so that could be it. Maybe whatever business he and Baxter had to discuss was more important to Willit than another marriage. It didn't matter much to K. John — so long as they got away safely.

The land ahead leveled out into a red-dirt, sage-stippled desert flat.

'Where's she going?' Tremaine, still riding close to K. John, asked.

'The Oxhead. There's no place else to go except for Crossroads, and she sure wouldn't want to head there.'

Flower continued to slap the flanks of the bay with the reins. Justine had no option but to jounce and sway beside her, clinging to her hat, eyes fearful. Flower had only one intent; she was driving like a stagecoach driver passing through Indian country with a hostile party of Comanches in pursuit.

'Tell her to slow down,' Tremaine said, as they continued to trail the buggy. 'There's no great need for speed now.'

'I doubt she'd listen to me. She's pretty determined.'

'She's downright feisty,' a hoarse Warren Tremaine called back. 'Did you teach her to act that way, K. John?'

'Not me,' K. John said, with a suppressed smile. 'It must be something she's come by naturally.'

Tremaine wanted to yell back, but couldn't come up with a rejoinder.

Now K. John Landis decided that it was time to take a hand. A furious Justine was screaming unintelligible things at Flower. The big roan K. John was riding had tired, as had Tremaine's animal. The bay pulling the buggy had been run nearly to death. K. John angled his horse toward the buggy, leaned forward in the saddle, and touched Flower's arm.

'That's enough, Flower. No one's after us.'

'They will be!' a furious Justine Masters shouted at him. 'A dozen men, fifty! Clyde will never let you get away with this.'

The girl had done so much shouting at Flower that her voice was nearly gone. Thankfully, K. John silently remarked on the fact that Justine had referred to Willit as 'Clyde', not as most women — especially a new bride — would as 'my husband'. He doubted, without knowing for certain, that the ceremony had been performed. Clyde Willit had apparently left Justine sitting out in the buggy while he conducted some business with Judge Baxter, and this was why she was so angry when they had first come upon her.

But that was of no importance right now. Flower had slowed the bay to a reasonable pace. Ahead, K. John thought he could see a corner of the Masters house, just beyond the oak trees that grew in the yard there.

'That's it, is it?' Tremaine asked, relief evident on his face if not in his words. 'A nice-looking spread!'

'I wonder if Emerson Masters is back?' K. John said. It would sure make matters easier if the rancher had returned from Albuquerque. They could hand Justine over to him and then K. John and Flower could depart for . . . for where? K. John shook his head. That was a problem to be faced later.

Any place that was away from Crossroads — that shabby, infected, little desert town. They no longer owed anyone there anything. K. John's thoughts stumbled a little. Did they owe someone something?

How would Flower feel about that? Surely she must have had some wild thoughts about trying to help the other lost girls who lived at the Double O. She had known these young women for a long time. At least some of them must be friends of hers — and all of them were not as fortunate as Barbara, who had her little ranch to go back to and a crew of men to stand by her. The others still had nowhere to be and no way to get there.

Well, no one could save the world. Would Flower agree? K. John had once thought that the girl had more common sense than courage. Now he was not so sure. He wasn't sure of many things concerning Flower Tremaine.

They trailed into the yard of the Oxhead Ranch, the horses all dragging their hoofs in the dust. From the shadows of the big oak trees, K. John was watching the house with careful eyes. They had come this far; they needed no surprises now.

But the only person K. John saw was Olive the cook on the porch, watching them quite stoically as if she were just counting heads for supper.

All of the wild ride had been a picnic compared to the project of getting Justine Masters to return to her house. Unwilling to re-enter her home, she had twisted, squirmed, fought and screamed.

'I have to get back to Clyde! You'll not get me into that house!' she had yelled at Flower, who had been trying ineffectually to loosen the girl's grip on the side-rail of the buggy seat. Justine must have had some grip: Flower could not even pry one finger loose. The bride-to-be wanted her man, and she was fighting to remain free. That was the way Justine saw it, at least. The reality was that Clyde Willit had probably planned a quick marriage and an early demise for the daughter of the Oxhead owner. To Willit, it was the easiest way of acquiring land.

Watching Flower continue to struggle with the enraged Justine, her little white hat now tipped over to the side of her head, K. John decided that it was time for him to take a hand.

Stepping out of the saddle, K. John strode toward the buggy.

'Climb down now, or I'll bust those fingers one by one and carry you in over my shoulder.'

'You have no right . . . !'

'Your father left me in charge of this ranch. I have the right. Now get down before you get hurt.'

Flower looked nearly as shocked and upset by K. John's tone as Justine did. True, K. John would never hurt a woman, but he had thought that Flower, at least, would know that, whereas Justine couldn't know that he was incapable of carrying out such a violent threat. Warren Tremaine stood apart, separating himself from events. Olive peered out of the window of the house at them, her face as expressionless as always. Probably she only wished to know when they would end their games and come in for supper.

'Last chance,' K. John said, adopting what he hoped was a menacing voice and expression, and he watched as Justine's fingers slowly loosened their clutch.

'This won't defeat true love,' Justine said, stepping down from the buggy.

'No, it won't,' K. John said. 'Do you see that man over there?' he asked, nodding toward Warren Tremaine, who still stood aside, rifle in his hand. 'He has orders to keep you under his guard, his rifle at the ready for any unwanted visitors. That might not be enough to defeat true love, either, but it ought to be enough to slow it down.'

Tremaine, who had heard this, tried his best to look like a hard-eyed old man, and he succeeded rather well. In his sun-bleached clothes with his weather-cut face, Tremaine looked the part of a dangerous man.

'I don't understand why all of you are doing this,' Justine said, in a slightly calmer, still irritated voice.

'We know you don't,' Flower answered. 'I could explain it, but you wouldn't accept what I could tell you. You will understand one day; we just want to protect you until that day comes.'

'You talk in riddles!' Justine snapped.

'Life's a puzzle,' K. John replied, with little feeling. He really didn't like this woman and was wondering why they had gone to such lengths to protect her from herself.

They traipsed into the house one by one. Justine swept up to her room. K. John, feeling a hazy obligation, carried her trunk into the living room. Tremaine stood around uneasily, studying the big house, no doubt comparing it to his poor farmstead. Flower said, worriedly, 'I wonder if I should go up to her, try explaining things.'

'I doubt that she's in the mood to see you right now,' K. John said. 'All we can do for the next few hours is eat supper and watch the doors and windows so she don't try to get away again.'

'And keep an eye on the back trail,' Tremaine reminded them.

'And that,' K. John agreed. There was no telling what a man like Clyde Willit might try now that he had been thwarted in his plan. He was a hard man to deal with at any time. Now he would be furious. The man could afford to hire any number of shooters he wished, and they were still alone on the ranch with an unwilling prisoner.

Olive called them in to supper, glancing toward the stairway where Justine had disappeared, without commenting. She worked for Emerson Masters, for the ranch, but she was not paid for concern or opinions. She only had one job.

And she did it very well. Supper — as

to be expected on a cattle ranch — was beef. It was tender, juicy, and served with a rich, tasty, dark gravy, a huge bowl of mashed potatoes and thick hunks of cornbread heavy with melted butter.

Olive served and cleaned up soundlessly. Tremaine outdid himself, cleaning his platter twice. He looked appreciatively at Olive. Finished with her meal, Flower asked K. John, 'What do we do next?'

'I'm putting the buggy away. They won't have the use of that again.'

'Wait a minute and I'll give you a hand with the other horses,' Tremaine offered.

'Relax. Finish your coffee first.'

'The woman's a fine cook,' Warren Tremaine said. 'Don't talk much though, does she?'

With a long, careful look outside at the yard and the land beyond, K. John led the horse and buggy toward the barn. The bay horse had been ill-used that day, and it plodded on with its head hanging, not even the promise of rest and food brightening its demeanor.

Inside the barn K. John saw to the unharnessing of the bay. He used main strength to position the buggy in the corner; placed the bay in its stall and then went up the ladder to the loft to fork down some fresh hay, which all the horses would need. When he had dropped a bale and a half of fresh fodder, a sweat had built up across his brow, and he judged the job to be well-enough done.

K. John climbed down the ladder, wiped his brow and turned to find himself looking into the guns of Clyde Willit and Hammond. Working above, he had not heard their horses approaching. They must have left them some distance away.

Nor had there been a cry of warning from the house. Warren Tremaine had not proven to be the sort of sentry K. John had hoped for, but then K. John himself had told Tremaine to remain at the table, finishing his coffee.

'I didn't expect you men so soon,' K. John said.

'You should have,' Clyde Willit replied. His sharp, foxily handsome face was pale, but bright spots of fury stained his cheeks. 'I've come for what's mine. No man steals from Clyde Willit.'

From the corner of his eye K. John thought he detected a shadowy figure moving in the darkness of the barn. Maybe Tremaine had not been as neglectful in his duties as he had thought. He tried to keep the man talking while Tremaine fixed his position.

'You don't really want the girl anyway, Willit. Why don't you just ride off and leave her alone?'

'No, I don't want her, the stupid fool. But I will have her. Between the Oxhead and old man Tremaine's farm, I'll have half of the county in my pocket. Barbara Casey I have been considering, but she still has riders on her ranch. I'll get around to her when it's time.'

'Seems like a low way to go about business,' K. John said, and Willit's flush deepened. 'Using young women as leverage; even going so far as to marry some of them. Tell me, Willit, how many have you married and buried?'

'How would you know about . . . ? Oh, yes, that loose-lipped, scatterbrained Flower Tremaine. Landis, you're a damned fool, you know that? You work hard all of your life and end up with no more than you started with, maybe even less. Let the people in skirts get out working for you and it's a much easier life.'

'Let's just kill him and get out of here!' Hammond growled.

'That gains us nothing.' Clyde Willit scowled at his gun-hand. 'I don't want any shooting right now to call attention to us. First, we have to get Miss Justine out of here and back to the Judge's. It won't be long until her father is back, and I won't have him meddling in my plans to take over the Oxhead.'

158

'You plan on killing him, too, don't you?' K. John asked.

'Not until after the wedding is registered,' Willit replied, with an oily smile. 'First there has to be a wedding. Why don't you hitch a fresh horse to the buggy, Landis, then we'll see how we can figure out to get Justine out of here? Maybe,' he added in a menacing afterthought, 'trade Flower's life for Justine's release? Think the old man would go for that?'

He turned toward Hammond. 'Once we get the girl back to Judge Baxter's, you can — '

A woman screamed from the dark corner of the barn and Justine Masters rose up from her hiding-place where she had heard every word. All three men turned their eyes that way.

'I'll never go back with you,' Justine shrieked. 'You might as well just kill us all right now!'

The same idea had occurred to Hammond and, apparently, it appealed to him. He swung the muzzle of his gun around toward K. John once again and triggered off, the Colt's roar deafening in the close confines of the barn.

# 10

K. John dove for the poor shelter of the flimsy buggy, which was punctured by two rapid shots through the barrel of Hammond's gun. The man cursed as he fired and continued to curse as Clyde Willit grabbed his arm and shouted:

'Let's go! Back to town. That shooting's going to bring Tremaine on the run.'

K. John had risen to one knee and now he braced his own pistol to fire at the fleeing men. Astonishingly, Justine threw herself his way and clutched his wrist.

'Don't! Please, K. John, don't kill him!'

'After everything you now know?'

'After everything I now know, I mean to do the job myself!' the blonde answered in a tight murmur.

The shots had drawn Warren Tremaine and Flower at a run to the barn. Standing in the doorway, rifle in his hands, Warren Tremaine looked wide-eyed and ashamed. Flower rushed past Justine to K. John and asked with concern, 'Did you get hit?'

'No. It must have been one of Hammond's bad days.'

'And you didn't get either of them?' Flower asked, glancing down at the Colt in K. John's hand. He shook his head. Flower told him, 'We saw two men running out of the yard. Father wanted to shoot, but I told him we didn't even know for sure who they were.'

'Clyde Willit and Hammond. They didn't want to take the time to kill me.'

'Then . . . what did they want, K. John?' Flower asked, still obviously worried as she looked up at him.

'To get the buggy back and return Justine to the Judge's,' he told her.

'They'd have to put me in chains to

get me back there,' Justine said savagely.

'The lady's had a recent change of mind,' K. John told Flower, smiling crookedly.

Warren Tremaine shuffled nearer, rifle in hand. 'Where'd they go?'

'Back to Crossroads — safest place in the world for them. To the Double O. We couldn't pull them out of there with a dozen armed men.'

'Just lend me a gun,' Justine Masters said. 'I'll get Clyde Willit!'

'A woman after my own heart,' commented Tremaine, who had such ideas himself.

'No one's going to do anything crazy,' K. John said, firmly. 'We're away from the man now; let's keep it that way!'

'When my father gets back . . . ' Justine started to say and K. John interrupted her.

'That will be up to him. For now I'm in favor of holing up again — and keeping a sharper eye out for trouble,' he added, looking at Warren Tremaine, who shifted his eyes, guiltily.

'You told me to finish my coffee,' Tremaine protested, 'I got to sipping at it and talking to Olive a little longer than I should have, I expect.'

'Talking to Olive?' Flower asked with surprise. She hadn't heard the cook speak more than a dozen words since they'd been on the Oxhead.

'It's no longer important,' K. John said to the apologetic farmer. 'Let's just all be more watchful next time — if there is a next time.'

'But why would there be a next time?' Justine asked. 'I told Clyde that the wedding is off.'

'I don't pretend to know how Clyde Willit's mind works,' K. John replied, 'but I know he's not the sort of man who takes 'no' for an answer. Everyone stay alert.'

'What are you going to do?' Tremaine asked.

'Finish putting the horses up. I could use some help.'

'I'll help you,' Flower volunteered, and K. John nodded acknowledgement.

As Tremaine and Justine traipsed back to the house, Olive watching them from the porch, Flower and K. John gathered the reins of Tremaine's dun and collected the roan horse and the pony they had been riding. Both the roan and the pony were now finally back where they belonged.

The animals were all rubbed down and had fresh hay forked to them. All looked satisfied to be home and taken care of again. K. John sat on the wooden bench where he had been the morning after Clyde Willit's men had beaten him before they took the buggy.

Flower slid beside him on the bench. 'Are you still hurting?' she asked him.

'I've been in better shape,' he replied, honestly. 'I've taken two beatings in two days, and pretty skilled beatings they were. I'll make it, though,' he added with a smile to Flower, who sat demurely, clasped hands on her lap.

'You know what I've been thinking,

K. John?' she asked, lifting those dark-green eyes of hers to meet his.

'I'm afraid I do!' was his answer.

'I doubt it,' she answered. 'K. John, I was thinking about those young women who are still captives at the Double O.'

K. John nodded, turning his eyes away. His first guess had been a good one. For a minute he watched the red roan half-asleep on its feet with a stubble of straw whiskers on its muzzle, and smiled. Then he let his thoughts go back to what Flower was suggesting — a kind, sympathetic gesture with no possibility of success. Freeing the girls at the Double O and sending them . . . where? That was half of the problem that Flower had not considered, apparently.

The first half of it, presuming she had considered that, was simply impossible. No one could believe that Clyde Willit, if cornered, would not use all of his resources to prevent having his fortune in women spirited away — and, of course, that included the use of gunmen to shoot down anyone who would attempt such an audacious act.

K. John glanced at Flower. Her eyes remained hopeful, trusting. What could she expect of him?

On the other hand, K. John admitted, grudgingly, he was the only one not in favor of simply rushing the Double O and taking care of business with Willit. That was what Warren Tremaine had recommended right from the start. Justine, a recent convert, filled with a neophyte's fervor, only needed a gun in her hand to attack Clyde Willit. Flower was the brains behind the plot, the instigator.

That left K. John Landis — dumb, down-at-the-heels cowboy that he was — the only holdout. Was it because he was smarter than the rest of them, could see where this must lead, or because he had lost the fire and recklessness of his youth? He glanced again at Flower and walked away, brooding.

It was a stupid notion attacking the Double O, and could not work . . .

*   *   *

They started on their way shortly before sundown, after a long conference. K. John insisted that they needed more help and suggested that someone be sent to Barbara Casey's ranch to try to enlist her and whichever of her crew might be willing to accompany her to the Double O. There was no certainty, of course, that Barbara, now free of Willit, would wish to take a hand in punishing the saloon-owner. K. John nominated Flower to make the ride there, she being the only other one of them who knew Barbara. The young, hot-blooded Eric Styles, who wanted to marry Barbara, was capable of shooting K. John on sight, having warned him off the ranch in a jealous rage. Looking back, he was almost certain that it was Styles who had followed him nearly all the way to Crossroads, just to make sure that K. John was really leaving the ranch.

K. John's mood was dark as they approached the outskirts of Crossroads at the sundown hour when the sky showed as an orange backdrop to a few dark, wispy clouds. They had decided to wait in Tremaine's hotel room until Flower could reach them with word from Barbara Casey. K. John held no conviction that an extra five or six men were enough to overpower Clyde Willit's forces in his own citadel, the Double O Saloon, but they would be much better off with additional men than they were now.

If any of her men could be convinced to join the fight at all, that is.

Barbara obviously could not order her riders to storm Crossroads, but K. John was hoping the men would have enough sympathy for Barbara's recent travails and what others might be going through under Willit. Would they consider, imagining other women — perhaps their sisters or old school-friends who could be roped into Willit's stable of young women?

He could only hope. He had seen other cowboys boldly rush in when a woman was threatened. It was certain that Eric Styles would come along if Barbara decided to. Would that young firebrand be more of a help or a hindrance to the plan? Of course, this was assuming that Barbara Casey herself was willing to leave the safety of her ranch and again enter Crossroads, which was far from certain. K. John did not regret his decision to send Flower to talk to Barbara and her crew. Flower's words would carry more weight than his own.

A heavy unease settled around them when they finally reached Warren Tremaine's room. K. John was eager for Flower's return, watchful for any of the Willit men who might approach the hotel room. He paced from the window where he peered out frequently to the open door to look up and down the empty hallway. Justine was simply too spoiled, too wilful to be confined to a small place, inactive when she had already made up her own mind what she must do, and seemed to be clinging firmly to her murderous thoughts. She had brought a Winchester repeater from her father's house and now sat at the foot of the bed, rifle propped up beside her.

Warren Tremaine, his eyes dull, sat in the corner, occasionally licking his dry lips. Now and then his gaze would drift around the room, search the walls and settle on the table where he had formerly kept a bottle of whiskey. K. John could almost hear Tremaine's mind working.

'It won't be long,' he said to Tremaine. 'You're showing Flower a lot more strength this way.'

'I don't know what you're talking about,' Tremaine said, a little roughly. But he knew all right — the need for drink was reflected in his eyes.

Tremaine was silent for a minute or two and then said a little too loudly,

'I'm a man who should never come near a town. I think after this is all over, I never will again.' Neither K. John nor Justine replied.

Peering out the window once again, K. John felt himself stiffen. In the alleyway below and beyond he saw a group of horsemen dragging their way up past the hotel. Flower with Barbara and her crew? It could be more hired Willit men, or simply a group of local cowboys out for an evening's entertainment. At this distance, with heavy shadows all around, there could be no certainty.

'She might be back,' he announced nevertheless. It was necessary to bar Tremaine's rush toward the window. 'There's nothing to see,' K. John told him and the old man fixed bitter eyes on him.

Cooling, a disgusted Tremaine returned to his chair. He muttered, 'This is a hell of a way to go about things. I'd walk right over there and just shoot him. Get it over with.'

'I'd go with you,' Justine said, chipping in her two-cents'-worth.

'You two simmer down,' K. John snapped at them. 'It's going to be more difficult than that, and you know it.'

'But with Willit out of the way . . . '

Tremaine continued, 'Someone would take his place,' Hammond? Judge Baxter?'

'The Double O is raking in too much money for everyone to just slink away and forget about matters. Clyde Willit has to be taken care of, but that won't do much toward closing the Double O down or freeing the girls.'

Apropos of nothing, Tremaine suddenly blurted out, 'Are you going to marry my daughter?'

'The subject has never come up. Why would you ask me that?'

'She's already got you pretty well molded, doing everything she asks you to.'

'We were partners on a job,' K. John said, defensively.

'Watching the Oxhead!' Justine added, with a laugh. 'And what has this caper you have planned have to do with that job?'

K. John declined to reply; he had no answer. He returned to the doorway to keep watch for approaching visitors, hoping beyond hope that he would see Flower and not half a dozen of Clyde Willit's gun-hands.

He became aware of a series of soft steps coming up the stairway followed by a group of heavier clomps. Looking that way, tensing, he saw Flower's head appear and then that of Barbara Casey. As these two reached the landing K. John saw the grim face of Eric Styles, who was following Barbara closely. Behind them were three rough-looking, unfamiliar men. Flower waved at K. John as he stepped out into the hall and the visitors approached in a group.

'Hello again, K. John,' Barbara said. 'Can't get out of Crossroads?'

'Hello, Barbara,' K. John answered, seeing the scowling Eric Styles, his eyes fixed on him. 'Let's go into the room, all right?'

'Of course,' Barbara Casey said. 'Should I leave a couple of the boys out here to watch, just in case?'

'Maybe you'd better,' K. John nodded, after a thoughtful moment. 'Is this your whole crowd?'

'More men wanted to come,' Flower said, 'but Barbara said she didn't want to leave her ranch unprotected.'

'No, I did not!' Barbara agreed, hotly, crossing the threshold. 'Who knows what Clyde Willit might get up to next?'

K. John made introductions all around, pausing for Barbara's second ranch-hand to provide his name. Arnie Brewster was a tall man with a bent nose and a long scar down his cheek. Going by looks alone, K. John judged Brewster to be a man who had seen his share of fighting.

'Now, then, K. John,' Barbara began, sitting on the bed near Justine, 'why don't you tell us what the plan is? Flower acted as if she didn't know much about it.'

'The plan,' Justine Masters interrupted, wildly, 'is to kill Clyde Willit!'

# 11

The harshness of Justine's words was not unexpected, but it was a little unnerving. Warren Tremaine, his rifle propped between his knees, sat in the corner, nodding in apparent agreement.

Barbara smiled hesitantly. 'That's it? That's your only plan — to kill Clyde Willit?' She looked at K. John.

'No, and it's not my plan although I wouldn't shed any tears at Clyde Willit's funeral. Justine is still a little overwrought.'

'Oh, that's right,' Barbara said, 'Flower told me that today was to have been her wedding day.'

'Yeah — she's just a little peeved at the way things worked out.'

' "Peeved"?' Justine snorted. 'I'm mad as hell! Let me go first. I'll walk right into the skunk's office and shoot him dead.'

'And I'd go with you,' the vengeful Tremaine said, meaning every word.

K. John decided it was time to take charge of matters. 'We're not here to plan a murder,' he said, deliberately. 'We're here to put an end to Clyde Willit's way of doing business. After all, if Willit were to be killed, things would go on the same as before in the Double O, with someone like Hammond or possibly Judge Baxter in charge. Things wouldn't change a bit for the girls there.'

'So, what do you mean to do?' Barbara asked.

'Get the girls away from the saloon,' Flower said.

'And you have that all planned out?'

'Pretty much so,' Flower answered, 'or, at least, we hope we do.'

K. John listened as intently as the others. Flower had mentioned nothing to him of a plan to release the women. It must have been something she had dreamed up along the trail.

'Here's what I'm thinking,' Flower

178

said, perching on the other corner of the bed. Justine looked uninterested; everyone else watched Flower expectantly. There was a small sound of movement out in the hall, but one of Barbara's men looked in and shook his head to indicate that it was nothing to worry about.

Flower continued. 'The main reason I'm in this now is to rescue the girls living at the Double O.'

'They don't want to be rescued,' Justine said, as if that put her in a different class from the others.

'Some may not,' Barbara admitted. 'We'll let them make the choice for themselves. The second reason for the raid of the Double O is to break Clyde Willit's back — right?'

'To break the scoundrel's neck is more like it,' Warren Tremaine muttered, and Justine nodded her agreement. The unlikely pair shared a common thirst for vengeance.

Barbara Casey brought the conversation back to the relevant. 'Go on,' she urged Flower, 'tell us exactly what it is you want us to do.'

Flower took a deep breath and looked around the room. 'The first thing, Barbara, is we need your men to go into the Double O, drink for a little while and then start a ruckus. At some point I want them to break out their weapons and fire a few rounds into the ceiling.

'The girls will already have their instruction to rush upstairs to their rooms as if frightened by the fighting — your boys will have to get pretty rowdy.'

'Don't worry about them as far as that goes,' Barbara said, with a little tightness in her voice.

'I don't understand,' the scarred Arnie Brewster said. 'How's that supposed to help get those girls out of there?'

'Oh, it will,' Flower said, with confidence. 'By the time they've calmed you boys down, probably thrown you out of the Double O, the girls will be on their way.'

'I don't understand you,' Barbara Casey said.

'I think I do,' K. John said. 'There's a way out upstairs — a fire-ladder. I think that's what Flower has in mind.'

'It is exactly,' Flower said, wearing a bright expression as if she were proud of herself. 'By the time the uproar downstairs is ended, the girls upstairs will be down the ladder and free of the Double O.'

'Where you going to put them while they figure things out?' Tremaine asked. That question had been on K. John's mind as well.

'We'll gather them all together someplace and explain what's happening. Any of them who feels that she has a better chance sticking with Clyde Willit will be given the option to leave.'

'I asked where that was going to be,' Tremaine said, his mood growing no better. 'I don't like plunging into this with everything up in the air.'

'She means to gather them all like cattle in a holding-pen,' Eric Styles said, drawing a scathing look from Barbara.

'I know just the place,' Barbara Casey contributed, 'the old schoolhouse.'

'What schoolhouse?' Eric asked. 'I lived around this area for a long time; there ain't a schoolhouse.'

'Yes, there is,' Barbara insisted to her rash ranch foreman. Watching Styles, K. John wondered if he knew what sort of impression he was making on Barbara, the woman he hoped to marry. Styles seemed to have forgotten that Barbara had friends among the Double O girls as well. 'It's quite near, too. They began building it and then determined that they didn't want to spend the money on it and that there weren't enough kids in Crossroads to make it worth their time.'

'I never seen it,' Styles grumbled.

'It's just, past Nazareth Road,' Barbara said. 'Easy walking distance. We could all meet there and start working out the details for the girls who want to leave, who have a place to go.'

'Y'all seem to be forgetting that this

Willit is not going to be willing to just let these girls walk away,' Arnie Brewster said. 'What do we do if he decides to come after them, guns blazing?'

'Blaze back,' Tremaine said, sullenly.

'He won't be alive by then,' Justine Masters said, deliberately. 'Here's my part of the plan — when the ruckus starts in the Double O, Clyde Willit will be off his guard, distracted. That's when I'm going to march in and kill him.'

Flower and K. John glanced at each other. They had not come this far, done so much just to have Emerson Masters come home and find his daughter a killer. 'You'll have to re-think that part of the plan, Justine,' K. John told her.

Flower had what she considered another bright plan. 'K. John and I will be upstairs at the Double O; you obviously can't be a part of the crew making trouble downstairs — either one of you,' she added, directing her words to her father. 'And I don't want either of you shot.'

Justine asked, 'Are you telling me not to go along?'

'It would be the best idea,' Flower answered, 'but if you feel that you have to be around, it would be better if you two stick together. I don't want to lose either one of you. I think it makes more sense to have Father keep an eye on you and make sure you don't attempt anything hasty that might wreck the escape plan.'

Both Warren Tremaine and Justine scowled at Flower. They had their own plan and both were determined to give it a try. Flower walked to where Warren Tremaine sat slumped in his chair and hovered over him for a minute. When he was forced to glance up, she said, 'I'm counting on you, Father, to protect the lady — and keep her out of the way!'

Warren looked at Justine and then slowly, heavily, nodded his head. 'I'll do it although my sympathies are with her,' he answered.

'I know they are,' Flower snapped

back, 'but you'll have to control yourself — and her. I don't intend to end this night's work with a single fewer person than it began.'

'You're an ambitious lady,' the gloomy Arnie Brewster commented. 'For myself, with us busting into the man's own place trying to strip him of all he owns, I'd be surprised if a bunch of us don't get shot. He won't stop just because we've shown him that we have a few guns. How many men has he got?'

'A small army,' K. John replied.

'And us with a herd of his prime heifers.'

None of the women looked happy about that characterization, but none of them answered back. It was no time for hurt feelings or petty differences. K. John announced:

'It's time we were going, folks.' Speaking to Arnie Brewster and not to Eric Styles, who seemed to consider that a snub, K. John said, 'We'll need a good half of an hour to get in position and get word to the Double O girls.'

'All right then,' Braxton answered. 'The boys and I get to go drinking and raising a ruckus — best work assignment we've had for a while.'

'Arnie,' Barbara Casey cautioned, 'don't let any of the boys play their parts too well.'

'No, I'll tell them that it's only acting drunk that we're interested in.'

'One other thing,' K. John told the scarred man. 'I wouldn't let anything slip about you working for Barbara Casey. Someone will catch on and remember that she and Willit still have matters between them that aren't settled.'

'Half an hour. We'll take care of things,' Eric Styles said to Barbara, as if trying to regain ascendancy in her eyes. With a sour look at K. John Landis, he stalked out the door, Arnie Brewster on his heels. K. John let his eyes flicker toward Barbara, whose own expression was one that said 'I know.' K. John had no idea of how far things had gone between Barbara and her foreman, nor was it his business, but the man hadn't done his cause any good on this night.

'All right, K. John,' Flower announced as the cowboys trooped away, 'we'd better get going too.'

'Do you want me to come along?' Barbara asked.

'I think not. Perhaps you could make sure that your men's horses are where they expect them to be when they come out of the Double O, and then ride out to the schoolhouse ahead of us just to make sure there won't be a problem there.'

Instead of looking as if she felt left out of things, Barbara appeared slightly relieved. This was not so for others in the room.

'What are we supposed to do?' Justine demanded.

'Stay out of our way for the next half-hour,' Flower said. 'And try to stay out of trouble.' She looked at her father with a firm expression. 'You'll see to that, won't you?'

'I'll see to it,' Warren Tremaine answered in a mumbling voice. 'Whether I like it or not.'

Flower looked like she had more to say, but time was pressing now, and K. John took her elbow and steered her toward the door. Once downstairs they started working their way on foot toward the Double O. The alleys were dark, empty and still. They passed not so much as a dog, saddle-tramp or derelict drunk. The heavy, sultry calm remained as they neared Clyde Willit's place of business. It was as if the town was mourning its own demise.

Soon, from the Double O they could hear drunken roistering, but that did not mean that Barbara's riders had arrived. It was seldom that the Double O was not filled with rowdy crews doing their best to get drunk.

'I don't see the horses,' Flower whispered. 'Where do you think Barbara had the boys tie up?'

'Right out front, I'd wager. If something goes wrong, those men might have the need to leave town quickly.'

'What could go wrong?' Flower asked with anxiety.

'A dozen things that I can think of. Maybe one of the other customers recognizes them and knows that they ride for Barbara. Maybe your father doesn't manage to restrain Justine and she walks in, shooting. Maybe . . . '

'That's enough, K. John. I don't need any extra worries — we've enough of our own.' Her dark-green eyes were wide and star-shimmered. K. John wanted to say something else, but he simply nodded. Flower was right. They had enough of their own troubles, no matter that they had brought this all on themselves.

Reaching the cross-alley on the far side of the saloon, the side that was not lighted, they made their way through the sparse shadows of the broken elm trees there and worked toward the back of the building. K. John breathed a sigh of relief — the fire-ladder was still in place. That had been one of the other concerns he had not shared with Flower. He had considered it possible that Clyde Willit, in a fit of rage, might have had it torn down so that he would lose no more 'birds from their nest', as Charlie the bartender had put it.

'Gloria's still up in her room,' Flower said, pointing toward the second-floor window where a light burned.

'Is that important to us?'

'You bet it is. She's the one I was going to ask to go down and spread the word among the girls in the saloon.'

'If she doesn't want to . . . ?'

'I'll do it myself,' Flower said, firmly. K. John stepped back a little and looked down into the girl's star-bright eyes. That was the last thing he wanted Flower to attempt.

'Let's hope that Gloria is willing, then.'

'I hope so, too,' Flower responded. Her words were now emerging on short, tight breaths. She was frightened and had the right to be.

'If we're going to do it, let's do it now,' K. John said, stepping away from Flower to look up the wooden ladder to the lighted window. 'We put Barbara's boys on a schedule, let's keep to our own. You'd better go first,' he advised. 'She sees my ugly face creeping in from the darkness, she's liable to start screaming before you have a chance to talk to her.'

'I don't think so,' Flower told him.

'Gloria's not the shy type?'

'That's not what I meant. I . . . I meant that I don't think your face is ugly at all.'

'Oh!' K. John said, rather stupidly. He could think of no other response. In the darkness it was difficult to read Flower's expression. She seemed to be smiling faintly.

About what?

'You're right,' Flower agreed, 'we'd better get moving, The saloon is getting awfully noisy. Barbara's cowhands might be beginning their act.'

Having said that, Flower Tremaine

started up the plank and rungs of the ladder. K. John held back a minute, then followed after her. By the time he had made his entrance over the windowsill, Flower and the woman who must be Gloria had fallen into conversation. Gloria, a tall, robust woman with dark eyes and wearing a green satin dress, glanced at K. John without interest as his boots thudded against her floor.

'You really mean to get everyone out of here? Right now?' Gloria was asking.

'We have to. Everything is set up, and we can't spoil the timing.'

Gloria was poking at her hair energetically, obviously uncertain.

'Please, Gloria, you know how important it is,' Flower pleaded.

'It's all so sudden,' the woman stuttered. She said with some embarrassment, 'I'm not really sure I even want to go away.'

'You can always return if you choose,' K. John said. 'We're not going to hold you prisoner.'

'Please, Gloria, think about April and Sadie. Other girls like them who are frightened and desperate.'

'You know that this is a crazy idea, don't you?' Gloria responded.

'We know,' Flower answered, 'but it has to be done.' Downstairs it was growing louder still, although no gunshots had yet rung out.

Gloria sagged on to her rumpled bed looking uncertain. 'What if I refuse, Flower?'

'Then I'll have to do it myself,' Flower said.

'You! What if Clyde Willit sees you?'

'We'll find out afterward, I guess. This has to be done, Gloria, can't you see that?'

'I suppose I can,' Gloria said, rising again with some determination now showing on her face. 'Is it all right if I run a brush over my hair first?'

'We're running short of time,' K. John said in what Flower had termed his grumpy voice. She shot him a quelling glance.

'Fine,' Flower told the other woman, her eyes still flickering toward K. John, indicating — he thought — that he should know that a woman needs time to fix herself up, no matter the urgency of the situation.

When Gloria had done, she rose, slapped her hairbrush down on the bureau top, smiled without amusement or pleasure at K. John, and then went out, her long skirts rustling through the doorway.

'Thanks, Gloria,' Flower whispered, holding the door. 'Do come with us; you're too good for this place.'

'We've started it now,' Flower said, settling on Gloria's bed. She looked worried, as she had the right to be. K. John drew his Colt revolver, briefly checked the loads and stood beside the bed waiting for the night of the guns to begin.

# 12

The roar of gunfire racketed through the night. K. John felt — or perhaps he just imagined he did — the vibration of bullets thudding into the flooring of the room. Minutes later, Gloria appeared in the doorway, looking frightened, wild-eyed, her hair displaced.

'They're coming!' she panted out, and for a moment K. John froze, gun in hand, not knowing who she meant. Then he realized who she'd meant. There was the sound of little heels against the planks of the hall floor, many of them, and they burst into the room in a flurry of yellow silk, scarlet and black.

Espying Flower across the room, they fluttered that way and clustered around her, all chatting at once — a group of flocking, panicking birds. K. John backed away instinctively; gatherings of many females had always made him a little nervous. He telegraphed a look at Flower, which said, 'Let's get going!'

She apparently received the message for within minutes while the shooting continued downstairs, the brightly colored flock of females was assembled near the window and the first bird was descending, chattering back at the rest of them.

'You'd better ask these girls to quiet down,' K. John said, feeling that he was an intruder in their secret female ritual. A few of the women glared at him. Others seemed to understand the importance of silence.

'There's time enough for talking later,' Gloria said at K. John's shoulder. All of her earlier indecision seemed to have vanished. She looked now like a woman set to take charge of the fledglings. With more or less obedience the girls moved nearer the window in whispered near-silence. Flower had already gone out the window and disappeared into the night. K. John now caught the sounds of many horses — four or five — pounding their way toward the west end of town at a gallop. Barbara's men making their departure, he believed.

So far, so good. He moved forward now with a tight expression on his face, hurrying the girls along. Some appeared hesitant to leave at all, others seemed merely afraid of the height and insecurity of the weathered ladder. When the last woman had slipped out in a ruffled flurry of petticoats, K. John paused once more to look around the room and toward the door.

'I'm next, I guess,' Gloria said. In all of the to-do, she had managed to shed her dress and now wore a rather baggy pair of jeans and a dark-brown man's shirt.

'I guess you are,' K. John replied. He had a strong urge to open the door and peer out into the hallway, but he did not surrender to it. Men would be arriving, no doubt; someone would be wondering what had become of the saloon girls, but there seemed to be no rush to find the women.

When Gloria's manicured hand had moved downward in her descent, K. John blew out the lamp in the room and moved to the ladder himself.

He paused once on the third rung as Gloria's door was opened and voices from her room reached him in the night.

'Gloria's gone, too!'

'Where do you think they've gotten to?'

'Did anyone have a look in the kitchen?'

'That's where Sadie would choose to hide . . . ' A muffled laugh followed, the door was closed, and then the room was silent again. K. John continued on his way, a cold sweat now coating his neck and back.

The night was quiet, warm, as K. John dropped from the ladder in the midst of the gathered females.

'Keep moving,' Flower encouraged

the women in a whisper.

'Where?' a trim little blonde asked, not quite in tears. Flower took the girl's arm, turning her.

'West along the alley. We're heading for Nazareth Road.'

The girl continued to show reluctance until Gloria took charge and moved her along, not too gently.

Flower lingered beside K. John as he watched the women flutter away, some still exchanging whispered chatter.

'What are you thinking, K. John?' she asked. K. John let his eyes drift to the starry sky before answering.

'Too many women.'

'You don't like them?' Flower asked with an imp's smile.

'I like them fine in small clusters . . . or alone,' he replied, lowering his gaze. Then, surprising himself more than Flower, he bent his head and kissed her full on the mouth.

'What are you thinking?' she asked as they proceeded arm in arm after the others.

'Nothing. Just something your father asked me.'

'What was that?'

'I said it was nothing,' K. John asked, returning to his grumpy voice. Flower frowned, her pleased smile of a minute before vanishing.

'Should we check on them? Father and Justine, I mean.'

'I know who you meant. Do I think so? No. Whatever we might wish to know about, it's probably already over. Let's take care of our end of the business.'

\*   \*   \*

They reached the schoolhouse half an hour later, following the weaving, multicolored cavalcade of confused, excited saloon girls. K. John had insisted that they take the time to recover their horses before following even though that meant more risk of being noticed and captured.

'I won't be left afoot if something

200

goes terribly wrong here,' K. John had said, and Flower had agreed that it was something that must be done. While they walked through and lingered in the awakened town, Flower kept her eyes open for her father.

'Where do you think those two got to?' she asked. K. John could only shake his head.

'They've been warned. Maybe the sense of what we were telling them finally sunk in.'

'They were both pretty determined to do Clyde Willit in.'

'That doesn't mean that they were capable of busting in and actually doing it. Flower, I know you want to take care of everybody, but we just can't do it if they wish to be reckless. Let's turn our attention back to the young women.'

She nodded with unwilling agreement and they found their horses, mounted and began riding the western trail out of Crossroads. The school-house, when they found it, was lantern-lit, filled with mingled murmuring. Barbara Casey met them at the door as they stepped up on to the porch of the unfinished building. Gloria seemed to be in charge of maintaining order inside.

As they entered the schoolhouse there was a small group of girls holding an impromptu dance in one corner of the room, a few standing around looking simply bewildered by events, and some who set themselves apart, sobbing softly.

'Well, Flower,' Barbara said. 'It's your party. Better try to take charge of it.'

'I will — let's sort them out,' Flower answered, her face a little grim now. She ascended the small, stage-like area apparently originally intended for a teacher's desk and called out so that everyone could hear her, 'Listen to me, please!'

When she went on the room was quieter; everyone was listening. 'Those of you here who are sure they wish to stay with the Double O may leave right now. All we ask is that you do not inform anyone where we are. Those who are undecided are invited to stay. Those who wish to leave that dirty rat Clyde Willit — welcome!'

A couple of the girls gathered their skirts and immediately started toward the door. Beside K. John Gloria also shifted and turned that way. 'That's Rebecca Piggott,' she said to K. John, gesturing after one of the two girls. 'I'll follow her along and impress upon her the need not to reveal our presence out here.'

The women obviously had some kind of history between them. K. John did not try to guess what it might be or question Gloria's judgment. He did notice as his eyes shifted that way that the four riders Barbara had brought with her had drifted in out of the darkness, two of them looking a little too bright-eyed, probably from liquor, and quite pleased with themselves. Eric Styles stood to one side, leaning against the wall, his arms crossed, his expression tight. Arnie Brewster stood near him, his face reflecting a different sort of grimness. His, K. John guessed, was the knowledge that as Brewster had expressed earlier, they would not manage to finish this business without gun-play. Clyde Willit just wasn't going to stand for it.

One of Barbara's cowboys watched the girls leave and then lingered in the yard, listening. K. John returned to the inside of the school where Flower was still trying to field questions from the gathered girls.

'I want to make my break,' one of them was saying. This was the quite-young blonde K. John had now identified as April. 'I can go back to my father's farm, but how am I to get there? And what if they come after me?'

'At least you have an idea of where you'd like to go,' another woman spoke up. This dark-haired, slightly plump girl was named Daphne. 'I don't even know where my family is. I may have an aunt over in Las Flores, but I can't write her and expect a reply in a week's time, if that! In the meantime, what am I supposed to do?' Daphne demanded. 'Camp out like some plainsman?'

There was a small murmur of agreement from some of the other girls. Flower tried to stem the tide of unrest. True, she knew, she had planned this all too hastily — or not planned it at all. She looked desperately toward Barbara, the one person who did have space to take in a few of the girls until they could find their way home, but K. John saw Barbara shake her head regretfully. She was not willing to take in any boarders at her ranch, filled as it was with unmarried young bucks; not with Clyde Willit on their trail.

Justine Masters, similarly, had space to offer lodging to a few of the girls for a time, but Justine was not even there, and there was no telling what her reaction would have been — probably negative.

One of the girls, more rebellious,

more fed-up, and bolder than the others, spoke out. 'Give me a horse and I'll be on my way tonight. Damn Willit and his men!' This one, a brunette called Theresa, was the exception. But, as with the others, they could not offer her more help. They just didn't have a horse to give her.

Flower continued to plead with the girls, to try to convince them that their freedom was more important than another night of comfort at the Double O. They wanted to believe her, K. John saw, but they had been yanked too rapidly from their cozy confinement into the cold world outside, and now they found themselves lost and confused.

Flower's plan, noble though it might have been, seemed doomed to crumble in front of her eyes.

Gloria spoke up. 'If I could hide out until the morning stage; if someone would trust me with the price of a ticket east . . . I'd be gone.'

But she did not know where to go

until morning, and no one was in a position to offer her money for the coach. In the corner of the room, one girl began to sob softly again. Flower was doing little enough to comfort them.

Standing near the door beside Arnie Brewster, K. John himself felt that the cause was nearly lost despite Flower's good intentions. The young cowboy with the red mustache who had lingered outside came in and spoke a few hurried words to Brewster. The scar-faced man turned toward K. John and asked:

'What is this place supposed to be?'

K. John was baffled for a moment. 'Only a place to halt temporarily for refuge and conferring.'

' 'Temporary' is the right word,' Arnie Brewster told him. 'This man is Carl West. He tells me he hears horsemen approaching from not far away.'

'That woman — Rebecca — must have told them where we were.'

'S'pose so,' Brewster drawled. 'The

question is, what do we do now?'

'We fight!' Eric Styles, who had been on the edge of the conversation, stepped forward. His face was young, tough and looked eager for a gunfight.

'Bad idea,' Arnie Brewster told his boss, and K. John agreed.

'Well,' Styles said, stiffly, as he studied the assembled women gathered around Flower. 'What would you suggest? We can't just gather the herd and start driving them.'

'You'll get these women hurt if we stand and fight here,' K. John said, although the others were aware of that. 'If we try to flee with this bunch, there's no way at all we'll reach any place safe.'

'You eliminated all of the choices,' Arnie Brewster said. 'The only option is to let Willit have his girls back and we run to safety ourselves — assuming we can.'

'No, that can't be done. We can't desert the women.' K. John shook his head. Not now, not when they were free. The question was what, outside of a wild, unwinnable bloodbath, was their choice?

# 13

By unspoken consensus the decision seemed to have been left to K. John. He was, after all — in their eyes, at least — one of the organizers of the breakout from the Double O Saloon. Not liking the responsibility, he nevertheless fell to the task with vigor. Mentally counting heads and horses, he decided that they had enough to make do.

'OK, boys,' he said to the gathered cowboys. 'You don't have the time to pick your partners for the ball. Grab your ponies and find a woman. There's four of you — strike out in four different directions. Now!'

Eric Styles, no doubt wishing to remain near Barbara, hesitated. The other men followed K. John's hasty instructions. K. John made his way to where Flower, bewildered, was still trying to hold forth. Arnie Brewster and

210

Carl West had both already taken hold of a different saloon girl and were heading them toward the door. The girls' faces were wearing different levels of surprise and concern, but they were accustomed to being grabbed and ordered around and at least these men seemed to be moving with sure intent.

'What's happening here?' Flower demanded as she rushed to K. John, her own eyes wide with startled unease.

'We're dispersing,' K. John said, as if he himself had no doubts about the wisdom of their actions. 'Willit's men are on the way.'

Gloria was beside them now, listening anxiously along with the girl named Theresa who had asked for nothing more than a horse earlier. 'You take one of these girls with you,' K. John said to Flower. 'The other can ride double with me.'

'No,' Flower said, without pause to think. 'Gloria — take my horse and you and Theresa get out of here. I'm riding with my man.'

'You might be sorry about your choice,' K. John told Flower as they mounted his red roan, she riding behind him.

'Why?' Flower asked, her voice seeming muffled, far distant in the night as she spoke to his back.

'Because I'm planning on heading back to Crossroads and the Double O. There's nothing more to be done out here for anyone.'

'That's twice the reason to ride with you,' Flower said. 'I think we still owe it to my father and to Emerson Masters to see this through.'

Neither of them mentioned the way Flower had spoken up when she had made her intention to ride with K. John clear to the others. What had she meant by that? Was he truly 'her man'?

K. John did not dwell on it as they circled wide of the trail out of town where he thought he saw a man or two heading toward Nazareth Road, and headed back toward Crossroads through the warm, unsettled night.

'Where do you think they'll all head?' Flower asked, still thinking of the girls.

'Well, those boys all being Barbara's cowhands, I think Miss Casey is going to end up with a few uninvited guests on this night.'

'She'll be sorry she ever offered to help.'

'I imagine so. It's not the worst place the girls could end up. Barbara has a few more hands to help out.'

'And to maybe get themselves shot over something they had no part in,' Flower said.

'I don't think Willit would willingly try to attack that ranch even if he suspects his girls have been taken there — and there's no reason he should.'

'Where is Clyde Willit? We don't even know that.'

'That's what I intend to find out,' K. John answered. 'I find myself leaning more toward your father's and Justine's way of thinking. It was stupid to ever think that this could have been done without spilling blood.'

'You can't be thinking of finding Willit and gunning him down yourself!' Flower said, her horror plain.

'I don't plan anything like that. I won't have the choice. As soon as Willit lays eyes on me, he'll want my hide. He'll know who was behind this.'

'You're sure?'

'I'm sure,' K. John replied. 'Which means I'll never be able to leave Crossroads alive so long as Willit has the strength to pull a trigger, or someone who can do it for him.'

'And you're riding back to town!'

'Where else can I go? Let's end it now! For all we know Tremaine and Justine already have finished it.'

'Or gotten themselves killed!'

'That's what we're here to find out,' K. John said as they reached the town limits.

He guided his roan up Main Street, noticing the activity in town which was combined with a peculiar silence. Men were grimly preparing for some battle; there was no time for the hell-raising for which the Double O was famous. These men, not so hastily organized as the first of Willit's troops, were determined to do their job. Probably, a reward had been offered for K. John and the return of the girls. K. John mentally apologized to Barbara Casey for delivering trouble to her door. The number of the men who seemed to be gathering were easily enough to overwhelm Barbara's small crew. It was time to put a crimp in their plans.

'Where would they have gone?' Flower asked, meaning her father and Justine Masters.

'I don't know. It depends on whether they actually tried to attack Willit and how they fared.' Either or both could be dead, K. John knew, but rather than voicing his thoughts, he suggested, 'Let's try your father's hotel room first.'

He felt her grip on him tighten. Flower was hardly a stupid woman; she knew as well as he that her father's grudge against Clyde Willit could have resulted in his death.

The roan, now tired, dragged its hoofs toward the hotel as uptown there was still more activity. The men of Crossroads were preparing for a night of blood sport. At the hotel Flower jumped down nimbly, although her heart was far from light. She was expecting the worst. K. John swung heavily from the saddle, loosely hitched the roan and followed her into the hotel lobby.

As they crossed the room no one seemed interested in their arrival. The door to Tremaine's room was slightly open. There was no light within. Flower hesitated for a fraction of a second before she swung the door in.

There he sat, froglike in his appearance against the unmade bed, his shirt front bloody, his hand gripping an open bottle of whiskey. Warren Tremaine looked up without expression, his eyes glossy and hard as if they had been removed, polished and placed back in his skull.

'Put that bottle down!' Flower

ordered. 'You know what you promised me. You don't need a crutch.'

It was hard for her to get through that little speech. When K. John had lighted the lamp again it was obvious that there was an unchecked flow of blood from Tremaine's shoulder and that his face was sagged down as if weighted by invisible sorrows. K. John took charge.

'Get that shirt off and let me have a look,' he told the old man, gently.

'I didn't think you two would be back.'

'Well, here we are. Can you get that shirt off yourself, or do you need a little help?'

'A little help wouldn't be amiss,' the old man admitted.

'I assume you haven't seen a doctor.'

'I was afraid he'd be followed over here.'

'What happened?' K. John asked as he gently peeled the bloodstained shirt from Tremaine's scrawny chest.

'About what you warned us against,'

Tremaine said. 'When Barbara's boys started that shooting ruckus, me and the girl slipped into the back where Willit has his office. Justine meant business, and so did I.' He winced as K. John finished separating his shirt from the scabbing wound.

'Go on,' Flower said.

'Someone — that one they call Hammond — laughed out loud as we burst in. He just grabbed Justine's rifle and tossed it aside. Behind his desk Willit rose with a nasty little smile and plugged me while I was looking toward Justine. My nerves just went numb and I couldn't hold my own rifle any longer. The pain was terrific.'

Flower, listening, winced in sympathy.

'They told me 'Run, old man!' and I realized that's exactly what I am — a useless, old man.' His head bowed. 'And I ran,' he said, 'bleeding like a stuck hog with no weapon — I just ran.'

'What happened to Justine?' K. John

asked, throwing Tremaine's bloody shirt aside.

'Her, I don't know,' Tremaine said, with shame. 'Last I remember seeing her she was sitting on the floor of Willit's office, legs splayed.'

'You couldn't have done any more,' K. John forced himself to say although he felt like scolding Tremaine for his irrational decision.

'Now what?' Flower asked as K. John washed her father's wound with lye soap and water. The old man had passed out — from loss of blood or his intake of liquor, there was no saying which. 'We have to go after Justine again?'

'It looks like it. He'll force the girl to marry him if she has to be carried bound hands and feet to the altar.'

After K. John tended to Tremaine's wound as well as possible, Flower helped him place her father into the bed. Full of regret, she said, 'Taking that job at the Oxhead wasn't the most brilliant thing either of us has ever done.'

'No, but we did. And it's still not finished.' K. John stood up, hands on hips, looking down at Tremaine, whose mouth was slack, eyelids fluttering.

'What are you going to do?' Flower asked.

'The only thing I can think of. Willit's riders are all pulling out of town. I'm going to the Double O again. Willit has to be stopped. Everyone else was right: there's only one way to stop the man — with a bullet.'

'K. John, please, don't! You can be stopped the same way, you know.'

'I know,' K. John said. 'You can stay here and watch your father in the meantime.'

'I am in this too, K. John,' she said stepping nearer, those dark green eyes looking up. 'This is no time for me to be quitting on the job.'

'Maybe it is,' he said, carefully.

'Maybe it is,' she responded, 'but I won't.'

'You are a hard-headed woman,

Flower Tremaine.'

'Am I not? Let's get going.'

'You know, Flower,' he said, holding her up briefly, 'that promise you made to Emerson Masters — no one could expect you to follow it this far.'

'I expect it of myself. What about you, K. John?'

'I think that you expect it of me,' he answered.

In the lobby K. John asked her, 'Have you any money left?'

'Some.' She fished in the pocket of her jeans and showed K. John. 'Six dollars in folding money plus the fifty-dollar gold piece I was saving for escape money.'

'Escape . . . from what?'

'From everything, if it just got to be too much.'

K. John nodded. 'Let me have the six dollars. Keep your escape money. You still might need it.'

K. John, knowing the way of hotels, walked to the desk where a lazy-looking man with sagging jowls stood. 'Sir?' the clerk asked, looking up with unhappy eyes.

'I'm thinking of a pistol,' K. John said, leaning on the counter.

'Not again! No more taking a man's pistol in lieu of his unpaid hotel bill.'

'No, sir. I want to buy one — I'm sure you have a few back there.'

More than one cowboy had come to town, gotten drunk and forgotten to set aside some money for his hotel bed, K. John knew. The only way out was to pawn their pistols and promise to come back to redeem them.

'Buy one?' The fat man's eyebrows drew together.

'Yes, show me what you've got.'

'For two dollars,' the man said, 'I can let you have this.' Placing a rusty piece on the counter, he smiled hopefully at K. John.

'No wonder the man didn't come back for that one,' K. John said, disparagingly. 'What else have you? I have six dollars to spend.'

Returning to Flower with an accept-able .44 Colt in his possession, he gave it to her. 'If you insist on going along, I thought you'd feel better with this in your hand.'

'Now I'm a quick-draw artist!'

'Nothing of the sort. Just wave it around if necessary. The sight of a gun can be pretty intimidating.'

'What if they aren't the sort to be intimidated?' Flower asked, uncertainly examining the Colt in her hand.

'Then it'll be up to me. Come on; let's get going before I lose my own nerve.'

Stepping out into the night, now oddly silent since most of the Double O riders seemed to have gone, they started directly toward the saloon, K. John leaving his horse behind. One way or another he did not think he'd be needing it again on this night.

The walk seemed long to the Double O. Every moving shadow caused K. John's heart to skip. No man walks willingly to his death.

They finally reached the door, opened it and scuffed their way across the dead-appearing saloon. There were few able-bodied men inside: perhaps a dozen. Most of these were clustered around the roulette wheel where still men played, jibed and groaned at a losing spin of the wheel. Besides these there were a few who looked as if they would have to be uprooted by force from their chairs, and were too old or drunk to care about running around dying to round up a bunch of runaway females.

Behind the bar Charlie still served drinks. When he caught sight of K. John, saw the deadly intent in his eyes, Charlie's hand dropped below the bar toward where his shotgun was kept. Seeing Flower directly behind K. John also carrying a pistol, Charlie's hand fell away from his weapon. He turned to polish his glasses, which needed none of it, and slightly inclined his head toward the back room.

K. John glanced at Flower, his mouth

tightly set, and taking one last deep breath strode toward Clyde Willit's office. K. John swung open the door and stood there, gun drawn, startling the tall Willit, who stood behind his desk in shirtsleeves. His Smith & Wesson revolver lay on the desktop in front of him.

'Where's the girl?' K. John asked, deliberately cocking the Colt.

'Which one? Landis, is it?'

'That's right.'

'I wondered when we'd finally meet. What girl is it you're looking for? I'm sorry to tell you that I'm temporarily short of that particular commodity.'

'Justine Masters,' the voice behind K. John said. 'We're responsible for her, and we want her returned.'

'Oh,' Willit said with an amused smile. 'Little Flower — you've come back again! What's that big gun in your hand for? You want Justine? I do too, but she's vanished again — after a little squabble.' He touched his cheek where four lines of crimson were visible. 'If you want to sit down and wait, I'm sure that I'll have her back shortly.'

'No,' K. John said, stepping forward. There was determination on his face now as he said, 'You're through in this town, Willit. It didn't have to be that way, but you've pushed it to that point. You're through, and I'm finishing you.'

'I'm not alone, Landis,' Clyde Willit said.

'You seldom are. Who is it, that low-life Hammond? The mood I'm in now it would be a pleasure to see him. What's he doing? Hiding under your desk?'

'Damn you, Landis!' Hammond's voice exploded as he appeared from an inner room. 'I'll show you 'hiding'! You should have taken your warnings.'

K. John, who had been expecting it, triggered off and his bullet caught Hammond in the chest, driving him back against the wall. Now with a panicked expression on his handsome face, Clyde Willit lunged toward his revolver. He snatched it from the desktop as K. John switched his sights in the saloon-keeper's direction. Willit might have been the first to trigger off, but from beside K. John a second pistol was fired and, after a moment's standing there, shocked disbelief on his face, Willit slid slowly to the floor, fingers clawing at the desk.

K. John whirled to find Flower. Her face ashen, staring at the dying Willit, her Colt curling smoke.

'I was just waving it to frighten him,' Flower said in a miserable voice.

Apparently, she had waved it in the right way. K. John heard Willit's body thump to the floor, felt Flower's nearness as she rushed into his arms. 'What have we done, K. John?' Flower murmured, clinging to him.

And what exactly had they accomplished with all of their running about? The saloon girls were still lost, homeless. Justine Masters had gone missing again. K. John pushed away from Flower, who was trembling violently.

'Let's finish our job. We have to find

Justine and get her back to the Oxhead again.'

It was not that K. John was so eager to do the job, but he knew that it would distract Flower from her present sorry state of mind if she were given something to accomplish.

'All right,' Flower said. She stepped back, sniffling. She rubbed the heels of her hands against her forehead, nodding. 'Let's do that before the Double O riders get back bringing more bad news.'

They walked back into the saloon where all was silent. Men stared at them with wondering faces, questions they dared not ask. Charlie still stood motionless behind the bar. As K. John watched him the big man's face went red, and he lifted his shotgun to his shoulder. K. John had no time to cry out; he pushed Flower to one side, then hit the floor himself as the double-twelve shotgun thundered across the room.

No buckshot tagged K. John, nor had

it been intended for him. Looking back at the sound, K. John saw the body of a man thump against wood as it slid down along the staircase. He was already bandaged across a bare torso. Halfway down the flight of stairs, the body stopped its slide. All motion had ceased for him. He had been waiting at the head of the stairs, rifle at the ready. K. John looked his thanks at Charlie, who shrugged and muttered:

'A man's got to choose his side sometimes.'

K. John walked to the bloody body of the fallen man, kneeling briefly beside him.

'Who was he?' Flower asked in a wavering whisper.

'Bean,' K. John said, rising from the staircase. 'His name was Bean. I once gave him his life back. It seems he didn't value it all that much.'

'There has to be an end to this!' Flower said, finding her voice at last. She was not hysterical, exactly, but she waved her hands in an overwrought way and her eyes seemed a little wild to K. John.

'There's Justine,' K. John reminded Flower, putting his arm around her shoulders. 'We have to find Justine.'

'Yes,' she said more quietly, almost numbly. 'We have to find Justine. We have to finish our job, don't we, K. John — come hell or high water!'

# 14

Flower was in such a fury that K. John could not have controlled her even had he been so inclined. He understood her anger against events, men with their guns and the entire corrupt town of Crossroads, but he had never seen this side of Flower before. It seemed as if the shock had brought it on.

'I'm appealing to you!' Flower announced with a room-filling voice. 'All you drunken bums and rowdies! The ones who liked to ogle me, and others like me, and turned your heads when you finally saw that we were little more than slaves held here for your dirty little pleasures — help me now! I need your help. There's a missing girl and we have to find her. Spend a few minutes away from your whiskey glasses and your gambling to help us!'

Flower had strode across the room to

stand next to the roulette table. Not a man had spoken or moved. They seemed to be hoping that she would just go away. Now she spoke up as loudly as ever. 'I can pay you! If that's the only thing that will motivate you to finally do the right thing. Look!' she said, angrily slapping down the fifty-dollar gold piece she had retained on the baize of the roulette table. 'That must be enough to encourage some of you to do the right thing. Help me find Justine Masters!'

The silence in the room was heavy, disheartening. Men returned to their drinking and gambling. No one seemed to have paid the least bit of attention to Flower's outburst. Someone laughed in the back of the room; the roulette wheel spun again, the men gathered around it intent on the whirling wheel, the bouncing ball.

Beside K. John a familiar shape appeared. It took him a moment to recognize Gloria.

'Came back, did you?' he muttered.

'I've got Flower's horse,' the dark-eyed woman said. 'What's she doing?'

'Waiting for hell to freeze over, it seems,' K. John replied without humor.

A roar went up from the roulette table and a few men walked away cursing. Flower decided to try speaking to them again. 'I'd better see what's happening,' Gloria said. But K. John wasn't listening.

'All of you men, what's the matter with you? You each must have a sister somewhere, a daughter you wouldn't want to see treated as the women in this saloon have been, held prisoner. All I ask now is that some of you spend a little time helping me find a poor lost girl who's run away from Clyde Willit.'

Again, a roar went up from the men crowded two-deep around the roulette table, but they were not cheering Flower's speech, that was certain. K. John saw Gloria push through the gathered men to reach Flower.

'My Lord!' Gloria said. Flower

233

looked at her, perplexed. 'Don't spin that wheel again, Mort!' Gloria shouted to the man operating it.

'I couldn't if I wanted to,' was his answer. 'What would I pay out with?'

'What is it, Gloria?' Flower asked as if returning to earth from the far reaches.

'You won!' Gloria told her.

'Won what?' Flower asked, still confused as K. John came to stand beside her, his arm around her small waist. Around them men were moaning, murmuring, laughing and cursing.

'Honey,' Gloria told her, 'you walked over here and slapped down fifty dollars on Double O, and it came up on the wheel.'

'I wasn't intending to.'

'Nevertheless, you did. For that the banker here has to pay you thirty-five dollars to one.'

'That's a tidy sum,' Flower said, staring at the table, the money stacked on Double O.

'I'd say 'tidy',' Gloria, who was good

with numbers, said. 'Seventeen hundred and fifty dollars, to be exact. But you were too busy talking and you let it ride.'

'What do you mean?' Flower asked.

'What do I mean? The banker was probably happy to see you so inattentive, but then the improbable — impossible — happened. Your number came up again. Double-nought twice in a row, with your money riding on the green number.'

'Do you mean I won again?' Flower asked.

'Won?' Gloria said, hugging Flower. 'Honey, you broke the bank! Thirty-five to one on that seventeen hundred dollars' wager. How much is that, Mort?' she asked the man in charge of the roulette wheel.

Mort, a small, perspiring, balding man who had the concession in the Double O, was busy with a pencil. 'Sixty-one thousand, two hundred and fifty dollars,' he said, with an expression of utter desolation. 'Of course, I can't pay you off at the table. You'll have to take this to Mr Willit.'

'Mr Willit has taken a long journey,' K. John said.

Mort nodded. 'Then it will be up to Judge Baxter to find a way to pay. He purchased half of the saloon from Willit a few months back, For now,' Mort said, untying the apron he wore, 'I'll give you my chit for your winnings. No more roulette tonight, boys!' he said more loudly. 'I don't know if I'll be seeing you again. For now, meet the new owner of the Double O Saloon.'

He briefly placed a hand on Flower's shoulder, let it slide away, grabbed his black derby hat and shuffled toward the door, putting his coat on as he went.

Some men gathered closer, some drifted away. From behind the bar Charlie stared at them, his face expressionless.

'Is the saloon really mine?' Flower asked Gloria.

'Until and unless Judge Baxter comes forward and pays you that sixty-one thousand dollars.'

'I hope he does,' Flower said. 'I don't want a saloon — especially this one.' She turned sharply on her heel, and addressed the gathered men, hands on her hips. 'I just want to tell all the men who were so willing to help me out with a minor matter of saving a girl's life — this saloon is closed for the night, and I mean right now!'

The three of them lingered a while as the saloon cleared, letting Charlie finish up with his work, then decided to go to the hotel diner to discuss matters. They stepped out into the warm night and Flower, with the keys given her by Charlie, locked the doors to the Double O Saloon, perhaps for the last time.

★　★　★

'Well, that solves a big share of your problems,' Gloria was saying. The three of them were drinking coffee. Gloria had informed them that they had fresh hot donuts there at this time of night;

however, K. John and Flower declined. Neither's stomach was feeling quite right. That didn't stop Gloria from ordering a pair of fat, risen donuts with maple frosting.

'What are you talking about?' Flower asked. She had been aimlessly stirring her coffee.

'The Double O,' Gloria said, waving a half-eaten donut in the air. 'I plan on staying there until I can get organized. That gives all of the girls a place to be until their relatives can come; they can make plans to get themselves to where they want to be.'

'I suppose so,' Flower said, numbly. She still did not seem to grasp the idea that she actually owned the saloon.

'And that money that was left on the roulette table — how much was that?'

'Something like seventeen hundred dollars,' K. John said.

'Seventeen-fifty — now I remember,' Gloria said. 'That's surely enough to help some of the girls out — if you're feeling generous. Remember — all that

238

I wanted was stagecoach fare east. Theresa — all she wanted was a horse.'

'I suppose you're right,' Flower said. 'The money was won by accident anyway. I can afford to share it. But as of now, K. John, what can be done about those men attacking Barbara Casey's ranch?'

'We don't even know that that's where they went,' he reminded her. 'That was our fear, our idea because we knew where the girls were probably headed.'

'Whatever direction they went in,' Gloria said, 'they won't be riding long — not once word reaches them that there's no longer any pay in it, not with Clyde Willit gone.'

'I suppose not,' Flower said. She was still in low spirits. Behind them the door to the restaurant opened and closed again and a shaggy, big-nosed man stood looking around the room until his eyes fixed on them.

'Who's that?' K. John asked.

'I don't know his name,' Gloria said,

'but I recognize him as a regular at the Double O.'

'What's he want?' Flower asked, fearing still more trouble.

'Let's wait and see,' K. John said, touching her hand across the table.

The man, holding his hat in both hands, inched their way. When he stopped beside their table, it was Flower who asked, 'What is it you want?'

'I was there tonight,' he stammered, 'at the Double O, that is. I heard what you were saying. All of the men there aren't as bad as you painted them. Some are, maybe most are, but we ain't all that bad.'

'Is that what you came to tell me?' Flower asked, now sounding weary.

'Part of it. The other thing is that I know where that Miss Justine is.'

'You do?' Flower said, coming halfway to her feet in her excitement. 'Where?'

'There's a shed out behind the blacksmith's place where he keeps his bar iron and such. A friend of mine, a boy I know, told me that he had seen a woman with her clothes all disarranged, crying, go into this shed to hide.'

'Would she still be there?' Flower asked and the man answered:

'Miss, I don't know why she'd come out and risk walking around this town any more.'

'No,' Flower agreed. As the man traipsed heavily away, Flower rose. 'What do we do, K. John?'

'Go get her and take her home. That's the job, isn't it? Then we can finally be done with this.'

# 15

'The way I see it,' Warren Tremaine was saying as they sat gathered around the kitchen table at the Oxhead Ranch in the morning, 'is that with Olive living on the farm, we won't have no need for Flower, and she'll be free to go off and spend her fortune as she likes.'

'That's assuming a lot,' Flower said. Her father answered.

'No, no it's not. Olive and I now have what you might call an understanding. We reached it while she was nursing me back to health. We just have to wait until Masters can find a replacement for Olive. Justine tells me that it's possible that the girl Sadie, who used to work at the Double O, might want the job. The girl seems to have a liking for kitchens.'

'None of that is what I meant,' Flower said. 'What I meant is that everyone is suddenly assuming that I have a fortune. No one has yet heard a word from Judge Baxter about his intentions.'

'He'll come around — the Double O is the biggest money-making business in Crossroads by far. He's just trying to drive your price down. Besides, you've still got over seventeen hundred dollars in cash money. It wasn't so long ago that you'd consider that a fortune.'

'Oh, you're right,' Flower admitted. 'The Double O is still almost paying its own way despite the restricted drinking hours. Charlie's a good man; he's handling all that for me.'

'And the girls?' Tremaine asked.

'Except for Rebecca and Sylvia, they've all gone home. We did have one wedding.'

'Yes?' Tremaine lifted an eyebrow.

'Yes, it seems that April and that red-headed young cowboy from Barbara's ranch, Carl West, almost didn't come back from their ride that night at all, but instead he returned to Barbara

243

Casey's, where the two got hitched.'

'By Judge Baxter?'

'Who else? The man will always find some way to get along.'

'As will we all,' Tremaine nodded. As Olive returned to the kitchen, K. John and Flower made their way outside, leaving the two to each other's companionable conversation.

It was still early in the morning with the low sun angling prettily through the oak trees. Standing on the porch they saw Emerson Masters on his red roan and Justine on her pinto approaching them.

'Father and I are going out to look the new property over,' Justine said. 'Would you like to come along?'

'You really should see it,' Masters said. 'It's going to make me a fortune.'

That property had been all that Masters wanted to talk about since returning from Albuquerque. He had traded a thousand acres of dry land for five hundred bottom-land acres and gotten some cash on top of that.

Masters' belief was that the land company's appraiser had only visited the property after the spring rains and made his determination by its appearance then. 'Either that or some big land dealer was only looking at the numbers and figured a thousand was better than five hundred. People who work with their noses stuck in ledgers all day can't seem to realize that the land's usefulness changes with the season.'

During the same conversation the beaming ranch owner had asked almost as an afterthought, 'Everything went well here while I was gone?'

'Yes, Father.' Justine had been quick to answer. 'Fine, thanks to K. John and Flower.'

'I'm happy to hear it. I had a few doubts at first as to whether I'd done the right thing hiring these two.'

'I'm sure you couldn't have done any better,' Justine said.

On this new morning, Emerson Masters was still pleased with himself and the world in general. 'Are you sure you don't want to ride along and have a look?' he asked K. John.

'Not this morning, sir. There are a few odds and ends Flower and I have to take care of before we leave.'

'You're determined to leave, then?' Masters asked.

'Yes, sir. Sorry to put it this way, but I believe we've seen just about enough of the Oxhead Ranch.'

'Restless sorts, huh? I can understand that, too.' Before riding out he added, 'Don't leave without saying goodbye. By my calculations, I still owe you two a little money.'

They said they wouldn't and then stood and waved goodbye as Masters and Justine rode away together, both smiling.

Warren Tremaine came out on to the porch just then, holding a fresh cup of coffee. He was a little stiff, but well on the way to mending, which Tremaine attributed to Olive's fine cooking.

He hobbled up to K. John and said in a low voice, 'You haven't forgotten what

I asked you a few days ago?' His eyes flickered briefly to Flower, who was listening while trying to appear not to.

'No, sir,' K. John answered.

'Well, I don't think you ever gave me a real answer. Do you intend to?'

'Yes, sir,' K. John said.

'Fine.' Tremaine patted K. John's shoulder and returned to the house.

'What was that about?' Flower asked after her father had gone.

'Nothing — just man-talk.'

'Man-talk, again? From what I know of man-talk, it generally involves a woman.'

'Does it?' K. John asked, with a vague expression. Squinting into the new sun he told Flower, 'Think we should borrow the buggy? We can drive out to Judge Baxter's. We still have some business to conclude with him.'

'Do we?' Flower asked with those dark-green eyes sparkling.

'Of course — that is, if you haven't changed your mind about selling him back the Double O?'

'No, I haven't changed my mind about that.' She was thoughtful for a moment and then announced, 'I think I'll open up the saloon today.'

'Really? Whatever for?'

'Let the whole town join in and raise a toast to us,' Flower said. The woman always was one step ahead of him, K. John thought.

We do hope that you have enjoyed reading this large print book.

Did you know that all of our titles are available for purchase?

We publish a wide range of high quality large print books including:
**Romances, Mysteries, Classics**
**General Fiction**
**Non Fiction and Westerns**

Special interest titles available in large print are:
**The Little Oxford Dictionary**
**Music Book, Song Book**
**Hymn Book, Service Book**

Also available from us courtesy of Oxford University Press:
**Young Readers' Dictionary**
**(large print edition)**
**Young Readers' Thesaurus**
**(large print edition)**

For further information or a free brochure, please contact us at:
**Ulverscroft Large Print Books Ltd.,**
**The Green, Bradgate Road, Anstey,**
**Leicester, LE7 7FU, England.**
**Tel:** (00 44) **0116 236 4325**
**Fax:** (00 44) **0116 234 0205**

# WYOMING BLOOD FEUD

## Dale Graham

Neither Rafe Charnley nor his son Jeff could have foreseen how quickly their family tensions would escalate when Jeff falls in love with the daughter of the sheepherders with whom the family have a long-standing feud. Rafe cannot see his son's actions as anything but a deeply personal betrayal. Jeff is desperate to prove his feelings to his father — but when his beau's brother is accused of violating a land boundary, Rafe threatens to have him strung up. Can the hostilities between them be rectified without blood being spilled?